Kathleen McCaul was born in 1981 in London. She read English at Oxford University before travelling to Baghdad in 2003 to help begin Iraq's first post-war English language newspaper.

As a journalist she has lived and worked in Kashmir, Iraq, Qatar, Finland, the UK and India – where she freelanced as a radio reporter for the BBC World Service and wrote the occasional article. She most recently worked as a news producer for Al Jazeera English. This is her second novel.

Also by Kathleen McCaul:

Murder in the Ashram

GRAVE SECRETS

in

GOA

Kathleen McCaul

Piatkus
An imprint of
Little, Brown Book Group
100 Victoria Embankment
London EC4Y 0DY

An Hachette UK Company
www.hachette.co.uk

www.piatkus.co.uk

piatkus

PIATKUS

First published in Great Britain as a paperback
original in 2012 by Piatkus

Copyright © Kathleen McCaul 2012

The moral right of the author has been asserted.

A CIP catalogue record for this book
is available from the British Library.

ISBN 978-0-7499-5368-3

Typeset in Sabon LT Std by Palimpsest Book Production Limited,
Falkirk, Stirlingshire
Printed and bound in Great Britain by Clays Ltd, St Ives plc

Papers used by Piatkus are from well-managed forests
and other responsible sources.

MIX
Paper from
responsible sources
FSC® C104740
www.fsc.org

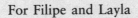

For Filipe and Layla

PART 1

1

The head of the bull had been hacked off cruelly; it looked like the work of a chainsaw. The neck was jagged with new, sharp edges. Fine, black sawdust lay all round its feet. I didn't think you could kill a statue, but this really did look like murder.

The camera zoomed out of the close-up, to a mourning crowd, gawping at their bull in mute shock. A doe-eyed reporter, gripping an outsize red mike, swung into view.

'Goa. Paradise Lost. We're getting used to news of drugs, Russian gangs, murders of foreigners, corrupt land deals. But this crime is entirely new to the state. Idol Theft.'

The reporter walked backwards slowly.

'These Hindu villagers woke this morning to a terrible scene. Their precious murti, a twelfth century Nandi, had been decapitated. The Holy bull had guarded the entrance of Goa's oldest temple for centuries, but could not protect itself from these barbaric thieves. I spoke to the son of the temple priest earlier and I asked him, how – and why – this had happened?

A small trim man, well-dressed, with a neat grey beard and bright, angry eyes, flashed up.

'It's money. Pure and simple. Like every crime here in Goa, money is at the root. Our Nandi is a legend, a legend not just in Goa, across India. Its beauty, its age, its survival. It's survived colonisers, invaders, evil missionaries. It protects the order of lives. It gives us meaning. This isn't just a theft, this is a crime against God. Against our land and our way of life. They must be found,' he said.

Back to the studio. A middle-aged presenter in what looked like a wig.

'And we've news in just now, the Archeaological Survey of India have requested the National Idol Squad – the crack team responsible for waging and winning the war on the Tamil Nadu temple thieves – handle this case. We'll be back with more on the Goan bull's head later but first let's pay a visit to Delhi Art Fair, where curators predict a record year of sales for India, who's economy continues to shine. But in a country where ancient art is valued and worshipped – does anyone really care about the modern stuff – or is it simply a fashion statement?'

A tinny tune from inside my rucksack. My phone. I scrabbled and got to it just in time. It was always right at the bottom.

'Hello?' I answered.

'Hi, hi Ruby . . . it's Josh from CultureClick.'

'Hey. How are you?'

'Good. Good. Wondering if you know much about Delhi Art Fair?'

I'm actually watching it on TV right now.'

'Could you do a piece for us? Usual price – 250 for 1,000 words.'

'Ah, sorry Josh, I can't this time.'

'Just something quick? A bit of colour; couple of quotes?'

'I'm at the airport Josh. I'm about to go on holiday.'

'Oh. OK.'

He sounded pissed off. Freelance journalists weren't supposed to go on holiday, I suppose. Editors think their lives are an eternal holiday.

'I really need a break. It hasn't been easy these past few months.'

That softened him up a bit.

'Yeah, I can imagine. You going anywhere nice?'

'Goa.'

'Goa. Cool. I spent a bit of time there, must be ten years ago now. Intense partying. Don't think I was ever the same again.'

'I'm not going for the Full Moon Parties. I'm just going to relax, get some perspective on everything.'

'Yeah, well, anyway. Have a good time. When are you back?'

'I dunno actually. I've given my flat up so I could be down there for a while.'

'All right. Well, let me know if any good stories crop up. Culture. If there's any left in Goa.'

I got off the phone and leant back in my chair. The café was fairly empty. It was an imitation of Starbucks and made milky, sugary coffees. Flies flickered heavily from surface to surface. The groaning air conditioning system was working so hard to simply stay alive it generated more heat than cool. Two small birds had somehow got into the airport terminal and ended up in here too, twittering and crying out and banging their heads on the small windows. They had no idea where they were or how they could get out and were pooing all over the tables in fright. I felt sorry for them. The manager became bored of the news and changed to MTV India, blaring out some Desi pop.

I rummaged through my bag to find my iPod. Sticking my headphones in and shutting out the world had been my default reaction to almost everything since Stephen had died. I couldn't work out whether the obsessive listening habits I had developed were an antidote to depression or a symptom of the black hole I found myself in, but I knew it was weird. I would become addicted to certain songs and listen to them over and over and over again until I was sick, completely sick on a three-minute song, but couldn't help listening just one more time. I was greedy for chord changes and choruses that made me vibrate, made me feel something, touched the lonely bits inside me. Other people's emotions, other lover's stories, which filled the empty space where my own relationships, my own friendships should have been.

My latest choice was Prince, a song about a three-some gone wrong. I was into my fourth play when I felt a hand on my shoulder. I turned around to see a skinny guy in a hoodie and baggy jeans with deep bags under his eyes. I took out my headphones.

'Hey,' I said.

'Hey. Sorry. Excuse me. Sorry. Sorry. I just saw you had a phone and I want to use the wireless in the

6

airport but you need an Indian phone number to get the password texted to you. I got a US number but I don't have an Indian one. Could I get a password sent to you? Is that OK?'

He was American. He gabbled his words.

'Sure. Er . . . Have you got a pen?'

'Yeah, yeah.'

He patted his trousers down with jerky movements but couldn't find one.

'I'll just type it in my iPhone,' he said, pulling a new model out his pants.

'OK – it's 9739024182.'

The guy gave me a tight smile.

'Thanks man. What's your name?'

'Ruby Jones.'

'Nice name,' he said, typing the number in.

'Thanks. What's yours?'

'Zim Moon.'

'Great name.'

'A lot of people take the piss. It's short for Simon. My dad's Raoul Moon.'

Zim suddenly closed his eyes and shuddered. He looked like he might vomit.

'Is your dad really that bad? Or are you ill?' I said.

He opened his eyes, surprised. Looked at me properly for the first time. Laughed.

'A bit of both I guess. Anyway, thanks, will you let me know when you get the password? I'm just sat on the next table, on my laptop.'

The text came pretty soon. I gave it to him and offered to buy him a coffee or something. He looked like he needed one. Zim accepted with a gaze that was more mournful than grateful. He poured five sugars into his already saccharine vanilla latte and took mindless gulps. I went back to Prince, though couldn't help but keep glancing at this guy behind me. He was fixated on whatever he was reading on the internet, flicking down fast, kept on running his hands over his head and then rubbing his mouth. He looked up at one point and caught me watching him. He came over.

'Do you know somewhere I can smoke in this place? I'm desperate for a cigarette.'

'There's a little kind of dungeon place by the toilets.'

'Sounds awful.'

'It is. But it's the only place.'

'Do you wanna come? Do you smoke?'

'Yeah, why not, I could do with one too. My plane's been delayed.'

I'd smoked a ton of cigarettes when I found out Stephen had died and I'd tried to give up after the funeral. It hadn't worked, there were whole days when I went without seeing anyone and the cigarettes helped me mark time, break up the loneliness.

I led the way to a tiny windowless room with two plastic-covered settees; a thin fluorescent light cast a green, ill-looking glow across both our faces. You could see the bones working through Zim's skin as he flipped out a cigarette and gripped it between his lips. He closed his eyes as he sparked his lighter but opened them again when he went to light mine.

'This country is shit,' he said.

I laughed and took in a drag of smoke. It was a US brand, much better then the cigarettes I smoke here.

'It's not that bad.'

'It's dirty and the people are mad. They're nuts. I stopped in Delhi but took two steps out of the airport and came straight back in again.'

'Why?'

'I got mugged.'

'No.'

'OK; not exactly mugged. But I don't like being touched. There were all these taxi drivers, pulling my luggage, getting in my face, shouting at me. I couldn't handle it. So I just came back in and re-booked my ticket to Goa.'

'I'm going to Goa . . .'

'Oh cool. Which airline?'

'SpiceJet.'

'Yeah me too. Delayed by five hours. Five fucking hours? The flight's only two and a half. I mean what is that about?'

'You get used to it. The flights are cheap at least.'

Zim put his head in his hands and then leant back in a sigh.

'I just didn't need it today. I'm crashing badly.'

'What's happened to you?'

Zim stubbed out his cigarette. 'Is there anywhere to get a beer round here? I need something to take the edge off.'

A new bar had opened up at the airport and it was full of people who looked like they were on the way to Goa; women in strappy tops, guys with pints of Kingfisher. Zim paid for our beers with a credit card painted with a large moon. It was the most beautiful credit card I had ever seen.

'That's a cool card.'

'Yeah. This trip is on Blue Moon. If you want champagne, go right ahead.'

'Blue Moon?'

'Blue Moon Gallery, Los Angeles. Off Sunset Boulevard. You know it? It's where all the stars go. I can't say who, but a very famous, Hollywood actress bought a bust from us recently. White marble Roman with a shot to his head, blood dripping down. I loved that.'

I shook my head.

'I don't know it.'

'Really? You never heard of it?'

'I've never been to the US.'

Zim widened his eyes.

'Shit. That's crazy. You came to India before America?'

'So?'

'I dunno . . . it's just . . . this place?'

He screwed up his face, looked around him.

Despite understanding exactly how he felt, I was offended on behalf of the country. I was sure America did Starbucks better. But large coffees weren't everything.

'What are you doing here?' I said.

'I was supposed to be going to the Delhi Art Fair. Finding some new Asian artists. Visiting a new client of my dad's, in Goa. A businessman. Paulo Mendes. I just couldn't handle the fair though you know? After the week I've had. I'm just going straight down to see Paulo. I shouldn't have had that stop-over in Thailand. You ever smoked Crystal Meth?' he said, putting his head in his hands.

'Er, no. My brother tried it once with a prostitute

10

in Cardiff. He got caught by the police round the back of the bus station. He didn't look good when we picked him up. Went to bed for days.'

'I've been vomiting periodically since Bangkok airport.'

'Well you don't smell too bad,' I said, for something to say.

I was clearly out of practice of conversation, but I thought this was obviously a joke. Zim took me deadly seriously.

'I took a shower when I arrived. I can't stand being dirty. I hate it. I hate bad smells . . .'

'My brother's room stank. He puked the whole day after we got him home. My parents completely freaked out. They banned him from leaving the house for a month. Took his car off him, he'd just got it too, for his birthday. My dad's a teacher, said he'd never seen such behaviour, etc. etc. Lasted forever. I felt sorry for him in the end.'

'God. I know how that feels. I've been banished. I'm supposed to be staying out of trouble. I'm supposed to be redeeming myself.'

'Why?'

'Ah . . . you know, I had some girlfriend trouble. They're well-known. They didn't like the fuss. Didn't look good.'

'Girlfriend trouble doesn't sound as bad as smoking meth.'

He shrugged his shoulders. 'Depends on the girlfriend doesn't it?'

Zim took a sip of beer and began peeling off the bottle label.

11

'What do you do?' he asked, more out of routine than interest.

'I'm a journalist.'

Zim lifted his eyebrows.

'Oh really? Really? That's cool. I'm like, addicted to twenty-four hour news. I can't stop watching. I love it.'

'Oh God. I hate it.'

'What kind of stuff do you do?'

'Print mostly. Freelance. Culture. Arts. Delhi and sometimes a few trips.'

'You working now?'

'No, this is a holiday. I needed to get away.'

We sat drinking beer in silence. Zim looked at me and began ruminating my name slowly round his mouth.

'Ruby Jones. Journalist. Sounds like you could be famous.'

'I'm far from that. Only just make a living.'

We wasted the hours drinking beer. Zim would often put his head in his hands. He felt sorry for himself, needed his suffering to be obvious. He made me laugh, something I hadn't done for a while, with his desperate face, his wretched expressions, his lack of any grip on reality. It helped he was good-looking, though not much, because he was far too aware of it. He explained that his face had been in his only saving grace.

'People have called me everything. Everything. People have been so mad at me, they've had to be held back from smacking me down. But no one has ever called me ugly. And believe me, if I was, they would have said it,' he joked.

I told him he was an egotistical cock. He seemed like the kind you could say what you liked to. He took it on the chin.

'But not ugly right?'

I shrugged, gave up, laughed. What could you do?

Zim spilled his life out to me like I was his best friend. He was here in India to make a new start, make amends for his misspent years.

'I'll admit. I've acted badly. I dropped out of college and pretended I was still there. Went everyday. I gambled my fees and snorted it up my nose. I begged for a job at the gallery and then started massive arguments with clients at openings. I've just been a shit. I think it's all been a cry for attention.'

'Did your therapist tell you that?'

I thought I was being mean, but he didn't even blink, just took a serious sip of beer.

'That's what she says. She says I have issues with my father because he's talented and successful and I'm scared to be compared to him, so I rebel instead. I have Developmental Trauma Disorder. This trip to India, I'm supposed to be confronting this and recovering. I'm supposed to *behave*.'

He pronounced this word carefully, like a foreign concept.

'Sounds like you're a spoilt little rich kid to me.'

'I'm rich. I'm not spoilt. My dad swears I was his one bad sperm. My mum always says I must have been abused, not that she sounds too worried about it. She replaced any filial bond with botox a long time ago. She's just not as interested in me as she is in preventative ageing technology.'

13

He looked so dismal as he said this, genuinely hurt. I actually felt sorry for him. I put my hand on his shoulder, the most emotional gesture I'd made in a long time. He looked up at me, shook off his family and half-smiled.

'I guess you're got a great family, loving, normal. You seem one of those really together, over-achieving types.'

He wasn't too far off, except I was the furthest from together I had ever been.

'My dad, he's a teacher, he's pretty normal. My mum. She's pretty crazy, she's a minor poet. Not really successful. Likes to write about blood and wombs.'

'Gross.'

'I know. You know she read us Sylvia Plath as bedtime stories? That was probably the most warped part of childhood. She's not bad though, just wrapped up in her own world. My brother's kind of like her. I take after my dad.'

'So how did you get to be a journalist, travelling all over the world?'

He sounded so much more impressed than he should have. I didn't travel all over the world, I was stuck in India. I'd come over with wild ambitions to dig up seminal stories, become a great writer of the new century. In reality I was stuck doing colour pieces on Delhi Art Fair. Still, it was nice to be appreciated.

'I dunno . . . I guess I do take after mum a bit. I like writing. I just didn't want to write crazy poems that went nowhere and didn't mean anything to anyone. I wanted to write something concrete, something that would make a difference to people, something people would actually read. I went to university, started work on a local paper and then somehow got out here. I'm from Wales originally.'

'Wales. Is that North England?'

'No. It's a whole fucking country. Have you not heard of Dylan Thomas?'

He looked at me blankly. I was about to start explaining rugby when the tannoy buzzed. Our flight was finally leaving. There was no seating plan and the usual scrum to get a seat. I skulked at the back of the plane for a bit, not knowing whether to sit by this guy or not. Sitting in close proximity for another two hours would be a commitment, would suggest that I liked him maybe. And there was a risk he might vomit. But he was really fun to talk to. I enjoyed listening to him, he was weird but at least he made me feel less of a fuck-up myself.

Zim took the decision out of my hands, calling loudly to me across the plane.

'Hey, I saved you a seat. Come on over.'

I smiled weakly and grabbed some napkins from a sullen air-hostess, just in case things went wrong. There were TVs bedded into the backs of our seats and Zim immediately tuned to CNN.

I pulled out my book, *Strangers on a Train*.

'Hey, hey,' he said, pulling his headphones out for a moment. 'It's like we're Strangers on a Plane!'

Zim seemed a lot happier now. He chuckled at his own joke, even though it really was not funny. He was still smiling as he watched some footage of a bomb going off in Afghanistan. He was the kind that recovered from hangovers by getting high.

I tried to concentrate on my book, but I couldn't. I took out my iPod again.

'What are you listening to?' asked Zim.

'Prince.'

He shuddered. 'God.'

'What have you got against Prince?'

'Ah, it's personal.'

'What?'

'I told you, it's personal.'

I couldn't just drop it. Even in the depths of depressed self-involvement I was still nosy as hell.

'Oh come on, tell me. I won't tell anyone will I?'

Zim shook his head.

'Oh come on, I love a good story.'

'OK, but you got to promise never to tell anyone. Or I might have to kill you.'

He looked at me with no humour in his eyes. I tried to match his seriousness.

'All right I swear.'

'My ex-girlfriend, Melissa. She was obsessed with 'Purple Rain'. She would only come when Prince was on. I don't know who was turning her on more, me or him. I got a little jealous in the end. I smashed up all her Prince CDs.'

'God, that's a bit extreme.'

'I'm not proud of myself. I'm not. I just kind of saw red. She was so upset. One of them was signed. And there was a first print too. I felt terrible after. We didn't last much longer.'

'No wonder. That's a shit thing to do.'

Zim frowned like a dog who'd just been kicked for no reason.

16

'I didn't want to tell you. I told you it was personal. You insisted. Now you think I'm crazy and all I was being was honest. Damn.'

'Don't worry about it. I don't think your crazy. I'm not listening to "Purple Rain". I'm listening to "Dirty Mind".'

'OK, that's not so bad.'

We arrived at Panjim airport late. It was dark and hot as we stepped out the plane and there was a salty breeze.

'I booked into the Majestic Panjim online at the airport. Don't know if its any good, but its supposed to be the best round here. Do you fancy coming with me? Get a margarita at the bar?' he asked.

'Ah, thanks, but I've booked somewhere. Fernando's guesthouse, in the old town.'

Zim shrugged his shoulders. 'OK. Suit yourself.'

He didn't seem bothered either way and that made me regret refusing. Now all I had to look forward to was lying on a bed and listening to my iPod. Why didn't I say yes? Why couldn't I just relax? Make a friend?

A crowd of drivers were waiting for holidaymakers at the entrance of the airport. One man dressed all in white was holding a decorated white board with the name 'Zim Moon' neatly written.

'That's my ride. Do you wanna lift?'

'Ah no, don't worry. I'll get a cab.'

He looked at me. He had bloodshot eyes with very pale-blue irises. They would have been lovely if he hadn't just spent the whole of his Bangkok stopover smoking weed.

'You're independent aren't you? You had your fingers burnt by someone?'

I laughed. 'I guess I've had my fingers burnt but I don't know if it was by anyone but myself.'

'I know all about that. I think I've become a master in the art of self-combustion . . . well . . . look after yourself.'

'No worries. See you. You know, I really have got something to do tomorrow. Or I would have come with you.'

'What's so important?'

I was embarrassed but I wanted to explain. I didn't want him to think I was some ice queen who couldn't hang out and drink a margarita.

'I'm going to a festival.'

'A music festival?'

'No . . . it's the festival of a saint.'

Zim looked shocked then faintly worried. 'Are you religious?'

'No, no. God no. Ah. It's a long story.'

Zim's driver had taken his bag and had started the engine of his car. He clearly wanted to go.

'Well, look I got your number. I'm going to call you.'

'OK.'

He looked at me fixedly.

'I'm gonna call you Ruby. Is that OK with you? I'd like to hang out.'

'Yeah, sure, it is. I said it was.'

He smiled, reached out to stroke my hair, but thought better of it. Maybe it was the expression on my face that stopped him. Maybe it said 'don't touch'. We

18

hovered for a moment, his hand mid-air. I balanced myself in the night, eventually leant in. But he'd taken his hand up in a wave and then he was away in his car.

2

I woke up the next morning with an aching back and clammy skin. My mattress felt like it has been badly beaten up. The bathroom smelt of sewers.

Fernando's guesthouse had seemed old-fashioned when I arrived the night before, with a wooden veranda, dim lights and plaster walls. In the morning my over-whelming feeling was that it was dirty. I wished I'd taken up that margarita with Zim.

I found Fernando sitting in his mouldy bar, surrounded by the debris of last night's orders, watching football on TV. I asked him for a taxi into Old Goa. He didn't seem keen to move and just rubbed his tight, round belly.

'What do you want to go there for? Very busy today. Crowds. The feast day of Saint Francis today. Better to go tomorrow.' He said, not taking his eyes of the screen.

'Tomorrow when the football's over? I *want* to go to the feast day. That's why I'm here.'

'It'll be dirty.'

I couldn't quite make out this comment. Whether Fernando was being a hypocrite or the feast of Saint Francis was truly filthy. But I'd travelled thousands of miles down here to see this saint; I wasn't going to give up now.

'I don't care. Just book me a cab.'

He swiped a fly away from his face and looked up at me with new eyes. I was weirder than he'd realised.

'You're religious? OK. I'll get it for you.'

I didn't bother protesting. I'll admit it was a strange way to start a holiday, but it was a start at least.

It had been hard work freelancing in Delhi, but I'd been doing all right, I'd been having some fun. Then Stephen, my flatmate, my best friend, my only real friend there, died. I'd pretty much lost it after that. I couldn't work, hardly at all. Most of the time I lay on my bed listening to the wailing train horns from the railway station nearby.

I tried to muster the usual discipline, searched myself for the glint of hope that got me up in the morning, made me write lists, send emails, make calls. But I couldn't find it. I think it was the guilt more than anything.

Stephen had been pulled out of the Yamuna River and at first we thought it was murder. But it wasn't. He'd been off his face on heroin. He'd fallen in. I found it all out and wrote about his death, my first article for a national newspaper. A big break. Now his family won't speak to me.

Before this, journalism, writing, had seemed simple. The only problem was getting commissions. I loved it, believed in it, saw the truth as all-important. Now, I wasn't sure. I sneered at my old self; naïve, over-enthusiastic, self-righteous. I'd lost my vocation and didn't know how to get it back. Or if I ever would.

I discovered the festival of Saint Francis Xavier at Saint James', church in Delhi, where Stephen was buried. I visited the grave most weeks. It was November, getting cooler now winter was setting in and I took my time, sitting in the sun outside the church porch. That's when I saw the poster. A picture of a red coffin, in which lay a gnarled brown body, dressed in golden robes. Across this were information banners.

YOUR PRAYERS ANSWERED BY SAINT FRANCIS XAVIER
WITNESS THE MIRACLE OF THE SAINT'S SURVIVAL — OVER
FIVE HUNDRED YEARS OLD
HOLY EXPOSITION OF BODY — DECEMBER 14TH — BASILICA
OF BOM JESUS — OLD GOA
SPECIAL PRICE — 10,000 RUPEES — CALL FATHER JONATHAN
FOR TOUR DETAILS — 9786445683

I googled the old saint when I got home. Founder of the Jesuits. Zealous missionary. I wasn't sure if this was a totally good thing. But the legend of his death hooked me. Saint Francis had died of a fever while trying to sneak into China to convert yet more apparent 'heathens'. He was buried on a deserted island and coated with quicklime to hasten decomposition. When his grave was re-opened three months later, the corpse was in perfect condition. Reburied, Saint Xavier was exhumed again after five months, fresh as a daisy according to his fans. The body was sent by sea back to Goa, where Saint

Xavier had made his home and was more successful in his mission than on the ill-fated trip to China. An examination was made to ensure that the corpse had not been artificially preserved and a Jesuit priest was asked to stick his finger into a hole in the chest. The finger came out covered in fresh blood. Since then his body had been exposed once every three years and was said to have miraculous powers by supplicants to his shrine. Pilgrims gather from around the world to have their prayers heard by the saint.

Saint Francis didn't look so fresh now. A few centuries had definitely battered his body. But I liked the idea of having a few prayers answered. I needed some way out of the paralysis I found myself in.

It wasn't just work. Sadness had spread into all corners of my life. I couldn't sleep. I hated where I lived; around an old shrine to the Nizamuddin. I'd enjoyed living in a holy place, but now the Muslim saint left me cold. He meant nothing to me. Stephen and I had revelled in the mayhem, the pilgrims and their food and their wailing hymns, but without him all I could see was the dirt, the mutilated beggars, the kids with their ribs poking out, the scraggy rabid-looking dogs.

It would have been easier if I had someone to talk to, to help me laugh at myself, to put a mirror to my wallowing. But everyone I knew in Delhi had disappeared, our good times disintegrated, too forced after the horrible way we lost our friend. I emailed, I Skyped home, but it wasn't the same as real-life. All I had was this damn iPod Stephen had bought me for my birthday.

Somewhere in my confused and botched up head,

Saint Francis Xavier and his screwed-up old body appealed to me. Maybe he could help. Maybe he would cure me. I could at least witness a miracle even if I didn't experience one. And Goa had beaches.

3

I wasn't the only one desperate enough to think Saint Xavier could solve their problems. Fernando wasn't joking about the crowds. As soon as I got on the road to Old Goa people poured round the taxi. Four-by-fours with stickers saying 'God's Gift' and buses called Saint Anthony belched out petrol and inched forward slowly. Families dressed in satin sped past on scooters. Traffic fumes and best clothes.

A market lined the way to the church and hemmed in the pushing, shoving crowds. A dirty, religious Glastonbury. Heavy smoke wafted from pans frying oily, red sausage; mixed with the sounds of rattling bells and the low whir of a sugarcane crusher. CD stalls competed with one another, blasting Bhangra and gut-busting hymns. Religious vendors sold plastic Rosary beads and metallic stickers of the crucifix. Fernando had insisted on writing the address of the guesthouse and the phone number on a piece of yellow paper before I left. I'd been impatient – he'd wanted to show off his arduously joined-up writing and his felt tip calligraphy pen – but I was grateful for it now. Shoved it further down into my pocket.

Masses of pilgrims, thousands of black heads, queued in a snaking line under cloth canopies to get into the Basilica. Middle-aged women in peach polyester skirt suits, babies in pink ball gowns, shrunken old men in sunglasses and sheeny waistcoats. Women from the countryside were in their special saris, glittering with sequins. It all looked incredibly sweaty. Hours it would take, hours, to go in and see the body of this saint. I didn't know if I could do it. I was feeling sick. The sweat poured off me, and worse, I could smell it pouring off everyone else too.

The power of this saint was medieval. Thousands of people; whole families, cripples, the terminally ill, young couples, old couples, groups of friends, all pilgrimaging to see if Xavier could help them. Industrial picnics with vats of rice were laid out for big parties. A nun was making a mint on cold mango drinks and ice-cream. Camps had been set up in the shade of the cathedral museum. Tourists picked their way gingerly between men sucking from a beer can and women cutting vegetables with their legs splayed, oblivious to the lack of privacy.

I didn't have their faith. Miracles just didn't happen in my world. I'd come to this festival on a grievous whim, not burning with love of Saint Xavier like these people clearly were. Men offered me wax models to give to the saint, heads and hands, babies the size of a foetus, hearts inscribed with crosses and simple candles. They didn't inspire me. They were ugly. I shook my head.

26

I stopped in at a nearby church for some quiet, to gather my thoughts. Shrines flanked the long nave, leading to a grand altar. I looked around for a place to light candles and sit. But families were lolling all over the altars, camping out in the chapels, eating rice on steps meant for kneeling in prayer. Men napped in pews. A baby was stood up on the tomb of miracles and smiled for a photographer. Guys with their hands around each other leant over a figure of Mary, grinning. There was smoke near the altar, not from incense, but oil and frying spices. White-haired European women in salwar kameez knelt by the altar saying the prayers of the Rosary. The place had a party feel. Everyone was having their own kind of fun with their own friends and family. Except me. I was on my own and I wasn't enjoying myself.

It wasn't much different from the place I'd run away from, Nizamuddin shrine. This was Christianity, this was supposed to be my world, but I felt left out. I wasn't sure what I was doing here at all now. It didn't matter the religion, I was still thousands of miles away from home. I still stuck out as a lonely foreigner.

But I guessed giving up at the last minute wasn't a great start. I should at least go and see Saint Francis, even if it did mean a wait of hours. I rummaged through my bag, found some sun cream, applied it all over my face and set off for the queue.

Lodging myself firmly in the cattle-like queue stalls, between a family with four children and a tiny, bent over man, I estimated two hours till we reached even the door of the church. I got out my iPod again. I scrolled through to 'P', but thought again. I really should listen to something other then Prince. I wondered what Zim's girlfriend was like. I put on Ryan Adams. Multilated Country music. American.

Finally, I reached the door of the Basilica. It was getting exciting now, I put my music away. I craned my neck to try and see the body's casket.

It was much calmer inside. People were awed and shuffled along clasping their gifts, heads down. Just as well, the floor was marble inlaid with jewels, the roof and paintwork were peeling. The silence thundered with the thousand thoughts and prayers every pilgrim carried. I glanced around. Eyes were all lowered in hope and anticipation. This was a serious, serious business; being healed, witnessing a miracle.

Wax figures and wilting marigolds piled up around the casket. People knelt with their heads closeted, hands clutching unlit candles. Flames were forbidden round the shrine. Saint Francis Xavier was pretty brittle by now and the priests couldn't be completely confident of him having the miraculous ability to survive fire.

Finally I reached the shrine. In a dark recess of the church. Strong afternoon light streaked through skylights, hitting the pilgrims and showing up the dust. But you couldn't see much of the saint at all, resting high above the crowd. I thought I make out a claw of a hand, a couple of grey fingers but it was so shadowy, I wasn't really sure. I felt myself deflating. Did the ecstatic healing happen only when you knelt down to pray? I scanned the faces of the people walking away, but they were as closed as before. No one seemed to have blossomed with the experience. There were no smiles, no open joy. Perhaps it was all fireworks on the inside.

Then it was my turn. I hadn't bought candles or wax figures or even flowers. I wasn't sure what to do. I knelt self-consciously, asking the saint to help me find a way out of this mess in my head, to unfreeze my fingers and clear up my eyes. I searched myself for some spiritual experience, some Damascus moment, but I turned away shortly afterwards, hardly enlightened.

I began to shuffle towards the exit. The experience had not been earth-shaking. It was then that I heard shots. They echoed and rung out around the church. A jolt of shock ran through the people. More shots, confirming our collective fear. This wasn't a car or a firework, but a gun. The repeated crack, the vicious weight on the ears, the sudden rush of fear. I looked round for police, the army, security. There were none, just some officials in badly fitting shirts and large crosses ducking and crying.

My stomach dropped. Strangled screeches, animal fear, came from around the shrine. More shots, more screams, no room to run. People around me began to scream and cry, struggling and shoving to get towards the entrance, knocking over pews. Another round of shots, in the central aisle of the church, closer to me. Terror rippled from around the gunman. Was he going to shoot us all? Was I going to die here? I heard myself scream and began to claw my way out with the rest of the crowd. My thoughts were fast and very slow. My mum, my dad. My brother. I had to stay on my feet. I had to keep seeing the door. I had to get away from the gun.

There were swells and crushes. My bag got caught and I was sucked down to waist level, smelling fresh and stale sweat mixed. Wet, frightened, bodies. I couldn't breathe. My arm, caught in my rucksack, yanked away from my body. Intense pain jarred through me. I yelled; no one minded. The damp sari of a woman nearby me began to strangle her, the ends trampled on, she pulled it off her, ran in just her underwear.

I had to let my rucksack go. Either that or my arm. But I really couldn't lose it. It had everything in it. My passport, my wallet, my phone, my iPod, photos; of Delhi, of Stephen. Despite the fear, I clung to it. It contained all the things I needed. I couldn't lose it. I would have to lose it. I let go and pulled my arm back towards me, grabbed on to one man's shoulder to haul myself up. I whipped back round to grab but it was gone, sucked down into the storm.

There was nothing I could do. I concentrated on keeping my feet moving forward, in the thick of the crowd, slippery and unsteady, crunching on debris, making my way towards the strip of blue above the large entrance. The sound of crashing glass as one window fell. More screams. Blood splatters mixed with flickering rainbow lights reflected on the plaster from the smashed stained-glass. Then, all at once, I spurted out of the Basilica into bright light and air. The crowd fell on the ground, scrambled up and started to run. Chaos. Screaming mothers searched for their children. An old man had collapsed, his wife sobbing and moaning by his side. He wouldn't survive. There was no one to help. My shoulder was shot through with mind-numbing pain. I crawled, crying, to the side of the Basilica, to a palm tree hooked round the side of the entrance. I gulped air and choked on my sobs. I heard myself moaning.

'Here, drink some water. Try to breath normally, deeply.'

A plastic cup held by a fine wrist was suddenly in front of me. I looked up to see a handsome woman, green eyes and thick black hair streaked with grey. I couldn't say anything, my chest shook up and down.

'Calm down. Sip this slowly,' she demanded.

I took the water from her. Became conscious of my breath, tried to stop my hands from shaking.

'That's better.'

She watched me drink, crouched down in front of me, put her hand on my shoulder to steady me.

'What's your name?'

'Ruby.'

'Is there anyone looking for you here?'

I shook my head.

'There's no one here worried about you? Tell me. We'll need to start a list of people.'

'No. No, I came on my own.'

I started to cry.

'The police have arrived. They're going to put emergency buses and ambulances on soon. You'll be OK Ruby.'

'I lost my rucksack. It's got everything in it, my wallet, my passport, my book, my iPod. Everything. I haven't got anything.'

This woman's eyes narrowed slightly.

'Why on earth would you take such important things to a festival like this?'

'I didn't know this was going to happen.'

'It's the largest Christian festival in Asia . . . oh look. Never mind. Listen, I need to go and help. You stay here. Rest. I'll keep an eye out for your bag and come back later with it.'

'Thanks, thanks. What's your name?'

'Michael, Sister Michael.'

'Sister? You're a nun?'

She didn't look much like a nun, she was slim, wearing black trousers and a grey cotton shirt. A gold crucifix around her neck. Sister Michael rose to her feet and looked down at me.

'Ex. I'll be back. Could you looked after this for me?'

She handed me a plate-sized shard of old glass with the face of an angel.

4

Even Fernando was watching the news now. The TV was off the football and on to NDTV. A constant scroller updated the latest on Saint Francis.

'Breaking News: head of saint stolen in Goa. Vatican to send own investigator. Saint Francis Xavier founder of Jesuits decapitated at festival.'

The same reporter I'd seen yesterday, covering the stolen bull's head up in the north of Goa, was now standing amid the mangled grounds of the Basilica. He was wild with excitement, he'd been sent down here on a minor story and hit the jackpot.

'What is happening in Goa? First the Tambdi Surla bull and now – its beloved patron saint, Francis Xavier! The most visited Christian shrine in Asia is now in chaos. Questions on security and how this happened will come, but for now, the Catholic Church in Goa and millions of pilgrims from across India and around the world are simply reeling in shock. Is this a crime against Christianity? If so, it's on a scale not seen since the destruction of the Babri Mosque. The Vatican released this statement earlier today.'

The screen flashed to a black-robed, red-capped Cardinal standing outside a heavy marble church. He read from a piece of paper.

'The Roman Catholic Church and Jesuit order are shocked and saddened to hear that the head of Saint Francis Xavier has been stolen by thieves in the state of Goa, India. Saint Francis Xavier was one of the founders of the Jesuit Order and his missions to India shone the light of Jesus on new lands. Not since Saint Paul did a man work more zealously, converting millions to true knowledge of Christ. His body, until today, has been a miraculous testament to the Lord, surviving uncorrupted since the sixteenth century. The Vatican will be sending two Papal investigators to Rome . . .'

'Aw man, these priests, they go on. Can't we have a bit of cricket Ferny?' asked Jake, the curly-haired Australian sitting with me and Fernando in the bar. The only other guest at the guest house.

Fernando didn't respond, didn't flick his eyes from the television.

'What do you think Rube?'

I got up. 'Sorry, I'm out. I'm going to check the internet. Is it all right to use your machine Fernando?'

He nodded vaguely, clutching the remote control. I got the feeling Jake wasn't going to see the test match here, maybe not anywhere in Goa. The whole state had gone into shock. Flowers were piled high round the saint's statue in the square outside Fernando's, crowds of people lighting candles and praying and hugging each other and crying. It was like when Princess Diana died.

Yahoo! India was all over the story. Eyewitness accounts of the gunmen, dressed in black with black cloths over their faces. One man claimed they had diamonds in their ears. An interview with the Idol Squad's Inspector Srinvasen, who had arrived in Goa just before the head was stolen. He was going to use every resource in his power to find the bull's head and the head of Saint Francis. Yes, he welcomed cooperation from the Vatican and the Goan Police, although the Idol Squad's expertise was unique in this field.

Twitter alert available for breaking news on the head.

I logged on to my own gmail account. Not much. My mum, wanting to know what I was doing for Christmas, whether I was enjoying the holiday, had I heard what had happened in Goa? My bank. They'd send the cards to their Panjim branch. Five to seven working days. My passport was more of a problem. An unsympathetic fifth secretary at the Consulate, Claudia, had emailed to say I either needed a personal permanent address in Goa and a witness, or I needed to come up to Delhi to collect my passport. It would take up to two weeks unless I wanted to pay an emergency passport fee. I checked my bank account. I didn't have enough to justify that. And I couldn't fly up to Delhi without my passport. This was turning into the holiday from hell. At least my arm hadn't actually been dislocated. All I'd suffered from was shock, a few cuts and bruises. That old man I'd seen outside the entrance, he'd died from a heart attack.

I was about to delete the rest of my inbox as junk when I saw something else. Subject: Hello from Touchstone.

Dear Ruby,

It's David Dryden here – I do hope you remember me. We were in seventeenth century Satire together at university, with Magdalen Hepworth. I still have nightmares about that woman. Shockingly bad teeth. It upset me.

I was a very good friend of Stephen Newby and I followed your stories about him last year. Devastating news. Though it sounded exactly like the way Stephen would have wanted to die. 'Drowsed with the fume of poppies'. He always had the air of the fated around him. Maybe that is why we all found him so exciting.

I'll get to the point. I thought I saw a picture in The Times *yesterday, outside the Basilica of Bom Jesus in Goa. You were sitting under a palm tree, looking rather dishevelled, I'm afraid. Were you at the festival of Saint Xavier? If you were, I may have some work for you.*

I've just been made editor at Touchstone. Have you heard of it? Long-form journalism, in the American Style. Quality paper, colour printing, illustration, once a month. It's aiming to be the British equivalent of the New Yorker *with some Film Noir thrown in. We want big pieces with an investigative edge, seminal arts pieces, journalism that tackles the over-arching concerns of our time. That kind of thing. Rather large ambition, I know, but that paper's got money behind it.*

It's the baby of Peter Bukowski. American, but based in Britain for decades, one of London's most successful investment bankers. Huge philanthropist, he's given millions to Tate Modern. Now his youngest daughter has decided she wants to be a journalist he's dedicated himself to creating a magazine just for her.

She's only just 11 so I've got the top job for a few years yet.

Peter's a devout Catholic. Lourdes at least once a year. Audience with the pope on his visit to the UK in August. Jesuit educated. He's told me he wants the story of Saint Francis's head covered from every angle. Would you be interested? We'll need something, 2,000 words say, by next issue. We go to print in two and a half weeks. The pay isn't bad – £1 per word. Four times what the Guardian *offers.*

Let me know as soon as you can. I hope you can do it. I like your writing and you'd be helping us out enormously. Couldn't quite believe my luck when I saw you. Peter would say God moves in mysterious ways, but I couldn't possibly be so bold. I'm more inclined to believe 'providence in a watchful state'.

Best and sincerest wishes,

David

David Dryden. How could anyone forget that guy? A flamboyant queen, velvet jacket and steel core. Fiercely clever. Passionate poet. Political. Dangerous.

He wafted around Oxford on a cloud of decorum and satire, as if a direct descendant of King Charles II. But he wasn't. Far from it. You wouldn't know it from his dramatic delivery, but David was from the West Coast of Wales, Rhyl. David would paint the place in romantic, rosy shades. But I was from Cardiff, I knew better. Concrete estates staring blankly at the grey sea. Poverty of the kind that London didn't understand. Simply empty: a few old bananas outside the shops, desolate stretches of tarmacked promenade.

If he was editing a magazine, with money behind it, it must be a lot of money. This guy wasn't some dedicated campaigner. He famously hated the *Guardian*. There would be possibilities. It would an experience too, working for him. I'd learn something at least. And the pay, it was far more than I was used to. It would more than make up for the bad start to the trip. I got a small rush of excitement at the thought of writing. The first for a long time. Perhaps Saint Francis was answering my prayers, even without a head. I hit reply.

Hi David,

Well spotted. It was me. Dishevelled is a polite way of putting it. I'd just escaped from the Basilica and wasn't handling the shock too well. I'd lost my bag and everything in it, my passport, my wallet, phone, everything. It seems now that the gunmen weren't shooting to kill, just to cause havoc and steal the head. But no one trapped in there knew that then. It was terrifying.

Thankfully I had some kind of guardian angel come to rescue in the shape of an ex-nun. She lent me some money – told me she would make sure the police looked out for my bag.

I'd be really interested in writing something for you on the head. The whole state is devastated, they really love this guy. It's wall-to-wall coverage on national TV but nothing is clear yet. No one can understand why anyone would want to steal the head of a crumbling corpse, albeit a saint.

There's been cases of over-zealous pilgrims stealing bits of Xavier over the years. Apparently one Portuguese woman bit off his right little toe. They found her by a trail of blood that was spurting from her mouth. This must have been a while ago now because there is definitely no juice in the old guy now. From what I could see he is little more then crepe paper . . . the miracle must be wearing off or something.

I don't know if you've heard about the Nandi, in the north of the state, that had its head hacked off and stolen? The Hindus here are fuming. But at least in that case there is a clear motive. It's a priceless statue. There's money to be made. The black-market for Indian antiques is apparently huge. They've even got a National Idol Squad dedicated to beating the trade. But the head of Saint Francis? Everyone agrees that it would be a very odd buyer who wanted that on their mantelpiece.

I'd definitely want to interview the head of the Idol Squad here – Inspector Srinvasen. He's done a short piece with Yahoo! India but he's said that he's only giving press conferences from now on. Maybe the best place to start would be with my ex-nun Sister Michael? She is some big shot in the church here it seems. I have all her contact details.

Let me know what you think. I haven't got a phone here but you can get me on Skype or Facebook if you want to chat.

All the best,

Ruby

5

It was a TV journalist's nightmare. A great story and an incredible setting. Beautiful old churches rich with banners and gold, priests and nuns scurrying back and forth between tropical vegetation. No filming allowed.

The public were banned from Old Goa until forensics had finished with the site. Crowds of cameras and reporters gathered at the police barrier, filming the latest news but no decent picture. Just striped tape and two trunkish Goan officers in khaki. All the journalists could do was wait for Inspector Srinvasen to appear for a brief statement with no further questions asked.

I recognised a few people from Delhi. The long-haired, delicious CNN correspondent, Delia. Christopher Michaels, BBC. Blue shirt, crumpled trousers, harassed. He waved to me, the frown of perplexed frustration never leaving his face.

A few words from Sister Michael to the guard on duty and I was let under the tape and on to the hallowed land.

'Who does she think she is? Just waltzing in there like that. We've been camped out all night?' said a blonde guy from ABC.

I shrugged at him, tried not to smile. In the end I'd got lucky, going to the festival, being rescued by Sister Michael. It turned out she was not only on the board of the Basilica but curator of the Museum of Christian Art too. There couldn't be a more perfect start to my story for Touchstone.

It was a tranquil early evening. The sun easy after a searing afternoon, warm against my skin. The tower of a ruined church stood ahead, glowing in light thick with pollen and insects. Old Goa, so quiet now, so different without the tourists, like a fairy tale.

We passed the buttressed convent of Saint Monica, white once, but blackened now by the monsoon. A sign warned visitors were not allowed. A grill-door locked out the world. Beyond this, two nuns in blue habits sat reading quietly on a bench leant up against a wall.

'It's so peaceful here, makes even me think about becoming a nun,' I said.

'Oh it is. It is. It's idyllic, convent life in Goa. A beautiful way of living. Serene. I remember sitting happily right where those girls are.'

'Why did you leave?'

'Misdirected passion.'

'Misdirected passion?'

'I've had thirty odd years to think about it and I have come to the conclusion that my problem has been misdirected passion, though I still cannot see clearly whether the misdirection came before I entered orders or after.'

Sister Michael didn't say anymore. I searched for the right question to ask.

'Are your family from Goa?'

'They were from the countryside in Rome originally, but went over to London in the nineteenth century.'

'Why?'

'We were a theatre family. They set up in Soho, around the old Victorian Playhouses. My grandfather was quite a well-known figure. I was always supposed to go on stage. My real name is Dorothea Sophia Caperelli. They all thought I was going to be the next Loren.'

'And you became a nun instead. That's teenage rebellion.'

'They should never have taken me to Rome. A sixteen-year-old girl, given to drama, wandering the Vatican. What else is she going to aspire to? Becoming a nun seemed like a lead role to me.'

We were rounding a point on the small island, looking out over a wide misty river and banks of jungle and palm. Great, rusting ships loaded with some mineral steamed out.

'What's in the ships?'

'Iron ore. From the mining. It's big business in Goa. I rather like the ships. I think they make the scene quite majestic. There's quite a few who are starting to get upset by them now though.'

'Who?'

'Environmentalists. They want the mining in the centre to stop. Say its destroying Goa. Of course it would be better if there were no industry at all here. But that isn't realistic. These people, *eco-warriors*, they

never get anywhere because they never seem to understand that people must make a living. They say we have
to protect paradise. But paradise doesn't exist. We've
all taken a bite out the apple. We must just get along
as well as we can. But here we are. This is my home.'

We had arrived at a white plaster bungalow with a
dark wooden roof. A veranda skirted round the length,
looking out on flowers and fruit trees dotted across the
lawn. As we opened the gate, two dogs bounded towards
us barking with excitement. I ran back out. I didn't
like dogs. But Sister Michael bent down and petted
them happily.

'These are my darlings. John and Luke. Come in;
it's OK, they won't hurt you. They are just looking
after me, aren't you? Come in.'

Shadowy steps led to a dark entrance hall. Sister
Michael flicked on lights to reveal a large and elegant
house.

'Maria?' called out Sister Michael. 'Maria?'

Wide doorways made it possible to see straight
through several rooms, filled with beautiful objects,
antique furniture and chandeliers.

'Wow,' I said.

'It's my husband's family home, such a solace to me
over the years. Why don't you sit down in the visitor's
room here, I have to make a phone call. There's cigarettes on the side table.'

It was a dark-green room stencilled with a border
of thistles. A crystal chandelier gave off heavy patinated
light. Taking a cigarette out from a carved wooden box,
I sat down on the sofa. I put my feet up, but then
thought better of it. I lit the cigarette with a silver

43

Tiffany lighter lying nearby. I coughed back up the smoke as soon as I inhaled. I hadn't tasted anything like it. I peered at the glowing cigarette. Murad's, it said on the filter.

An ex-nun, ex-actress who lived in a self-made museum and smoked heavy Turkish cigarettes. You couldn't make it up. I took out my notebook, reminding myself of the Google research I'd done on the head, the questions I wanted to ask, taking special note of what David Dryden had asked for. I could hear some faint murmuring from the room next door but couldn't make out what was being said.

There were a few photos on the wall. A well-to-do Goan family, some in suits, some in traditional Indian costume, all looking deadly serious. Another photo; a celebration. Europeans, smiling, sitting round a table set with wine and food and champagne. One girl stood out; large dramatic eyes, thick long hair, a melancholy expression. It was a young Sister Michael, Dorothea. She'd been a beauty.

'You found the Caperellis already. My cousin's wedding,' she said, coming upon me from behind, catching me unawares.

'Sorry to keep you waiting. The curate. He does go on sometimes, but I wanted to talk to him before I said anything to you,' she said.

Sister Michael took a cigarette, lit up and sat down.

'Now, what did you want to ask me? You're working for a new magazine. Touchstone?'

'Yes. That's right. Peter Bukowski is behind it. He's very keen on covering the story of the head. Devout Catholic apparently.'

'I know Peter. Very spiritual man. I met him when he visited the shrine. He donated to our Museum of Christian Art. Generously. I'm happy to help you out with this article if he's involved.'

I took a last inhale of my cigarette and looked around for an ashtray to put it out in. Sister Michael called out for Maria with such a level of impatience that, if she hadn't been such a refined woman, could have been classed as a yell.

'Sorry. My maid. She's not the most reliable woman. Hasn't put out an ashtray. Here, I'll get rid of it for you.'

She took the butt and lobbed it out the window, took a final drag of her own before throwing that out too. The environment clearly wasn't one of her passions.

'Now finally, we can begin. Fire away Ruby,' she said, settling herself on the opposite sofa, crossing her legs.

My interviews never went along the route I had planned. It didn't matter what you asked people, they knew what they wanted to tell you most of the time. What was most interesting was the space between your question and their response. I was looking forward to this talk. It had been a while since I had talked to someone so eloquent and so forthright. This woman liked talking and she seemed to enjoy making a dramatic effect, which was even better.

'I guess let's just start simply. What was your reaction when you found the head had been taken?'

Sister Michael turned her eyes to the ceiling before looking straight at me and began her performance.

'OK. Well, of course, absolute shock. Shock. It was

45

chaos after the shooting. Our first concern was the pilgrims. We thought we were in the middle of some kind of terrorist attack, though it seems now that no one was shot at. The Basilica was in ruins, pews overturned, windows, hundreds of years old, smashed to pieces. And then the shrine. No one could believe it. No one. The head ripped away so cruelly. The rest of the body hung down on one side, like it was nothing. No spirit, just a very old dead body. Awful to see. There was no blood. Just papery skin. It was like soot had rained down. All the marigolds were dusted with black. It was horrible.'

'You're on the board of the Basilica – do you or any of the other members have any idea who has taken the head? You must have talked about it?'

'Of course. We had a meeting with the police late last night – into the morning. None of us has slept at all. We have no real ideas. All I can think is that it is someone crazed in the mind. Someone who hates Saint Francis.'

'Why would they hate the saint?'

'He's a controversial figure, of course. Some of his conversion methods that have come to light recently were, let's say, a little extreme. And there are his letters which do not, to put it politely, talk well of the local population. The inquisition here, it's well, famous is the wrong word. Notorious. But the past is the past. Goans love Saint Francis, think of him as their protector. And he does help Goa. He's a huge tourist attraction. The most visited shrine in Asia. That could be another reason to steal the head. Simply from hate of Goa, to stop the tourists coming here.'

'There's no value to stealing the head? It couldn't be sold? Or even ransomed? I've read that there's a huge black market for Indian antiquities.'

'Ransomed – I hadn't thought of that. But sold, no. This isn't an antiquity. This is a relic. And even if this was stolen to sell, I really don't know any self-respecting Catholic who would want to buy such a morbid memento. It's the head of a corpse, for goodness sake.'

'A reporter on the TV said that this was a religious crime. Talked about the Babri Mosque. Could the stealing of the head be revenge?'

'Revenge? I don't follow.'

'Have you heard much about the bull's head in the north of Goa?'

'Sorry?'

'The Tambdi Surla Nandi? Apparently it's a well-loved Hindu murti. The head was sawn off a few days ago.'

Sister Michael stared at me blankly before answering.

'Ah, I think I saw it in the newspaper.'

'It's just an idea. I don't know. But these villagers were really angry, the one's I saw on TV. Talked about how the bull had protected them from missionaries – Saint Francis I assume. Is it just a coincidence that the stealing of one head came right after the other? Could this be a tit-for-tat crime?'

Sister Michael laughed, pulled out another cigarette.

'But that would suggest that someone from the Catholic Church went all the way up to that remote village to saw off the head of the bull for no reason. I don't think so. You haven't met the curate yet but I very much doubt it was anything to do with him. You'll see what I mean. No, I don't think so.'

'You sound very sure of that. There's no tension at all between the two communities here?'

'No. Look, Goa is a very unusual place. It's known for incredible tolerance. It always has been. There were hippies dancing naked on Anjuna beach when showing an ankle was considered the height of immorality in the rest of the country.'

'You make it sound idyllic. But it's not is it? That was the sixties. Goa now – it's known for drugs and corruption and mafia and murders. There's a lot of crime going on, a lot of money going through the state. Smuggling is a problem down at the port.'

'I'm afraid I don't know anything about this. We're rather isolated up here.'

She shook her head, pulled on her lower lip. Despite this lost look Sister Michael didn't seem like a woman who lived in isolation, who knew nothing of the outside world. She was too clever.

But she was getting tired, I was talking her out. She looked relieved when the door swung open. A large Goan woman with long grey hair strode in, probably around the same age as Sister Michael, this woman had not had the time, money or determination to keep herself so well. Her skin was furrowed around the brow and cheeks. Her middle had spread into her sagging breasts to make one large, shapeless mass. Perhaps what aged her most was her mouth, which pulled down at the sides like an angry fish. She had a brief conversation with Sister Michael in Konkani. Neither of the women looked like they particularly enjoyed each other's company.

'Maria – and myself – would like to know if you are staying for dinner,' said Sister Michael, smiling to me, recovering her composure.

I didn't have anything else to do. I didn't fancy another night in the bar with Fernando and Jake. I wondered whether Zim Moon had tried to call me. Maybe he just gave up when he heard a dead line on my phone. If he'd called at all.

'I'd love to. Thanks.'

'Excellent. We usually eat at half past seven. We have an hour or so. Are we done with the interview now?'

'Just a couple more questions.'

Sister Michael's eyes flicked out to the side. I saw she was losing patience, despite the Bukowski millions. I would have to be quick. I could always come back for more.

'Do you have any idea who the actual gunmen were?'

'There's plenty of gangs in Goa now. Local boys run by mafia types. The Israeli mafia, but more often the Russians now. If you pay them enough money they'll do anything, work for anyone. They're not loyal. If I were the police I would simply take up a big case of money to Anjuna and see who bites. Someone around there knows something about this. But who is really behind it? Whose idea this was? I'm not sure. I don't know. This crime took a lot of imagination and those young local boys, I don't think they're that creative.'

'OK. Maybe I'll go up to Anjuna myself. If I find anything out I'll let you know. Final question. Security. Have you got any? Did you have any before this happened?'

'We have, of course, hundreds of steward volunteers

to help with the festival. They keep a close eye on the shrine. Unfortunately we didn't think to arm them.'

'No, why would you? This was a unique crime. But what about the rest of the year? And the rest of the churches in Goa? You have some beautiful antiquities, some very precious gold and silver. What's done to protect these?'

'Ah – well – the best pieces go into the Museum of Christian Art right around the corner here. It's temperature controlled to make sure these pieces are preserved in the best possible way.'

'And the rest? Does the church have an inventory of what it owns here?'

'That I'm afraid, is out of my jurisdiction. Each town and village has a council that I assume looks after this.'

'There's not a central list? Or a central system?'

'No, no I don't think so. I don't think it's been an issue. But I'll have a think should I? Rather tiring talking so much. I'm not used to it. Would you like me to show you round? I've spent the last thirty years restoring this place. A labour of love if ever there was one.'

With that, she introduced me to her house; her companion, her solace, the place she built up in her strong moments, to console her when she was weak. The rooms and the objects which filled up the hole her husband seemed to have left.

6

Sister Michael took me from the entrance hall, re-painted every two years because of the decaying effect of the humidity, to what she called the conversation room. A long, delicate chamber containing three love chairs covered in blue velvet. Fresh flowers stood in tiled vases. A statue of an angel, wings spread, held out scales.

'That you will gather the souls of the righteous and the wicked, place us on your great scales and weigh our deeds. That if we have been loving and kind, you will take the key from around our neck and open the gates of Paradise, inviting us to live there forever. And that if we have been selfish and cruel, it is you who will banish us,' said Sister Michael.

I looked at her blankly. I had no idea what she talking about.

'Saint Michael. One of the archangels. He's usually depicted with a sword, he's known for fighting satan, protecting the church. He's also known for weighing up our deeds, saving our souls at the hour of death. We're all given a chance to repent our sins by Saint Michael; before the devil can get to us. I love that about him. He stands for real justice, when it matters. So many men appear so holy when they are the least. I found this statue, in Rachol Seminary, in the south of Goa. One of the first pieces I found after my husband died. I took it as a good sign; that I was meant to stay here. That my namesake was here by my side, protecting me, looking out for my soul.'

'Is that why you took his name? Because he saves souls?'

Sister Michael gave me a short smile.

'No. I have to confess the reason I took his name was very shallow indeed. I was in Rome, in love.'

'With your husband?'

'Good God no. I was about to take orders. I was just infatuated with the city, the history, the beauty of it all, like a lovesick teenager. I spent far too long gazing up at the Sistine Chapel. That's why I choose Michael. He's up there, you see. Perhaps, secretly, it was a nod to Michaelangelo too. Of course I've grown up since then.'

She laughed a tinkling, controlled little laugh and led me into a small ballroom, blazing with light, reflected off large gilt mirrors, held by stone hands. Sister Michael turned her head away from me and suddenly stamped on the floor.

'This is Indonesian ship wood. Hard as nails; nothing can eat it; no damp can ruin it. I had terrible trouble with termites at first. The roof was completely rotten. I replaced it with fibreglass and painted it, you wouldn't know it was anything other than original. But the floor needed to breathe, we're in touch with it every day, you see. It needed to be wood. It was the biggest expense of my life I think, shipping the wood over here. My God, I had to find clever ways of paying for this. Do watch yourself though; I've just had it polished, for Christmas. It's rather slippy.'

I could feel my feet sliding around slightly and held on to a grand piano in the corner of the room for safety.

'The chandeliers are Belgian crystal and the floor is Italian marble and that vase on the piano? It doesn't look much but it is actually Ming. Luckily these were all still here when I arrived. No one had stolen these.'

'Stolen?'

'My husband came from an old Goa family. His father was a well-known newspaper editor, one of the main agitators for independence. Early on in the struggle, his newspaper offices were raided and he was sent into exile in Portugal. Francis's mother was left with three young sons. She fled to Bangalore with her family and left the house for the maids. They looted the place. You couldn't get decent staff even then. No one was there to stop them until Francis returned to restore the house.'

'He's the reason you left the convent?'

'Well, it's rather hard to be a nun and be married,' she said, icily.

She was annoyed I had bought it up. I tried to think of something to appease her. I fixated on the Ming vase, a gentle turquoise colour with gold leaves skirting it. The base was the size of a large, heavy head, which spouted up into a tall funnel.

'I don't think I've ever seen a Ming vase so close.' I said, touching it gently.

'Please – don't,' cried Sister Michael.

I leapt back.

'I'm sorry. I don't mean to be rude; it's just that. Well I am rather protective of it. Not just because of how much it's worth. The sentiment too you know.'

'I'm sorry. I didn't want to upset you.'

'No, really, I'm sorry. I have to let things go a little more. I've said I will host the Convent school's Christmas party tomorrow. I agreed months ago and for the past few weeks I've been having nightmares about this Ming Vase. I'm sure it's going to get broken. But I can't really back out of it now. I'm picking up the decorations from the Basilica tomorrow.'

'It sounds fun,' I said weakly.

A grandfather clock chimed seven-thirty.

'Mings are much sturdier then they look. Perhaps we will be fine. It's time for dinner. I usually dine in the kitchen but I asked Maria to serve us in the dining room. It's so little used; a guest is a good excuse.'

The dining room was at the end of the house. A long table carved with fruits and dragons and vines stood on a tiled floor. Two places were set formally with soup bowl, side plate and heavy silver. The porcelain all had JB engraved upon them in blue.

'Joseph Braganza. It was Francis's mother's father. Her family were big landowners here, made their money in coconuts. They had many things imported. This dinner set was for forty people, shipped from Wedgewood in England. Most of it had been sold when I got here. I scavenged every antique shop in Goa to find the missing pieces. It's not at all complete, but I can serve ten people,' said Sister Michael.

The ever-working Maria came in carrying a large soup tureen.

Sister Michael flicked her eyes up to her maid and said something in Konkani. Maria smiled and served me a white soup flecked with slithers of nut.

'Cream of almond soup.'

'It's delicious.'

And it was. I dived in straight away. Sister Michael waited with her hands in her lap for some moments before she picked up her spoon.

'Maria's an excellent cook. She doesn't get a chance to practise too much with me. I eat very little in the evenings. I used to have a huge appetite when I was younger, but one must adjust their habits with age.'

I finished my soup and watched Sister Michael carefully sipping hers. After a couple of mouthfuls she put her spoon down and began conversation politely.

'I've heard Delhi's changed a lot. It's years and years since I've been. It must be fun, living there, working as a journalist.'

'It was. Not so much anymore. A friend of mine died suddenly. We were living together. I've given up our flat now. I couldn't live there anymore.'

Sister Michael looked up from her plate.

'Oh, I'm sorry.'

I shook my head. Sympathy was awful.

'Was it, was your friend, a man?'

'Yes, but it wasn't like that. He was my best friend. We were so close, but we were just friends.'

'In my experience it's never that simple with men.

I'm sorry. One of the hardest things I ever did was pick up my life after Francis died. It was so sudden. I had nothing left of him, of anything. Just this house. I made it my vocation. It helps having something to focus on. You have your work.'

I smiled weakly. I wasn't about to go into my recent inability to put one word in front of the other with this woman.

'And your faith, Ruby,' she said, blowing on her spoon. 'The church, of course, helps enormously.'

I felt sheepish. She had assumed I was religious, Catholic; going to the festival of Saint Francis, working for Bukowski. In truth, I hardly ever went near a church, only to visit Stephen. But then, if I visited his grave, was that faith? I wasn't sure. I never prayed to God, not since I was a child. I had mostly believed in some kind of divine luck which always seemed to descend when I most needed it. Better to be born lucky than rich, that's how my father had described it, always said I'd got lucky. Since Stephen died that confidence had left me. Now I really did want patterns, some sense that there was a plan or reason in life. But that didn't mean diving head-first into the Catholic church. I would try anything with incense, it was all the same to me, meditating in front of buddhas, sitting in a temple, visiting the shrine of some famous imam, flying to Goa to see a miraculous saint. I tried to think of an answer for Sister Michael, something in me that was kind of Catholic, that would warm her towards me and help me get more quotes.

'Well, I feel guilty about a lot of things. Guilty. It's one of my main emotions at the moment. I feel guilty about Stephen. Maybe I'm worried about what God makes of me.'

Sister Michael snorted. It was the most un-ladylike sound she had made so far.

'You shouldn't. I gave up feeling guilty long ago. It's such an awful, useless emotion. It's one thing I hate about the Church, the way they force people to feel so bad, just for being human. It's what killed Francis I think. And I suffered terribly, for a long time. But I had to get over it, to survive. You should too.'

She was adamant. I felt rather offended. I'd carried my guilt round with me preciously for months, feeding it, tending it. It had become part of me; it filled some of the hole Stephen left behind. And I deserved it. She didn't even know what I had done.

'I did something bad. It's hard not to feel guilty. I wrote about Stephen's death, to help me get a byline in a national newspaper. I used him to get ahead. I found out he'd been taking heroin and his death wasn't murder at all, which is what people had thought. He'd just been completely gone.

He'd leant up against a fence he hadn't noticed was loose and fallen in the river. His family won't speak to me now. They hate me, they think I've ruined his name.'

Sister Michael mused for a few seconds, before giving a slight shrug and pushing her empty bowl away.

'No death is noble. You were just trying to make your living. Everyone has to make their living. This is the truth. You should clear your conscience, move on,' she said.

I was rather amazed. This woman didn't bat an eyelid at the crime I had carried around with me for so long.

And she was a nun, an ex-nun at least. Maybe I really was feeling too guilty.

Maria had cleared away our soup bowls and was now preparing to serve us the main course from an ivory tray. Setting down a rectangular dish and a bowl of green vegetables in coconut milk she cut her pie with a silver knife and served me. Creamy sauce oozed out from beneath the pastry.

'Oh. It's Braganza's Oyster pie. This is a real treat. And Maria must have used some white wine in it. We should have a glass.'

Sister Michael talked to Maria, who duly went off after serving us both.

'She has opened a good bottle. A Sancerre. I don't mind her using wine in the cooking. I know she doesn't drink herself and we have a whole cellar that rarely gets opened. I enjoy good wine, but I find drinking alone makes me morose or a little wild in the mind. In company I am fine.'

Maria returned carrying two small crystal glasses full of yellow wine. She set mine down first. Sister Michael leant forward as she was serving her.

'Oh there is a chip in this glass.'

Maria pulled back and caught her gold bangle on Sister Michael's cuff. I heard a rip and a splash.

'Oh,' cried Sister Michael in frustration. Her button had ripped off and had pinged into her wine. She began talking fast and hard Konkani to Maria, who looked apologetic at first, then upset, then obediently angry.

'I told her she shouldn't wear her bangles while serving dinner. She's upset. But it's not the first time something like this has happened. They are so heavy, they knock against the china and I am sure that's how the glass got chipped. I haven't said she has to take them off the whole time. Just when she is serving formally or cleaning the china.'

'It seems fair enough. Why is she so upset?'

'They're her wedding bangles. Every woman has them in Goa; Christians too. Even I had them. But it's not difficult to take them off for an hour. At least she still has a husband. And a family. Maria thinks I live like a fairy tale queen here. But really? A lonely old woman with only antiques for company? It's not the stuff that dreams are made of. Is it so wrong to try and protect the things I have, that I care for?'

7

The Garden of Eden. Adam and Eve, naked and smiling, surrounded by birds and fruit and plants and animals. Adam stared happily at Eve's gratuitously large bosom. Eve herself was holding an apple and giving him a knowing smile, as if she already understood sin and liked it. Snakes with glittering eyes watched the scene entwined, forming a border. I spread my hands out across the bedcover, a faded embroidered red.

I'd spent a night in Sister Michael's museum home and woke in her guest bedroom. She hadn't wanted me to leave alone so late the night before. The police had warned everyone in Old Goa to be extra careful. They were combing the area but couldn't guarantee it was safe. Roads weren't the only way up to the convents and the churches here. There was the river too. Crime was moving down the coast from the beaches. The stolen head could be just the start of problems in Old Goa.

'If we had a man in the house to walk you down it

would be fine. But we don't. It's just Maria and myself. Two old women,' Sister Michael had said.

I was happy to stay. The bed was a lot more comfortable then the sorry mattress at Fernando's. I'd called him to let him know where I was. He hadn't seem too bothered. I could hear the news on in the background. Still no cricket for Jake.

I lay back on the pillows. It was early. Small skylights flickered a thick grey light across my face. The sun wasn't up yet. I closed my eyes. I could sleep a while longer. I'd had a restless night, full of dreams. I'd been back at Delhi airport with the guy I'd met, Zim Moon, and the head of Saint Francis. We were all drinking beer. Saint Francis had to sip his through a straw that we managed to push through his papery mouth.

As I was just dozing off again, there was a knock at the door. Maria, looking unhappy, bringing tea on a tray. I took it, gave up sleeping and sipped it, watched a growing pattern of light dance across Adam and Eve and the snakes. Sister Michael had found the bedcover in the laundry room of her old convent.

'They couldn't bear to see those naked bodies. I had to help them out, take it off their hands,' she'd told me airily. It sounded more like stealing than helping, to me, but I hadn't said anything, just listened to the stories she delighted in telling me.

In the sixteenth and seventeenth century, Goa had been world famous for embroidery and the Saint Monica convent had been the centre of the trade. They sold to every royal court in Europe. At some point the designs got too risqué, the nuns too imaginative, too lascivious. The trade was stopped. I could just imagine the closeted nuns sitting in rows, sewing silently in the twilight; getting hotter and hotter, creating more and more erotic designs for royal households, until one day the mother superior had enough and ordered them all to start on the tea cosies.

There was a holler at my door.

'Ruby?! I'm taking the dogs for a walk. Down to the museum. I think you should come. Can you be ready in ten minutes?'

'Right. Of course,' I called out weakly. I wondered what time it actually was. It didn't seem reasonable to be getting out of bed yet but I thought it would be impolite to refuse. It clearly hadn't crossed Sister Michael's mind I wouldn't want to go.

It really was very early. A white mist clung to the road. The trees were black silhouettes against a just yellowing sky. The two dogs, Luke and John, mouths open, panting pink, were outrageously lively for this time in the morning. Their flesh and fur flew about them, trying to keep up with their jumping bodies. Their eyes were wet with stupid happy innocence, mostly fixed on Sister Michael, who they adored. Racing ahead of us, they couldn't help but leap back again to make sure she was still there; walking just behind, watching them, approving of their games. She constantly reassured them, rubbing their fat necks and chatting happy nonsense. I was surprised at how affectionate she was. She treated her dogs a lot better than her housekeeper.

'They really love you,' I said.

'Do you think?' she glanced up at me, flushed happy for a second. 'I love them so much. I just don't know what I'll do without them. I couldn't take them back to England. They wouldn't be free. I'll miss them so much when I leave . . . Oh. And this. Maybe I shouldn't leave.'

We had rounded the bend in the road and had come across the wide river, rippling pink and orange under the rising sun. Sister Michael stopped to drink in the scene, overwhelmed and emotional. She seemed like a girl, not the perfectly controlled ice-queen of the night before.

'It was such a fight, after Francis died. I swore I wasn't going to give in, I wasn't going to simply go back home to my parents. It was hard, to survive here, alone. Judged by everyone. They blamed me. I hated that. But Francis, he loved this place so much. He had so much passion for Goa. I wanted to stay here and keep that alive. Seeing all this always reminded me why I was staying. This was what stopped me going back. I couldn't go back to that closed-in indoor life. It would have been narrow, sad. I don't know if I can, even now. But, I've got to, I think,' she said.

'Why? Why don't you stay?'

'It scares me, getting old here. I just, suddenly, I'm too lonely . . . You know, when you lose someone, the pain, it changes you. It can destroy you, it can make you bitter. Or it can make you stronger. I've always been very proud – how I coped with Francis's death. How independent I became. You're like that too. I can see. But don't be too independent Ruby. Don't turn away from people who want to help. One day you'll need it and there'll be no one there anymore.'

I thought I understood. A strange disconnected

feeling from everything and everyone around me had hung about since Stephen died. I'd just wanted to be alone, wading through the misery in my own time. My parents had asked me to come home, but I wouldn't. I had a sense that the gnawing feeling of missing them, of missing my friends, of familiar shops and places, would simply be replaced by dead depression once back. Life closing in on me, ever smaller choices.

'*Saudade*. That's what the Portuguese call it. A constant feeling of absence, the sadness that something's missing. It came from the time of the Great Portugal Discoveries. Men sailed away to God know's where. Who knew if they would ever come back? Not their wives. The women just had to live with the loneliness, never moving on. *Saudade*. I've felt it for so long, for Francis, for Goa. I can't remember ever feeling anything else.'

'Goa? But you're still here. How can you miss it?'

'It's not the same place. It's not the way it used to be. I'm homesick for the home that I've lost, that was here. Staying isn't the answer. Better to leave and be content in London, my memories intact. Better to remember a man as he was when you first married him, young and fresh and kind; not the murderous old pirate he would become. I would prefer my husband to stay away. Not to return. Do you see?'

I nodded. I did understand, but I think I would have preferred my husband back, in whatever shape. He might even have made some money as a pirate. I wasn't idealistic enough to let myself suffer for too long. That's why I had come here after all. To try and work out how to bring myself back to life. Sister Michael was a romantic. She had enjoyed the drama of her own tragedy for so long, and now it was too late to change it to anything else.

She pushed her hands into the pockets of her jacket, shrugged her shoulders and shook her head.

'Come, I'm rattling on just because I see a little of me in you. I probably shouldn't. I'm getting old. Let's get to the museum.'

The Museum of Christian Art was a small building attached to the convent of Saint Monica. High ceilings, perfectly controlled air, artfully exposed beams, glass cases beneath spotlights.

'The best in Goan Christian art. The best in Asian Christian art, is here. Take a look around, I'm sure you could write about the displays here. It would be good for Bukowski to read about it I think,' said Sister Michael, switching on overhead lights. We were the first people here, before the attendants or any visitors.

I walked carefully from case to case, my footsteps making a hollow echo on the wooden floor. An ornate silver chalice found in the attic of Chandor church. One ivory statue of the virgin Mary dressed in a sari from the seventeenth century, found in Rachol Seminary. An image Saint Margaret of Antioch, riding the back of a fish, eyes closed, finger high, like a school mistress about to lecture her class.

The relics were artfully spaced and displayed. There just weren't very many. Where exactly were the Bukowski millions spent? Not on the actual pieces. Perhaps on the state-of-the-art preservation system.

'Ruby! Come and have a look at this. Tell me if it is in the right position.'

I found Sister Michael standing at the back of the room, regarding the display she had just fixed against the wall. It was the shard of angel glass, the one she gave me to look after, at the festival.

Thick lead shaped the face of a pudgy angel, eyes closed, cheeks blown out as if in a tantrum. His face was clear; of old, yellowed glass. Surrounding him were greens and blues and pinks. I liked the sharp shattered edges, they made the picture new. Like the angel was living in the real world, not simply part of an age-old myth. Sister Michael had an eye, had talent, to find such beauty in the midst of all that mayhem.

'It's amazing really. The Basilica was built in the sixteenth century. The Portuguese simply told the local workmen what they wanted, and they found a way to make it. They found a way to create stained glass without ever having seen it or learnt about it. And they made it their own. Look at the colours, those pinks and greens. They're tropical colours. And look what they've done to the angel. Can you see it has a tail?'

I looked closely. It had, Sister Michael was right. It had a green tail.

'More like a devil really.'

'No! Yes! You're exactly right. This is what I love so much about Goa, about this art. It's a mixed up crazy pot of beliefs.'

'People worshipped devils here?'

'No, no. But they worshipped snakes, you see. Nagas are holy in Hinduism. The angel here is a snake as well. That's what the man who painted this imagined. The closest thing he knew to a Christian angel was a Hindu Naga and this is what he created. A snake that was an

66

angel and an angel that was a snake. You find them all over Goa; nowhere else in the world.'

'Sounds confusing. Didn't Satan pretend to be a snake?'

Sister Michael turned to me, her eyes glittering and slitted.

'Exactly. He was an angel too don't forget.'

I had the feeling Sister Michael had a bit of both in her as well. A nun who left the church to marry a priest. Why had everyone blamed her for his death? Had she seduced him? She hadn't wanted to talk about it last night, but she couldn't stop talking about him. Twenty, thirty years later, this man was still constantly on her mind.

She traced her hand over the glass.

'Francis first showed me the snake, the tail behind the angel. After confession in the Basilica. He was the one who told me about the Nagas and the myths and the history. He seduced me with it all. He made me fall in love with him with his beautiful stories.'

'He made you fall in love with him?'

Sister Michael turned back to me. 'Of course, he didn't realise he was doing it. He believed in the church. He believed so much in his vocation. People said it was my fault. That I had used my looks to tempt him. That I was a snake. They called me that you know? But he should have been stronger than me. He was seven years older than me. It just amazes me how innocent men can be. And then, then he died. He died and left me alone,' she said.

There was a vicious tone to her voice. Despite her appearance, time hadn't worn down any of the edges to her unhappiness. It was as sharp as the shards of stained glass. It scared me, how she'd held on to everything. I could easily become like that. I was doing that now. Not forgetting Stephen, not moving on, going over everything that had happened in my head. Keeping myself apart and angry.

'Who are *they*? The church? Is that who you mean?'

'The church, Francis's family, Francis even. Everything, everyone, against me. They said he died of a broken heart. It's just rubbish. It was coronary heart disease. What his father died of and his grandfather too. But he was only thirty-four. He shouldn't have died that young. He died because he let the talk, the gossip, get to him . . . He couldn't give himself up to me.'

There was a banging sound. The front door of the museum was being opened up by the attendant. It jolted Sister Michael out of the past.

'Nine o'clock already. I have a meeting with the curate. Are you hungry? I'll get Maria to make you some eggs when we arrive home,' she said.

I waited in the kitchen for Maria while Sister Michael went to meet the curate. I was hungry. My stomach rumbled. Maria didn't show up. I wondered if I should just make something myself, but I didn't want to be rude. I decided to ask Sister Michael first if she would mind and wandered out to find her.

I smelt smoke and heard two voices coming out of the conversation room. Instead of knocking I listened at the door instead. This wasn't an admirable habit of mine but it was interesting.

'Rome have been on the phone all morning. And

68

journalists. All wanting an interview. The news is every-where. All over the TV,' said a shrill male voice.

'Just keep calm Father Jonathan.'

'Well, I have to talk to Rome! They are furious. They want to know about our security. They want to know what we've been doing to protect Saint Francis. They want to know if he's been kept in the right environ-ment. They want to do a forensic test.'

'And what did you say?'

'I said of course everything here is safe but we just, we just didn't ever think that this would happen. They're sending two cardinals over. Not one, two. What are we going to do?'

'When they ring next give them my number. I speak Italian; I understand them. It will better for me to speak to them.'

'And the Head of the Goan Senate has been down. He's had the Directorate of Tourism and Culture in New Delhi on the phone all morning. They are furious. Furious. Another blow to Goa. The state is becoming a publicity nightmare and they blame it on us.'

'Jonathan. Just keep calm. This is going to blow over. I can do interviews if you like, as the Basilica spokesman. I've done it before. You're not up to it. OK? The doctor has told you not to put yourself in stressful situations. It has a terrible effect on you. You nearly ended up in hospital after the last exposition. You need to look after yourself.'

'Yes, yes, you're right. I'm to give Rome you're mobile number and your landline?'

'Yes, yes.'

Sister Michael let out a long sigh. 'I suppose I had

better come with you now to pick up those ridiculous baubles for these children. I have a delivery being picked up at midday. I have to be back, it's important. I can't believe we're so close to Christmas. I'm already receiving cards and I've sent none out myself.'

They were coming towards the door. I slid through to the room opposite and found myself in the library. I pulled out a book from the shelf and plonked down on a chair, opening a page at random just as Sister Michael swung into the room. A greying, gaunt man with a puckering mouth stood behind her.

'Ah Ruby? *Tu parle Francais?*'

I looked at her blankly before realising she had said something about French. The book in my hands, I saw, was a copy of Montaigne's essays – not in translation. I wracked my brain for some schoolbook phrase with which to answer.

'*Un petit peau,*' I said, blushing. I hoped I looked humble, not guilty.

'*Tres bien,*' Sister Michael replied, approvingly. '*Et tu es ca va? Tu es faim?*'

This was painful. So painful. I nodded awkwardly. The man behind gazed on the scene gormlessly. I took affirmative action to change the conversation back to English.

'Ah – I was wondering – could I possibly check my emails? Have you got a computer here?'

'Yes, of course, it's the cranky old thing in the corner there. I'll turn it on for you. Have you had some breakfast?'

'Ah, no actually. I couldn't find Maria.'

Sister Michael sighed loudly. 'I don't know what

happens to her sometimes. She is so unreliable. I'll try and find something. You can have tea at least. Father Jonathan and I were about to have some.'

'Father Jonathan? Curate of the shrine? Would it be possible to have an interview with you? I'm writing an article about Saint Francis. What happened yesterday?'

Father Jonathan looked at Sister Michael, who answered for him.

'I'm afraid, Ruby, it's church policy that only the spokesman of the Basilica can speak to the media. I'm going to take that on as a member of the board and the curate of our Museum of Christian Art. You've got just about as much as you can get from the church right now, sorry.'

She was back to the business-like face of the church I had interviewed last night. Sister Michael went off to the kitchen and I waited as the computer jumped and buzzed slowly into life. It really was an old monster. The priest sat slumped on one of the chairs, staring silently into space. I didn't bother trying to make conversation.

'I've put the kettle on, it won't be long. Ah – Ruby – no don't use my profile. It has a password anyway; you can't get in. Just log on as a guest please.'

'Of course.'

Sister Michael bustled back to the kitchen and after some squeaks and hisses from the computer I eventually managed to log on.

Nothing much. I wondered if Zim Moon would get in touch. I'd told him I was on Facebook. He hadn't. A stuffy note from Claudia at the Embassy saying that she understood my dilemma but policy was policy and they were always inundated with calls for help from Goa. Passport trade was a problem down there, they were already working with the port police, they couldn't just hand a new one out to anyone who asked. I needed an address in Goa, the name of a resident there and a police report if I wanted to get my passport delivered. Or there was the train back to Delhi. Twenty-four hours. And nowhere to go when I got back. I didn't want to do that. Besides, I had this article to write now. There was an email from David.

Dear Ruby,

Well done getting the interview with the ex-nun. Quick work. I do hope she turns up something interesting.

I've been reading up myself and you're right – it looks like the man to talk to is Inspector Srinvasen. I know you said he wasn't doing one to one's – but could you try please?

Also, while you're in Old Goa, perhaps you could get a little colour? Some descriptions, atmosphere? What other treasures are lolling about? I see none of the TV stations have been allowed in to film. Our chance to prove that the pen is mightier than High Definition Z1 cameras.

Keep in touch and let me know if you need any help from this end.

David xx

'What are you doing?' said Father Jonathan in a thin voice. I'd forgotten he was there. I turned to find him craning his neck out of his thin collar, trying to look at the computer screen.

'Ah just checking my emails.'

'I'm hungry,' he said plaintively, casting his eyes down to the side. I wasn't sure if he was talking to me or simply complaining. I wasn't sure what to say, ended up just looking at him.

Despite his wasted appearance, he was a large man. He had the sallow, leathery face of someone who has lived in the tropics for years and a slightly jaundice colour. Maybe he was recovering from some equatorial disease. Sister Michael had certainly seemed worried about him.

'Here we go Father, I found some coconut macaroons Maria has made. Whatever else I complain about, I can't complain about her cooking. These are usually delicious,' said Sister Michael, returning with a teapot and tray of porcelain cups and saucers.

We drank our tea without much conversation. The curate was like a large black cloud, putting a damp chill over anything. At one point he looked up from slurping his tea and said 'We're all in trouble', but then just went back to mechanically working his way through the biscuits, stuffing them in his mouth with his huge hands.

Sister Michael, for the most part, ignored Father Jonathan and ate very little. She took small bites of a single macaroon that she left teetering on her saucer.

She sipped at her tea thoughtfully and continued to look at the bottom of her cup when she had finished. I offered her more but she refused, licking her finger and picking up some dry biscuit crumbs, placing them in her mouth carefully. I asked her if it was OK to get my passport sent to her. She agreed straight away.

'Of course. Father Jonathan and I really have to go now. We have to get these Christmas decorations. The party is tomorrow and I really have to be back here in the house for midday. I have someone coming to pick up a delivery. You wanted to look around didn't you? Come back later and we'll sort it out then.'

8

Old Goa is a ghost town. One of those haunted places, ornately established with mighty wealth and then deserted. The Portuguese built so many cathedrals and churches in the small port city it became known through the world as the 'Rome of the East'. It was where Xavier landed when he arrived in India. But plague came and the population fled, leaving the grand designs and the statues and the gold to the rats and the creepers.

It was eerily silent now, another world from the feast day, with only the odd nun scurrying past. I could have been roaming around another century if it hadn't been for the police tape wound round the Basilica. I sat down in the shade of a tree beside the church, watched some forensic officers work on the ground around it. It seemed a pretty useless task after so many people had trampled their way across this path.

David wanted me to talk with Srinvasen. That was going to be difficult. He said he wasn't talking to the press. I'd googled him and read previous interviews.

They didn't paint an easy character. Famously clever, he was known for solving the most difficult crimes and pursuing art thieves with bloody mindedness.

His most famous case was the Lokari goat-headed goddess, a 1,000 year old sandstone statue, stolen in the middle of the night from a temple in Uttar Pradesh. Srinvasen found scatterings of pink sandstone in the out-house toilet of a priest, the man who had apparently wailed the loudest for the loss of the statue. Through what inspector Srinvasen described as 'hard-nosed interrogation' he traced the statue back through implicit customs officials to a well-known British auction house. Srinvasen flew personally to London, stopping the India auction just as the goat-headed goddess was about to go under the hammer and came back a Hindu hero. He'd worn traditional Indian dress for the photographers at the airport; set the goddess down as soon as they'd reached the ground and bowed before it to cheers. It looked like he was busy creating his own myths, his own god-like status. Perhaps his inaccessibility was all part of the image.

A thin, moustached Tamil, he'd grown up in the shadow of the famous temples of Madurai, one of the oldest, continuously inhabited cities in the world. In a rare *Times of India* interview, soon after his Lokari triumph, Srinvasen recounted watching, as a child, the old priests of Madurai dress, bathe, feed and prostrate in front of ancient statues of Siva, Parvati, Ganesha. A deeply religious Hindu, the inspector believed that these were not lifeless bits of stone, but images in which the gods themselves lived.

'When someone steals an idol from a temple, they

are stealing a god. They are taking the life and the spirit out of that village. People are bereaved. Their lives are turned upside down. I've seen grown men bow down to a pile of stones in desperation. It hurts me very much,' he said.

He was also highly competitive and had a habit of offending every police force that he visited. In one press conference he claimed that the local officer in charge of the Lokari idol was a drunken, meat-eating Pandit who wasn't fit to step inside a temple, let alone investigate a theft. The man was sitting next to him. Maybe another reason he no longer did interviews was because some higher authority had decided to limit the damage he caused to state relations.

Either way, an exclusive interview with the man seemed just about impossible. But David's request for Old Goa colour? Atmosphere? That was easier. A small hill-like island, thick with jungle, dotted with churches and cathedrals; it couldn't be a more picturesque setting for a tropical crime. I would start at the top and work my way down with my notebook.

On the highest point of the peninsula stood Santa Maria Cathedral, about the size of a large village church. Whitewashed and unassuming, ship horns and bird calls echoed round the nave. It was completely empty except for a lonely altar and a small statue of the Virgin Mary standing on a snake. Where was everything? I needed more colour than this. I wanted banners and statues and altars. Gold and silver. The pieces in the museum were all very well, but why wasn't there anything in the churches?

Back at the Basilica, the forensics team were eating

lunch and getting yellow curry stains down their white overalls. I went on, to the Se Cathedral, where I had tried to find some quiet on the day of the festival.

The cavernous old building made Christianity in the tropics look like a losing battle; pale yellow plaster struggling against the monsoon, big patches of damp running down the walls. Creepers had begun clinging and suffocating the structure; vegetation was closing in. The air inside was dusty and dark. A couple of bats hung high in the eaves. I sat down on one of the rickety pews. At least they had banners here. And statues. Saint Francis of course. And another saint, nearby me, holding a small child. 'Saint Anthony, patron saint of lost causes' explained a sign above.

Two nuns, around my age I thought, neat and sad-looking, entered the church. They had a bag of candles with them and lit them all round the foot of Saint Anthony. It began to look like his feet were on fire. They placed little prayer cards with pictures of Saint Francis in the arms of the saint and knelt down to pray. I could just imagine them, lolling about the convent, so upset about their saint, hatching this plan. It was over-romantic, female, dramatic; the product of bored, suspicious minds. It put me off joining the convent.

I wandered further up the church. It was empty, apart from one figure, on the front bench, hunched over in prayer, a large hoodie covering his face. Who on earth would wear an oversized sweatshirt in this heat? I got a rush when I realised. Zim Moon, the guy from the airport, the guy from LA.

I sidled into the pew.

'Hey,' I said quietly. 'Is that you?'

He turned and pushed his hood away from his face. He looked as pale as ever, though the black bags under his eyes had faded to a slightly lighter shade of purple.

'Oh my God. Praying does work. They've just been answered. Here you are,' he said.

'Very funny,' I whispered.

'No really, I was looking for you,' he said.

He put his hand on my waist. I got a jolt. That feeling. That human touch. Not the touch of your mother, or your friend or even your boyfriend of years. I hadn't felt it for a long time, but I recognised it straight away. Unmistakeable. A poker heat spreading from the spot, moving down to your stomach. I wanted more of it straight away. It was never enough. It was a touch that wouldn't stop burning till you satiated it. It had nothing to do with your head, nothing to do with your heart even. It was bodily and unpredictable and always pretty dangerous. Much more effective than drugs or alcohol or prayer in making you feel alive – and completely inappropriate in a church.

'Let's go outside. We can't talk in here,' I said.

'I need to say some prayers first.'

'What for?'

'The usual. Can you wait?'

I nodded. He took longer than I thought he would. Fifteen minutes just sitting there, his head in his hands. We walked out into the sunlight together and made for the shade of a nearby tree. The same tree that had sheltered the nun selling mango drinks on the day of the festival. In the distance I could see the forensics back to work around the Basilica. A plain-clothes policeman on his mobile, gesticulating. I felt strangely light-headed, over-heated. It could have been the sun, making me suddenly so hot after the cool dark church.

'I didn't have you down as religious,' I said.

Zim shook his head.

'I'm not. I'm not. Just sometimes. I don't know. It's my mother. Catholic, Italian family. Always praying. She's got this black lace veil from Donna Karan. Any whiff of a funeral she's there, wearing this thing. She would love it here. Love it.'

'All the churches?'

'Not just that. The stolen head too. It's her two passions. Religion and nasty crime. All we've got in our house is the Bible, James Ellroy and Dashiel Hammet. That police tape. It would give her such a fizz. She watches all the cop shows. She likes the true-life crime stories, the murders, the shoot-outs. Though they're pretty much the same as the made-up ones. It all looks the same to me.'

'God, she sounds mad . . . I mean, sorry. I don't know her.'

Zim shook her head.

'No, she is. Problem is she was beautiful. Of course she was, my dad wouldn't have settled for anyone else but a beauty. But she's fifty now and she hasn't got anything else but God and her crime books. Oh, and botox. Those botox bills are through the roof.'

'I've got a theory, all mothers are mad. I think it might be childbirth that does it to them first. They put their whole lives to one side to look after their children, and then, when the kids leave, they go a bit bonkers. I've never met a normal, reasonable sane mother over the age of fifty. I just haven't. I don't think my mother

80

ever had a grip on reality, but her nuttiness got decidedly worse after my brother left. She's replacing Christmas with a pagan Winter Solstice this year. She's trying to get my dad to slaughter a sheep in the garden. He doesn't want to. Sometimes I think I should go back home and look after them a bit more.'

Zim laughed, which is what I wanted him to do. He still didn't look like he'd recovered from his trip to Thailand. There was a waxy look to his face, pale and sticky. His hands were shaking slightly and I could see his bones round his jaw. I felt sorry for him, wanted to cheer him up. It was horrible, being ill and alone.

'How did you get past the police barrier? Didn't you see all those journalists camped out? It's practically impossible to get in here,' I asked.

'I called up my dad's client Paulo. He's some big shot. Owns half the coast and a load of the port too. Said I wanted to get into Old Goa. He sorted it out. The guard on the gate knew I was coming.'

'Why though? What are you doing here?'

'I was looking for you. I wasn't kidding, in the church. I called you but the line was dead. Then I saw all that shit with the head on CNN. I thought something might have happened to you. I called your guesthouse – Fernando's right? He said you had stayed over here in Old Goa.'

I could feel myself flush. He'd come looking for me. He'd been worried about me. I never would have thought a stranger, especially a stranger like Zim, would make so much effort. I thought when I'd lost my phone that that would be it. I'd never see him again. I hadn't let myself think about it too much, but I'd been disappointed. He'd been good company. I didn't know what would come out his mouth, what he would start thinking about next. I liked that. It was fun, exciting. Unpredictable.

'Did Fernando give you the address?'

Zim shook his head.

'No, no.'

'How did you think you were going to find me?'

'I dunno, well. I started by praying. And look it worked.'

I laughed, flushed again.

'Magic,' I said.

He smiled weakly. 'Magic.'

He didn't seem particularly happy, despite all the effort he'd made to find me.

'Are you all right?'

He shrugged, looked away at the sky.

'I'm not very well I don't think. Maybe I caught something on the plane. I just, I really feel like lying down.'

He did look like he needed to go to bed. He needed some looking after, I thought. He reminded me a bit of my brother; always over-stretching himself, spending every last bit of his energy and then crashing terribly.

'Do you want to come back with me? I'm staying at this nun's house. Ex-nun. She's a bit odd but she's kind. I'm sure she'd let you lie down in her guest room. It's got this amazing bedcover with Adam and Eve and the Garden of Eden on it. She stole it from her old convent . . . can you believe it?' I said.

'No. No, I don't want to come back. Thanks. No.'

'Oh, OK.'

'I just wanted to see you. So you didn't think I'd forgotten. I said I'd get in touch.'

I shrugged. I guess I wanted him to come back to the house with me.

'I do want to see you again. I just, I don't feel so good right now. Can you take my number? Can you call me? I feel sick, tired. I need to go back to the hotel,' he said.

I took his number down in my notebook, watched Zim skulk down the hill towards the police barrier and then turned towards Sister Michael's. But I didn't feel like going back to the shadowy house just yet. Afternoon was coming along, the sun was getting gentler; it was a good time to be out. I passed the house and walked on to the crest of the hill, where one forgotten chapel stood.

A path was broken down in the long, chirruping grass and I followed it to the stone porch. The door was locked. I tried to look inside but sun-bleached material strung over the windows blocked out curious eyes. It was better sitting on the steps anyhow. I could see for miles around; the long river opening out to the ocean, banks of waving palms. Rusty ships, glowing orange now, steaming in and out with their loads. A distant clang came from a shipbuilding yard. Eagles floated just above, circling something they had found.

It was peaceful up here, a beautiful place to live. I could understand why Sister Michael had stayed. Why a lot of people stayed. But it wasn't such a paradise, not the innocent idyll it looked from up here. Beyond the river mouth, heading towards Panjim, I could see the Casino ships, frothy steamboats decked out in fairy lights. Goa was the only state in India you could gamble. Snaking past the boats was Highway 17, loaded with tour buses, motorbikes and taxicabs, crossing Panjim bridge on to the beaches and the parties and the drugs. And somewhere out there was the head of Saint Francis – and the head of the bull. And my iPod. And my story.

I heard barking. A dog bound through the grass, I picked up a nearby stone to throw, but then recognised it as one of Sister Michael's; Luke or John, I wasn't sure which. He was panting and staring at me.

'Hey what is it?'

I didn't really like dogs but this one seemed OK. He had a gleaming coat; he was well looked-after. He growled.

'All right, I'm coming back. Is the Christmas tree too much for Sister Michael? Can she not stand the needles all over her precious Indonesian hardwood floor?' I asked him, standing up and shaking myself down.

But it looked like Sister Michael been enjoying the decorating. Christmas stars of coloured paper had been hung in the eves of the porch already. A cuckoo cooed in the front garden of the house, in an apple tree, I think.

'You guys live a balmy life up here, don't you? Not much to complain about. Just a shame there's no decent men around. Apart from you,' I said to the dog.

The door was ajar and I pushed it open quietly, trying not to make too much noise. The old computer was buzzing loudly. I wondered if I had left it on. I blushed. I could imagine Sister Michael noting the wasteful use of electricity. I turned it off at the mains. Cardboard boxes were all over the floor of the conversation room, spilling out screwed up newspaper and decorations. Delicate pink baubles and silvery tinsel caught the deepening light. Sister Michael has threaded a string across the long room and already hung a number of Christmas cards along it. She said she was lonely old woman but she must know a lot of people to already have so many cards, two weeks still to Christmas. I hadn't received any for years.

'Hello?' I called.

No one was around. The ballroom door was ajar. I pushed open the door gently to see a nativity scene, half set out. The small stable was made of dark wood. The figures were ivory, half of them clustered around the stable, the others scattered about in a fright.

There, beside them, was Sister Michael, lying face down with a wise man in her hand. A line of red stretched to the wall, where the Ming vase Sister Michael had been so worried about breaking lay. But it was her skull not the vase that had smashed when the two had met. I didn't need to go closer to see she was dead, her skull dented and slowly seeping liquid.

I screamed once very loudly. Then just a shivering silence. A blank space cleaved itself into my head. I put my hand on my mouth. I walked out and into the conversation room. I sat down surrounded by glinting baubles. Who had done this? One of the thugs the police had warned her about? A robber. Was he still in the house. Where was Maria? Was she OK? I heard a creak and jumped up. Another creak.

'Who's there?' I shrieked.

No answer. No one. It must be the house. So old. Creaking Indonesian floorboards.

I needed to phone the police. Or someone. Where was her phone? I walked slowly round the room. I couldn't see it. Was it in her pocket? I couldn't look. She must have a landline. In the library. An old black phone. I dialled 999. A dead-tone. Had someone cut the phone line? Another creak. I heard myself whimper. I remembered. 999 wasn't the Indian emergency number. I didn't know what was. I tried a few different combinations, my fingers collapsing like jelly on the dial. None worked. I was a fool. A damn fool. How could I have lived in the country for two years and not know the emergency number? I took out my notebook and phoned the only number I had.

'Hello?'

'Zim.'

'Yeah?'

'Zim. Something's happened.'

I could hear my voice rise to a warble.

'What's happened? Are you OK?'

'I think she's dead. Sister Michael.'

'What? Fuck. Fuck. Are you sure?'

'Yes. Yes, she's dead. Someone's smashed her over the head. I need you to phone the police. I can't remember the emergency number. I used to know it but I can't remember it.'

I began to cry.

'Wait. Are you sure she's dead? Are you sure you need the police? What's going on there?'

'I don't know if he's in the house still. I keep hearing noises.'

'Listen I'll come over. OK? I'll find the house. Just wait there. I won't be long. I'm not far away.'

'It's up the hill on the left of the Basilica. You just go straight up. OK? It's a big plaster house on the lip of the hill. But, phone the police first,' I said.

All I heard was a dial tone. He'd gone.

I waited in the conversation room. The cuckoo was cooing. I sat still there for some time, I don't know how long. I saw the shadows lengthen. The baubles, they glittered like rubies in the light. After a long while there was a clatter on the stairs. I screamed. The door opened. It was Zim. I began to cry. I stood up to meet him, but my legs gave way and I sat back down again. All I could do was stare as he entered the room and knelt down beside me.

'Where is she?'

'Have you phoned the police?'

'I, I don't know the number.'

'You didn't say! That's why I told you to do it!'

'OK, we can Google it on my phone. But let me check on her first, OK?'

'She's in the ballroom – over there.'

He sprang up and headed for the ballroom. Then came a cry, guttural, bleached of anything good.

I found him standing over Sister Michael, closer then I could have got, mesmerised by her corpse.

'She's dead. Fuck man. She's really dead. Fucking hell. I thought she was just concussed, but she's bleeding. There's blood all over her head. It's all in her hair.'

'Zim. Where's your phone?'

He shook his head, the edges of his mouth pulled down in horror.

'My bag, in my bag, in the other room.'

I rummaged around his rucksack and pulled out a digital Leica camera, cigarettes and a book on Buddhism before I found the phone. I tried to load up the internet but it needed a password.

Zim was now by the Ming vase. He touched it gingerly.

'I didn't think a vase could do so much damage. It's heavy. But to kill someone? How can a vase kill someone?'

'Zim. I need a password, Zim. What is it?'

'Give it here,' he said, coming across to me.

I handed it to him but either he was shaking too much or I was. We dropped it. It clattered across the floor. It sounded like a gun battle on that hard wood. We paused, hearts in our mouths, waiting for the silence. The sound of a car arriving filled the space.

'The police,' said Zim.

'No. We haven't phoned them yet. No one knows.'

'Who is it then?'

Neither of us moved. The evening sun had begun to flood the ballroom with orange light, staining Sister Michael and Zim like ripe peaches, with patches of deep red. A few moments later, steps, a conversation from the conversation room, floating through to us.

'This is my crime scene. You can't just come up here and start interfering. I've got forensics all over the place.'

'We got a call to check on this house. Nothing to do with the missing head. I need to do a routine police check, Inspector.'

'You should have called me first. I'm commanding

officer here. I think you're trying to compete with my investigation. This check – it's just an excuse. This crime is huge. Biggest art theft in decades. You want the glory for the local police, for you and your team. You can't stand another police force arriving in Goa and doing a better job. You can't stand the thought that it's Tamils who will find the head of your precious saint.'

'Of course not. If central have decided that you're heading the case, that's it. I'm here to help.'

'If it was up to me you could have the case. Some dead body. Disgusting. It's a corpse, not a god. Christians. The problem is no one trusts you Goans anymore. You're an embarrassment. This place is just a bin of sin. Drugs, prostitution, smuggling. The police have no control. You don't care.'

'Of course we care. Of course we do. It hasn't always been like this. It's not Goa which is the problem. It's the people who come here. We're doing our best. We're doing our very best.'

There was a chuckle. 'Of course, you're doing your best. Everyone knows the police are paid off handsomely. It's a lucrative job, police-work in Goa. But you can't be trusted with any real crime investigation. Why do you think the Idol Squad was sent here?'

Silence. A low controlled voice.

'Inspector, I respect your work. Please respect mine. I got a call that there may be a problem at this address. Please let me continue with my check.'

A low grumbling continued until the door of the ballroom opened. Two men. One, middle-aged, soft-eyed and moustached. Goan. The other, slightly older, eyes like beady marbles, thin. I recognised him straight away.

'Inspector Srinvasen,' I said. 'It's not what it looks like.'

PART 2

1

A stocky policewoman with dimples and long hair tied in a bun led me away. Sweetie, her name badge said, and she was. Sweetie held my hand gently, took my fingerprints and my photo. She asked me for my watch and my phone but I didn't have either. She frisked me softly; patting me like a fragile puppy, then smiled and led me to my cell.

'You'll be questioned soon. Please wait in here,' she said, making the whole affair sound like I was about to get my hair cut.

Two benches nailed to the floor. A girl sat on one narrow plinth with her legs pulled up. I took the opposite side. Thin, bony, dark-haired, loose-eyed, this girl's clothes were put together like they're all she owned; stripy socks with cheap flip-flops, ripped off shorts and an OM T-shirt so worn it was transparent.

I said 'hi' but she kept her lean, loose look ahead. She began to tap her foot. I tried not to stare. After some time she registered my presence and asked me something I didn't understand. I made out the word 'Ruski' and figured she must be asking me if I'm Russian. I was vaguely pleased. Russian sounds a lot more sexy then Welsh.

'No, I'm Welsh, British. UK. Do you speak English?'

She tilted her chin up. 'Yes. Of course.'

The girl could speak perfectly, but she wasn't interested in me once she found out I wasn't Russian. We both waited with only the tapping of her foot for entertainment. After a while, Sweetie returned.

'You're lucky Saskia, Galina's here to pay your bail.'

A tall woman in a green minidress, emerald heels and large Chanel sunglasses pulling back her long black hair stepped into the cell. She began to berate Saskia in fast staccato. Saskia shrugged like an ungrateful teenager. The woman waved her hand in frustration and walked out.

Sweetie shook her head at Saskia before following out, locking the door behind her. Saskia began tapping her foot again.

'Is that your friend? Are you getting out?' I said.

Saskia shrugged, didn't say anything.

I lay back on the bench and looked up at the ceiling. A spider was making a web in the corner of the room, working hard, spinning delicate patterns. It was quite amazing to me that something, somebody, wanted to make their home in this airless, hot, prison.

'The police think I murdered someone,' I said after a while, turning to face her.

The foot stopped for a moment. Then started again. But I saw a small spark in her eye. I'd got her interest finally.

'Did you murder them?' she asked after a while.

'No, of course not?'

'Why of course?'

'I just, I wouldn't. What have you done?'

'The usual.'

'The usual what?'

'I'm just trying to make a living round Anjuna. I'm not hassling anyone. They don't bother the real criminals.'

'You live around Anjuna?'

She shrugged. '"Live" is kind of the wrong word. But yeah, I'm mostly up around Anjuna.'

'And your friend too?'

Saskia pouted with a childish petulance.

'Galina? She's in Goa. She's not my friend anymore.'

'Not anymore?'

'We don't live the same lives. She got lucky. I got unlucky.'

'In what way?'

'Men.'

'You're both Russian? How did you end up here? I've never met a Russian in India before.'

Saskia laughed. 'Where have you been? You know Morjim Beach? They call it Little Moscow.'

'Didn't get that far. Didn't get past Panjim,' I said.

The door to our cell unlocked and Sweetie held it wide. Saskia hadn't been deserted by her friend. The bail was paid; she could leave. She smiled a tight smile and got up, not bothering to say goodbye. I lay back down on my bench and watched the spider for a while, until Sweetie came back for me.

A small room with one table and two chairs. Sat at

the table was the officer with the moustache, the one who'd come to the house. He gestured for me to sit down and turned on a small tape recorder sat beside him.

'This is inspector Joseph Ferreira, December sixteenth at 10 PM, Panjim Police Station. I'm here with Ruby Jones, British national suspected of involvement in the murder of Dorothea Caperelli, another British national, resident in Goa for thirty years. About to begin her first interview.'

Inspector Ferreira looked at me. Flicked through some papers in front of him.

'I'm about to read the suspect the police report from the scene of death. The victim is a Caucasion female, aged around 55–60. Estimated time of death is between 2.30 and 3.30 PM today. The victim was killed by three heavy strikes to the head. Two by a large vase found at the scene of the crime. The third caused by falling hard on a wooden floor. Suspected cause of death: internal brain haemorrhaging. It took the victim around two hours to die.'

I flinched, thinking back to Sister Michael lying there on the floor, her skull crushed.

Ferreira put the papers down.

'It must have been a very frightening way to die. Slow and painful. I assume it was Simon Moon who hit her over the head. You don't look strong enough. What I want to know is why you both felt the need to kill a middle-aged woman like that.'

'No. I mean, I don't know. I wasn't there. We haven't got anything to do with this.'

'We found you and your boyfriend –'

'He's not my boyfriend.'

The inspector shook his head in irritation. 'Your friend. At the scene of the crime. Both sets of your fingerprints are on the vase. The evidence says you were there and you killed this woman. There are no other suspects.'

I took a breath. I wasn't expecting to be so clearly accused. I assumed I would be able to clear this up with a little explanation.

'No. Look, it's not like that. I touched the vase last night, I did. I was with Sister Michael, Dorothea. She told me off because she thought I might break it. She was worried about it.'

I remembered her poor frowning face and her dreams. I laughed at the horribleness of it. Her fear had been so right and so wrong. Ferreira stared at me as if my strange, nervous outburst had been a clear confession of guilt.

'I'm sorry.' I was. 'I didn't mean to laugh. I'm just in shock. She had explained to me the night before she had been having dreams, you see. Zim, he, came to help me today. I called him up and he came over. He went to check on Sister Michael. I saw him touching the vase. He shouldn't have done that, of course. But he didn't realise it had been used to murder her until he saw the blood on it. We didn't do the right thing. I can see that now, but it doesn't mean we should be punished for it.'

The inspector paused the tape recorder. 'I need this case cleared as quickly and simply as possible. I'm sick of foreigners coming into Goa, behaving like devils and creating hell here, giving us a bad name. This is a case containing three foreigners and will not go any further. No Goans are involved. You and your friend are the main suspects here. If you don't cooperate things will get very, very difficult for you. Now let's start again.'

The tape player was running. I got a softly burning feeling in my heart. He'd said 'No Goans are involved'. But he didn't know that, of course he didn't. That just wasn't the way he wanted the case to go. The inspector didn't want any more problems for the locals. Was he prepared to let Zim and me take the blame, just to prevent bad press? Framing us was low for even the most bent cop. We could end up with twenty years in an Indian jail.

'Why did Simon hit Dorothea over the head?' he said.

'He didn't. I've told you that. We have nothing to do with the case. I think you're trying to frame us. You won't get away with that. I'm a journalist. I know people,' I said.

I didn't really know anybody. The inspector sighed. 'OK. Let's start from the beginning. Why did you break into the house?'

'I didn't break into the house. I was staying there. I told you. You're not listening to me. You can ask the maid, Maria. I came back to find it empty. When I found Sister Michael I called Zim. He came over to help.'

'We can't find the maid. We're very concerned for her safety. Why didn't you call the police?'

'I couldn't remember the number.'

Ferreira lent back in his chair. 'You couldn't remember the number? How long have you been in this country?'

'Two years.'

He laughed blandly.

'It's quite amazing really, you come to India, you come to Goa. You mess around with drugs and crime and you don't even know how to call the police if something goes wrong. What is going through your heads, you people? One foreigner every week is dying here now. It's not reported any more. It's not news. Do you think nothing bad can happen to you under a palm tree? This isn't some fantasy paradise. This is reality. You do something wrong, you pay for it.'

He was pissed off. Not just with me, with every tourist who came here and fucked up; drugs, car crashes and drownings. There were several ways to die having fun here. Zim and I seemed to be getting the brunt of his anger.

'This case is so different though. It's nothing to do with the parties. I didn't come here to party. Neither did Zim. I was at Sister Michael's to interview her. We honestly had nothing to do with her murder. I just came back, the door was open. She was dead already. We didn't do it.'

'Who did then? Old Goa is monitored day and night now. There are no records of anyone coming in and out between those times.'

'But that's when Zim came up – so someone hasn't been writing up the log properly. People have been coming in and out. I came in the day before. Sister Michael just told the guard I was with her and he waved me through. He didn't make any notes of my name.'

Ferreira shook his head, pushed out his lower lip. It

wasn't a good move around here, blaming the police for anything, even bad gatekeeping.

'Wait, wait. I remember. Sister Michael, she had to go and get the Christmas decorations before midday, because she had to be back in for a delivery.'

'What kind of delivery?'

'I don't know. Maybe Father Jonathan knows. He was with her. Have you talked to him. Is he here?'

'The curate is in a very difficult position at the moment. He hasn't time to come to the police station. He's very upset. We'll ask him about the delivery. He didn't mention it and there is nothing in the police log.'

Ferreira started to flick through his papers.

'How long do we have to stay here?' I asked.

He looked up. 'As long as it takes. You have one phone call.'

I lay on my bench, alone, except for the spider. I didn't know who to call. I could phone England, my parents, but they would go crazy with worry. I couldn't do that to them. My friends, in London, in Wales, they couldn't do anything so far away. I wasn't good at keeping in touch anyhow. I didn't imagine they would react well to a call out the blue after months, saying I was in prison.

Delhi? Everyone I knew there now was an acquaintance, not much more. My friends were all gone. Rani was teaching yoga in the Bahamas right now. Eddie had gone to Singapore, he'd got the correspondent job he wanted. Stephen, he was buried in Saint James's graveyard.

The two people I had befriended since arriving in Goa were no good either. One was dead and the other was in custody. How did I get so alone?

Who the hell killed Sister Michael? She'd said she was waiting for someone to come over around midday. Was the inspector going to investigate that? It would probably mean calling up local companies. But he didn't want any Goans involved. He was probably going to ignore it, like he was ignoring the phone call to the house. Couldn't they trace that call? Maybe not. I guess they didn't trace routine crime reports. Someone knew what had happened.

I wondered how Zim was. If he was OK. He'd come to help me and ended up a main suspect in a murder case. But he'd been so stupid, touching the vase. Why hadn't he called the police like I told him too? Why had he taken so long to get to me?

Why hadn't I gone straight to the priests? Of course that would have been the right thing to do. It was all like a horrible dream. Or a curse. Revenge from Saint Francis, everyone who prayed at his tomb was destined for destruction until the guy got back his head.

I clenched my eyes and grabbed my head. What was I thinking? I couldn't start thinking such insane things as this. I needed to get a grip and think objectively. I was hungry. I hadn't had lunch or dinner. I heard the door unlocking. It was the lovely policewoman with thin brown blankets and a plate of curry. At least one thing was going my way. The food wasn't too bad, with bits of fish in it. A bit sloppy, but that was probably just as well as my only utensil was a plastic spoon. No one could say I wasn't seeing Goa from the inside.

2

The spider was already working on her web when I blinked my eyes awake. I'd slept a blank sleep and had woken up surprisingly fresh apart from a grimy film that clung to my teeth.

As I sucked them clean, I began to realise exactly where I was, what was happening to me. My teeth became less of a problem. Good God. Yesterday's adrenalin and shock had worn off; my mind was clearer and began to fill with rising fear. Deep panic. This was fucking terrible. Why on earth hadn't I called my parents? What was I thinking? How could I have just lain here letting a case against me build up? Who the hell doesn't use a phone call?

I got up and bundled my blankets into the corner. I went to the bars and called out, hoping Sweetie would help me. But she wasn't there anymore. It was now a rolling, grey lady with a frown carved indelibly into her forehead.

'What do you want?' she mumbled at me.

'I didn't make my phone call last night – can I make it now?'

My new woman grunted and lifted her lips in a smile before turning her back on me and walking off. I thought perhaps she'd gone to get the station mobile but after sometime waiting at the bars, I didn't know how long because I didn't have a watch, I assumed she wasn't coming back. It dawned on me that no one at all knew I was here – and no one would notice I was missing for weeks. I wasn't very good at keeping in touch with people at home. If only I had phoned my parents. They would have got me a lawyer at least. I'd watched enough police shows to know you weren't supposed to keep people for questioning more than twenty-four hours in the UK and the US – but that was on *The Bill* and *The Wire* I didn't know the rules in India, much less Goa, just like I hadn't known the emergency number. What exactly did I keep in my head? I hardly knew anymore. I slumped on the bench and began tapping my foot like Saskia. Maybe this would magic up some Chanel-branded Russian angel for me too.

It didn't, only my new guard, lumbering across to my cell. She unlocked the door and nodded her head towards the interview room. She needed a shave.

'This is Inspector Ferreira. December seventeenth, with Ruby Jones. Ten AM. Second interview.

'How did you sleep Ruby?'

'Fine, actually.'

'Why didn't you make that phone call last night? Because you don't want anyone to know you're involved in a murder?'

'I'm not involved.'

The inspector sifted through some of his papers. Didn't bother to look at me as he spoke.

'You're lucky. I spoke to the curate of the Basilica. He doesn't know anything about a delivery but he confirmed he met you yesterday; that you'd slept at the house the night before. He also mentioned that Dorothea – or Sister Michael he calls her – complained about you touching the vase. She talked about it in the morning with him. He said she was worried about it breaking, that everyone wanted to look at it, touch it.'

I deflated with relief. I heard myself let out a moan.

'I'm free to go?'

'No. I need to talk to you about Simon Moon. How well do you know him?'

'Not well. I just met him on the plane.'

'Are you attracted to him?'

'What?'

'Are you attracted to him? Is that why you're trying to help him?'

'No. Of course not.'

'But you agree you have no idea if he is capable of violent acts?'

I thought of the Prince albums, smashed up. 'What are you trying to get me to say? I don't know anything about him.'

Inspector Ferreira pulled out some sheets of paper and placed them in front of me. A print out from the *LA Times*. A photo of a beautiful, long-legged girl; sunglasses and black hair. Prada handbag and skinny jeans. Caption: Melissa Gomez leaves Beverly Hills Magistrate Court. Lawyer says family is disappointed with verdict and want Simon Moon to face serious punishment.

'I'll leave you to read this. Then have a think whether you are really so sure about giving this guy an alibi. Take your time, Rita will be here,' said Ferreira.

My new police guard sat heavily down on a bench leaning against the wall and stared grimly at me. I began to read.

RICH KID ROMANCE ENDS IN COURT

By Don Allen

Two kids who had it all but it wasn't enough. Melissa Gomez, granddaughter of Mexican mobile phone tycoon Jose Gomez, was in court today to hear the verdict on her former boyfriend Simon Moon, son of renowned art dealer to the stars, Raoul Moon.

Acquaintances say the affair between the two had always been stormy. Fights and parties; drugs and alcohol. They loved the drama but the last act in their relationship seems to have gone horribly wrong. Moon stood today, accused of slashing the Mexican artist and model's face in a fit of anger when she tried to finish the relationship.

Gomez was accompanied by her father, Mario Gomez, one-time Hollywood actor and owner of the much loved Beverly Hill's Taco bar. He told reporters before the court appearance that there could have been no worse crime committed against his daughter.

'She's was the most perfect girl in the world. Simon Moon didn't want anyone else to have such a beauty and took it away from her. He cut her face and destroyed

her soul. We're devastated. Simon Moon needs to pay for what he has done,' he said.

Another photo. Two portraits. Melissa before and after. The first picture showed a doe-eyed Mexican girl pouting for the camera. Golden skin, expensive make-up, black bodice hugging curves. The next picture, Melissa, red-eyed, hospital blue smock, swollen face; skin flapping, a red gash going from the top of her perfect cheekbone to just before the end of her small, peachy chin.

The court heard from Ms Gomez, who explained that the incident had happened in her artist's studio last Wednesday, where she had been making woodcuts.

'I wanted to break up with Zim. He couldn't handle it. He took up a Stanley knife and threatened me, grabbing both my wrists. I tried to struggle and he slashed my face.'

Ms Gomez went on to describe several incidents of jealous, obsessive behaviour, including the smashing of her entire Prince collection. When asked by the defence why she had continued to see Mr Moon if she found him so frightening, she reddened visibly and said it was personal. Simon Moon refuted his ex-girlfriend's statement saying that the cut was an accident. A fight that had got out of hand.

'I don't see what all the fuss is about anyway. It's nothing her doctor can't fix. She's already half plastic. You think those tits are real?' he said. The judge called for this comment to be taken back and told Mr Moon he was doing his case no good at all.

Despite the Gomez family's calls for a prison sentence, Judge Andrews said that the case was not clear cut, simply Ms Gomez against Mr Moon. He could not pass any custodial sentence without more evidence of what had actually happened. He fined Simon Moon ten thousand dollars and ordered twenty hours' anger management counselling.

'This trial was a sham. Why did it not go to a jury? Because Raoul Moon didn't want it to. If you pay a visit to Judge Andrews' house what are the chances he has some new Picasso hanging on his wall now? Anyone who knows Simon Moon knows his violent moods are getting worse and becoming a danger to those around him. It won't go away just because he has a rich father and a gallery of fine art. He needs to be locked up,' said Mario Gomez, after the trial.

I flicked the article away and leant back in my chair. God. He'd said he'd had girlfriend trouble. He'd slashed the girl's face. And worse he didn't seem to regret it. That was crazy. Could he have killed Sister Michael? The two things weren't connected. Ferreira was just showing me this to persuade me to help him out in his 'no Goans' policy. This hadn't got anything to do with the murder.

Rita shouted out to the inspector.

'Well? Are you ready to help us now?'

Inspector Ferreira came back dabbing his mouth with a napkin.

'I don't know what you want from me.'

'All I need is a statement from you placing Zim Moon near the house at the time of the murder. Nothing more. His fingerprints are on the vase and his hair and fingerprints are also on the body. He's got a track record of violence,' he said.

'I called him from the house. He came to help me. He got too close to the body, he touched the vase. He had a fight with his girlfriend. That doesn't make him a murderer. Why do you want to charge him so much? Why don't you trace the call? Or get some more leads? Why don't you interview the maid?'

Ferreira sat down. 'There are no other leads. Give me a new statement and you can be out of here in half an hour. Keep on like this and it's going to take a lot longer. Your prints are on that vase too.'

'I want to use that phone call. I didn't use it last night. After that I'll think about the statement.'

'Good girl,' he said.

3

They let me find the number in my notebook. Five hours difference. It would only be about 9 AM in the UK. God I hoped he got to the office early. The dial tones were high-pitched, long and unanswered. I didn't know if your one phone call counted if no one picked up. If you got a second chance? Probably not here.

'Hello? Touchstone magazine?'

As plummy and as devoid of Welsh as I remembered.

'David. Thank God. I didn't know if you would be in at this time, it's Ruby.'

'You're lucky. I haven't gone to bed. Rather a large party at Black's last night. Where have you been?'

'I need your help. I've been arrested. I'm in custody.'

'Good lord. What did you do? Rob the convent.'

'Nothing! I didn't do anything. The nun I interviewed was murdered.'

'Bloody hell. That's awful. What's it got to do with you?'

'The police, they found me – and a friend – in the house. The inspector in charge, he thinks my friend did it. He's not following any other leads. He's trying to get me to make a statement against him, says things will be difficult if I don't. Do you know anyone who could help us? Just at least let the police here know someone important knows we're in here? We need some kind of protection.'

'India? God. Not my patch really.'

'David. You won networker of the year at Oxford Union. You must know someone.'

Silence.

'OK, it's a kind of long shot but a girlfriend of a good friend, her father was Deputy Ambassador at the British High Commission in Delhi. He's not there anymore but he must know the Ambassador pretty well. Maybe I can talk to her.'

'Please? Could you? We're in Panjim police station, Goa.'

'I can try. But you owe me something special for this. I want something that sings from you.'

'I'm on it as soon as I'm out. Thanks David, really, you're a saviour.'

'Me and those beautiful bellini's last night. I'm never usually in before midday.'

Lunch was another sloppy curry, a different colour but very much the same taste. There were two small bananas for afters. I was touched that the police station cared enough for its prisoners to give them something sweet and healthy with their lunch.

I lay back on my bench, staring up at my spider, who was curled up sleeping it seemed. I wondered what time it was. I hadn't seen one clock since I arrived. I wondered if this was some kind of softening up technique the police employed. Take away any sense of normal life.

I rubbed at my hand. Sitting in the police car coming here, Zim had gripped it tight, begun to scratch my palm hard. I hadn't minded, the pain had helped to ease my mind. I still had the marks and they reminded me of him. Just a few days ago, we'd been sat drinking beer, talking about his girlfriend troubles. He'd been a stranger. Then some death spark had fused us together. We were in this together. I wasn't going to help Ferreira frame him for this.

The sound of the cell door. I looked up from my hand. Inspector Ferreira.

'You called the British Consulate. They've been in touch. You know the Ambassador apparently,' he said.

I nodded vaguely.

'Well you can assure the High Commissioner that we kept you here for no longer than the normal twenty-four hours.'

'I'm free to go.'

'For now. I haven't got time to go to the magistrate for you both. But you're still a suspect. You need to stay in Goa.'

'Is Zim out too?'

'Previous offences. The lawyer has got us more time with him. He'll need bail to get out.'

'How much is the bail?'

'Two thousand dollars. He wants to see you about it. You'll have half an hour with him.'

Zim didn't look good. His eyes were back in his

head and circled by deep black and purple. He itched his shaved head and frowned at me. He looked like a convict.

I put the article down in front of him. He glanced at it and pushed it away, turned his eyes to the ceiling.

'Violent mood swings. Danger to others. No wonder they think you did it,' I said.

There was a pleading expression in Zim's eyes and an air of tired exasperation, as if he'd heard this one hundred times before, had tried to explain a thousand times and had never been listened to once. He began to speak and then gave up, just shrugged his shoulders and leant back in his chair; exhausted before we'd even begun.

'Ferreira, he's read this and he thinks you killed Sister Michael. He wants me to confirm that you were around Old Goa at the time of the murder. All I told him was I called you when I found the body. You didn't tell him you were around before did you? I found you in the church.'

Zim put his head in his hands and shook it. No. He'd lied.

'But you were there before, Zim. You got through the police barrier. What if they find out? You'll look even more suspicious.'

'They haven't yet. I think they tried to find the policeman on duty. But he'll be scared stiff won't he? He wasn't supposed to let me in there in the first place. He's not going to volunteer any information.'

'Why didn't you just tell him the truth?'

'I didn't know what to do. Ferreira, he'd found the article. I don't know how, he must have googled me.

It freaked me out. It made me feel guilty. It's awful. Melissa. She's like some bad spirit, haunting me everywhere I go.'

'Did you knife her?'

'No. It was an accident. Not that anyone believes me. Not even my father believes me.'

'Did he give the judge a Picasso?'

'He doesn't love me that much. It was a very small Braque.'

'So what happened? Persuade me you're not a complete and utter maniac.'

'I'm not saying I'm not a maniac. But it really wasn't my fault. And Melissa? She might look like one but she is far from an angel. I loved her but I hated her too. I hated her. And she hated me.'

'That's weird to start with.'

'Is it? I think it's fairly normal. It's like this long drawn out dawn of weaknesses. Once we'd realised what we both were really like, we'd been eating and sleeping and fucking and drinking together for so long that we kind of loved each other anyway. And hated each other all the more for that.'

'What was so terrible about her?'

'She was a complete fake. She was only with me because of my dad. Because she thought she could use me. She said she was an artist, she'd walk around with a paintbrush in her hair, but she was terrible. She had no talent. She made these morbid self-portraits. Colours and perspectives completely distorted. Not on purpose. Because she couldn't paint. I didn't really care but man, she did. She was ambitious. She wanted me to get her a show at Blue Moon.'

'That's what you had the argument about?'

'No. No. I just strung her along for ages, pretending like I was talking to my dad about her and he was interested. It was shit, but you know I couldn't lose her. I was nothing without her. All I was doing was living off my parents, their name and money, using it to abuse myself. I'd dropped out of college, was supposed to be working at the gallery but I hadn't anything to do. I hardly went in there; just hung around the opening parties. We got invited everywhere, got high. Melissa's father let us help ourselves to his own supply. People liked having us around. We were fun. She was hot. We had some good times together. Despite everything.'

'So what happened?'

'I turned up high at her house one night. I'd been out, I think at a casino or something. Taken a load of coke. She was in the back in her 'artist's studio'. I'll give her that. She did try. She did more than I did. I wouldn't even try to work. She'd started doing these weirdly terrible Aztec prints. I made a comment about them, she turned on me with her cutting knife.'

'What did you say?'

'"Your looks haven't helped you turn into a decent artist; I doubt your ancestry will." She really took offence.'

'You smash up her Prince collection and then you piss all over her dreams. No wonder she wanted you put away. You were horrible to her.'

Zim screwed up his face in an ugly frown. 'They *were* terrible, looked like the work of a schizo toddler on acid . . . I was only telling her the truth. No one ever spared me; pretended I was any good at anything. She was mad as hell though. She couldn't handle being told the truth. She was spoilt, you know? By her dad.'

'And then you stabbed her?'

'No! Of course not. She pinned me down on her worktable with this Stanley knife and told me she'd never met such a *puta* and we were over. She said everyone knew I was a complete loser, I only had a job because of my dad and even he didn't even really want me there. She'd heard him joking about me at an opening two nights before, telling someone I didn't know a Picasso from a cave painting. Then I got mad. He wouldn't say that.'

Zim shook his head. He didn't sound convinced that his father hadn't said it. There was a quiver in his voice that suggested he could well believe it. And he was more upset now, about the idea that his father thought he wouldn't know a Picasso from a cave painting than about the fact that he was in jail suspected of murder. I remembered the shudder in the airport.

'Then what happened?' I asked.

Zim pulled his hands up in front of him, stared into the space between them, concentrating, going over the scene in his mind.

'I grabbed her hands and pushed her off me. I thought she was going to let go of the knife but she didn't. I don't know what really happened, I was high, I told you. But the next thing I knew she was on the floor screaming with blood all over her.'

'Fuck.'

'I know. The worse thing about it was we got her face. I wouldn't feel as bad if it had punctured her lung.

115

That girl needs her looks. That's what she relies on. She needs them. Boy, did they screw me though. They got a lawyer. My dad got a lawyer too. It was all over the place. Reporters loved it. Google my name and it's there. "Zim the Ripper", "Moon vs Melissa". Fucking hell. What a nightmare.'

'But you got off?'

'I got off. I cleaned up. I was ready to prove myself properly; to stop hiding behind the drugs and the girls and actually try for once. Even if it meant not doing as good as I wanted. It shook me up, you know? I didn't want to be a fucked up rich kid. I might not be a major art dealer, or an artist or anything particularly special, but at least I could earn my living properly. Dad didn't think it was going to last. He just kept expecting me not to show up. But I did. After a few weeks, he decided to send me here. Maybe I was bad for business, after all the fuss with Melissa. He still didn't trust me. His last words to me were "don't fuck up Zim. I'm not bailing you out again. You mess up in India, you're out." And where do I end up? In prison, suspected of murder.'

He wiped his eyes with the edge of his hoodie. He hadn't taken it off, despite the heat. It must have been thirty-five degrees in there. He tried to laugh but it wasn't funny. It was awful. Did I believe him? I thought I did. He didn't seem delusional. He knew himself. He knew he lived off his father and he couldn't stand it. He knew he wasn't as good as his father and he couldn't stand that either. He knew himself and he couldn't stand himself. Maybe he did get too angry. Have fits of rage. But he'd helped me out, and underneath all the show, he was kind, intelligent and quite beautiful, in a fragile, ill-looking way. He'd come up to Old Goa to find me after the festival, worried something had happened to me. He'd come back to the house when I called him, in deep trouble, a dead nun on my hands. I wanted to be on his side.

'Listen, don't worry. OK? You didn't do it – they have no evidence. It could all turn out all right. I called a friend and they spoke to someone in the British consulate. They know we're here. The police can't just pin some crime on us and keep us here indefinitely. You've got bail.'

'I know. Ferreira told me. He looked so pissed off.'

'So you're gonna be out as soon as you get it paid.'

'But I can't pay it.'

'Why not? What about your expense account?'

'What's that gonna look like? Panjim Prison: two thousand dollars. Dad's gonna know something's up.'

'Just call him. Explain what happened.'

Zim looked at me in disgusted frustration. 'Ruby, have you not heard one thing I've told you? I can't do that. He'll cut me off. He said this is my last chance. He meant it.'

'Come on. Talking to your dad can't be as bad as staying in here.'

'You don't know him. Look, I know it's a big thing to ask, I hardly know you, but could you foot the money?'

I sat back in my chair. I should have expected it. But I hadn't. I had never thought he was going to ask me to pay his bail. But I couldn't do that. It would take all the money in my account plus most of the overdraft.

I leant my elbows on the table, thinking. Zim took one of my wrists. His hands were clammy, his hold surprisingly strong. God. I felt that same jolt I felt in the church; a thump in my stomach. Equally inappropriate.

'Ruby, I'm really sorry to have to ask you this. I wouldn't if I could think of anyone else. But I can't. I'm on my own here. I'm scared.'

It was my fault he was in here. But I couldn't pay all that money out. Why on earth did he have to pick up the vase? How could anyone be so dumb? It's so basic, not touching a crime scene. I guess you don't know what you'll do in a situation like that. Things just happen.

'Zim, I'm sorry. I really am. I'm going to try and get you out of here. But I can't pay that bail. It's all the money I have.'

'You'll get it back. I didn't do it. You can't think I did it?'

He let go of my wrist, pulled back into his chair, his eyes boring into mine, horrified. I leant over, tried to touch him, but he was out of reach.

'No, no. Of course it's some robbers or something. But I just, I can't.'

Zim shook his head. 'I thought you'd do this for me.'

'I'm sorry.'

He tried to smile at me. 'OK, fine. Just don't let me rot in here OK? It's only you who know I'm here.'

4

The sun was blazing bright as I stepped out of Panjim police station. I had to shield my eyes from the force of its gaze.

'What was I supposed to do? I can't afford that kind of money,' I said to the waving air.

I turned back to take a look at Panjim police station. A jolly looking place, yellow plaster with flags waving around the entrance. You wouldn't know it contained a belly of scared people trying to get out. Appearances were always deceptive. Zim. God, I couldn't forget about him, locked up in there, scared. I couldn't get him off my mind.

I made my way gingerly out into the street, still keeping a hand on my forehead to stop the sun burning me up. I was in the centre of Panjim, a maze of rotting houses and dilapidated wooden balconies. I had come here in a haze of fear and handcuffs. I didn't know my way at all. I was disorientated. What should I do? Where should I go? I should get in touch with someone, tell them I'd been released. But no one had known in the first place, except David.

I needed money. I only had the clothes I was standing up in. The bank. I needed to find the bank. The address had been on that email I'd got at Sister Michael's. I vaguely remembered where, close to the ferry port.

A new Panjim branch, the air inside was cool and refined, the floors marble. And I was lucky; my cards had arrived. The letter delivering them said my credit card limit had been upped by 500 pounds. I pulled out two thousand rupees from the ATM and thought about Zim. He hadn't used his phone call either. Was he just going to have to wait it out till the police found another suspect? Would they? Would they just let him rot there indefinitely? But sooner or later his family were going to realise he was missing. Should I get in touch with them myself? But he wouldn't want me to. That was the last thing he wanted.

There was a small street market going on across the street. Small, wizened women with bags and clothes and hats. I bought a fake Reebok rucksack, a photo-copied Lonely Planet to Goa and a sundress. It was sleeveless, tie-dyed blue and white; too risqué for the rest of India and just too horrific for London. I wouldn't be seen dead in it usually but it was all right for now. There was no one around to laugh at me or for me to look nice for anyhow. I was on my own again.

I wandered some more, not knowing what to do, where to go. The sun beat down on me and gave me a headache. Most of the shops were shuttered up for the gaping age that was called lunch. Not a soul on those bleached streets but me and a few stray dogs, sleeping in the shade of cars. Get in the shade, that's what I should do too. I headed for the first place I saw.

Some old restaurant, Gordinho's, with black wooden chairs and red gingham tablecloths. A faded Portuguese flag hung on the wall alongside a portrait of a couple in European clothes, staring down at the diners with flat Goan faces. The man had his hand on his wife's shoulder. They looked very settled together.

A group of four local pensioners were tucking into a late lunch of biriyani and prawn curry, not caring about dropping leftovers on the tiled floor. A young Goan woman was staring into the distance and drinking a coke. She signalled to the waiter who bought over a shot of whisky that she poured into her glass. I'd never seen an Indian woman drinking alone before; especially not lunchtime whisky. I'd never seen any woman, anywhere, drinking whisky alone during the day. Wasn't she embarrassed? Didn't she care about drawing attention to herself, all by herself?

I couldn't shake off my aloneness. It was like a shadow that followed me around, stopped me relaxing. Prevented me from doing things like drink whisky at midday. It watched me and made me self-conscious. I tried to rebel, ordered a whisky myself and made an effort to enjoy the solitary drinking.

As usual I couldn't actually be bothered to read my guidebook and contented myself with looking at the photo highlights. A Full Moon party. Dreadlocked, bug-eyed girls stuck their tongues out for the camera. Rib-caged guys waved glow sticks and spliffs around in the light of a beach bonfire. It was a world away from this old restaurant, with its patina of colonialism and proper service. That old couple on the wall, they could never have imagined all this.

The next photos showed glistening sushi and tropical salads; fine dining at the latest six-star Taj resort. Kite surfing on Morjim Beach and hanging out with the hippies north of Arambol. It didn't seem like there were many hippies left from the photo. A few paunchy men with greasy grey locks, playing bongos half-heartedly. In the distance, catching the sunset, were high-rise apartment blocks, holiday homes I imagined. It was like the hippy trail had got lost and meandered into the Costa del Sol. Nothing appealed. I'd thought about taking a few days on the beach, to shake off the last week, the shock, the trauma. But perhaps I was better just to get on with the article for Touchstone. I owed it to David anyhow, I'd still be in there in prison if it wasn't for his power socialising.

The lone girl sat up and waved, smiling widely. I thought for a moment she was calling me over for some company. I began lifting myself out of my seat until I realised that wasn't what she wanted. I slunk back down, embarrassed. Her boyfriend had turned up. Sloping shoulders and large brown eyes, he murmured apologies as he sat down close beside her. They bristled. He downed her drink and ordered another one as they paid lip service to the menu, holding hands under the table. I sipped my own. Her whisky now made sense. Mine, less so. The two old couples had finished their meal and were smacking their lips contentedly. One woman counted out medicines for her husband carefully. I thought of Zim, spooning up the sloppy curry into his delicate mouth.

'Another one ma'am?'

The aged waiter, attentive by my side. I looked down at my glass. I'd finished it already. My head was beginning to hurt. I couldn't decide whether another would make it better or worse.

'Yes please. What do you have to eat?'

'Special today is fried snapper ma'am.'

'How much is that?'

'One hundred rupees.'

It was more expensive than I thought. But the alcohol had given me an appetite. Fuck it, I was going to get it.

'OK – I'll have that. Do you have a newspaper too please?'

I should at least get up to date with the case, before I got in touch with David. The waiter returned with a second tumbler and a newspaper threaded to a wooden pole. As he was putting down the glass he made a pernickety noise, somewhere between extreme annoyance and complete acceptance. He'd spotted a trail of ants in the far corner of the room. They marched from a small hole in one side of the room to the entrance of the restaurant, but missed by a few inches, bashing into the wall and scattering off into chaos.

'They always come back and they can never find the door. I wouldn't mind if they just went out the door,' he said.

I watched as he doused the trail with water. I felt sorry for them, wrong place, wrong time, but tried to ignore the massacre. I thought about mentioning that they weren't actually causing any harm, that he could leave them alone. But I didn't. I just let him scald and kill them all with water.

Had Zim slashed his girlfriend? Could he have had anything to do with Sister Michael? I went through the day she died in my head. I'd seen him in the church, round one or two in the afternoon. He said he hadn't been able to find the house. He hadn't looked good, he'd looked ill. He'd said he was tired. We talked about his mother. She loved crime shows, religion. It wasn't the kind of conversation you have after you've just murdered someone. At least I didn't think it was. I didn't know. I didn't know how one reacted to murder. I guess everyone was different. If he was innocent, in the end he would get out. How long could they really keep him in that prison? He would just have to call his father if things got bad. It wasn't up to me to rescue him. I hardly knew him. I was as alone as he was.

I took up the newspaper.

'Fucking hell,' I said, when I saw the headline.

They'd found the head. The head of Saint Francis, in one of the shipping yards down in the port, Vasco de Gama. The main photo was of the head, greyer and even more papery than I had remembered, displayed proudly on a velvet cushion. Inspector Srinvasen gave a press conference outside the warehouse where they had found it. Despite the success, he didn't look any happier in his photo; dour mouth, beady eyes looking past the camera.

'Smuggling through Goa has been a massive problem for years now. The police and port authorities here have colluded with criminals to turn a blind eye to imports of drugs that fuel the state's party scene. Now we see that the port harbours another kind of criminal: those who will rape and pillage their own country's cultural and religious heritage. The head of Saint Francis was traced to this warehouse by an anonymous tip-off. The church has their saint back but the Idol Squad will not rest until we find who is responsible for this crime,' he said.

I flicked over to the next page to see a photo of three Vatican Officials in purple robes next to a quivering Father Jonathan, whom I'd met only two days ago, at Sister Michael's. The men had arrived late last night and were thanking God for the safe return of Saint Francis. Jetlag and worry did not seem to have affected them. Well-watered and confident men, they smiled beatifically for the camera. A complete contrast to the poor priest of the Basilica, who was several shades paler then these blooming cardinals. He had not lost his look of fear, indeed, it had a wilder streak to it now. Father Jonathan looked beyond the camera, as if some ghost was shaking his locks at him. He must have learnt of poor Sister Michael's death only shortly before these men arrived. What a terrible time he was having. Sister Michael was supposed to have been the Basilica spokeswoman, Father Jonathan was too fragile according to her. But he had no choice now.

'Of course we are happy about the head. It's been very traumatic,' he said.

What now? I guess I needed to go down to Vasco de Gama, find out what was going on there. Try and find out what was in the warehouse, apart from the head. The police were keeping this confidential. Said it would be part of a wider investigation and revealing the contents could jeopardise this. Mounds of cocaine? God knows.

I flicked through the rest of the newspaper, trying to find something on Sister Michael. I couldn't see anything. The next news item was a double page spread debating a new tourist development in Arambol, in the north of Goa. It was going to be huge, worth billions of dollars. Towers of holiday apartments, golf courses, water parks, an international food court – even an aquarium. There was a letter by the minister for tourism explaining how many jobs this would bring to Goa, how much the complex could make over just one year. He said this was the new face of Goan tourism. Family holidays, all-inclusive tours, luxury and economy.

'We don't want the hippies. Whatever the hippies did here, they didn't spend money. We want tourists who spend money. This is what is good for Goa,' he said.

The environmentalists didn't agree. The Arambol complex was going to concrete over Goa's last remaining strip of undeveloped coast, around the Tambdi Surla temple. Before the Arambol complex had been designed there had been a proposal to turn the area into a National Park. One local NGO, SOS Goa, claimed that the man responsible for the complex, Paulo Mendes, had paid off the senate for planning permission.

'Paulo Mendes has already made billions of dollars, ruining huge strips of Goan coastline, building unsightly hotels, plying busloads of tourists along small country lanes and creating mounds of waste and pollution, which he ignores. The only reason he has got the go-ahead for this project is because he pours money into the tourist minister's bank account. Is there nothing we can do to stop the abusive destruction of Goa?' said the head of the NGO, Anita Alberto.

Paulo Mendes. The name rang a bell. It was the man Zim was here to see, the man he was supposed to sell a painting too. No wonder Zim got into Old Goa so easily. Why hadn't he rang Paulo for the bail? I guess he didn't want his father to find out. Could Raoul Moon be that bad, that his son couldn't phone him for help, when he was in trouble all the way across the world?

There was only a short piece, on page four, about the death of Sister Michael. The newspaper used her real name, Dorothea Caperelli. Police were investigating the death, but suspicious circumstances were not mentioned. There was a search on for Maria Lima, her housekeeper, whose family lived in the nearby village of Nerul and were said to be greatly concerned. The reporter brushed over Sister Michael's own work to concentrate on her late husband. A political activist and promising theologian, from a well-loved Goan family, he had left the church to marry, only to die of a heart attack soon after. I wondered if leaving the church had done that to him. Maybe he couldn't handle the guilt. It did seem to eat you up in a powerful way. There were two small photos, one of Sister Michael as a young, beautiful novice nun, the other of Maria's husband and grown-up children, laying candles at the shrine of Saint Christopher for her safe return.

My ant-hating waiter returned holding a plate of

sizzling fish, garnished with lemon and onion. It looked delicious. The young couple opposite me, who had ordered the same, must have found it good too, already making sounds and offering one another forkfuls. I took a mouthful and chewed slowly, before pushing the plate away. It was just as good as it looked, but I couldn't stop thinking of Zim, still spooning sloppy curry into his mouth. I couldn't eat this with him still in there. My palms were itching. I rubbed them against the table top, trying to decide what to do.

I would just have to pay it. I'd only met him a few days ago. But we'd got caught up in trouble together and I just couldn't walk away and leave him to battle it out himself. I made some calculations in my head. With my overdraft and credit card, I would have about 800 pounds left after I paid out the money.

It was worth it to have Zim around. I had my own reasons for wanting him out of jail.

Underneath my every thought ran a current of fear and shock; images of Sister Michael lying there dead lingered in the recesses of my brain. Had she sensed she was going to die? She'd had dreams about the vase. Those conversations we'd had, they were part of that. She'd wanted to tell someone about her life. She'd wanted me to listen to her, to take her advice. She'd told me I was like her. Not to make the same mistakes. I wouldn't ever forget her or what she told me. But who would understand this? I'd known her for such a little time. But she'd made such an impression on me. I knew that I was going to be haunted by her, just like I was haunted by Stephen.

I needed Zim here with me, to talk about it to, to

go over it, to try and work out what had happened. He was the only one I could share this with. He'd been there, he'd seen her. And maybe he'd understand my creeping fear too. My veins tightened with a tense sense that I was next. That whoever had come after Sister Michael would come after me. I was strung up like never before, only just managing to keep the fear from boiling over. It had been bubbling all day, under the trip to the bank and the sunburn and the whisky. And I knew, as soon as the sun was down and night was here, I wouldn't be able to stop it pulsing up into terror. I couldn't be alone now; Zim was my only choice.

5

Vasco de Gama was a strange place anyway, but especially weird for Zim and me – out of prison but not out of trouble – gliding around in a weird dream.

The city stood on a spit of land rolling down into the basin. Smoke spewed from factories surrounding the city, scattering ash on the sprawl of wasteland and slums that were suburbs. The lack of real buildings made for a strangely naked horizon and the sun set as on the ocean; uninterrupted, casting a glow over all the rippling poverty.

The port had been banished from the rest of the paradise state. My guidebook didn't mention Vasco. There were no tourists here. Our taxi driver wound through communist style blocks stained black with monsoon damp. Coloured saris and shirts waved in the dark holes of balconies. Gridded streets heaved with people. They at least softened the strangeness.

'This place is hell. It's like Russia in the sun, gone rotten,' said Zim.

It was the first thing he'd said since we'd got in the taxi. He'd been in some self-imposed silent meditation since getting out of prison, just staring out the window at the paddy fields and the river and the building sites announcing holiday homes for the gods. Was it guilt? Or shame? Or embarrassment at needing so much help from someone he hardly knew? Zim hadn't been able to look me in the eye when I met him in the lobby of the police station, just gripped me in a hug. He'd smelt bad but I didn't mind, I understood. We stood there for a while, locked in this embrace. He hadn't wanted to pull away it seemed. Eventually I did.

'Thanks,' he said. Looked down at the floor and smiled. 'I've always depended on the kindness of strangers.'

'Don't think quoting Henry Miller makes this any more romantic or cool. It's not. It's shit. I don't need it. You're still a suspect and I don't get the money back until you're found innocent or guilty. It's not a game Zim; you're still in trouble and so am I,' I said.

'Who's Henry Miller?' he said.

I rolled my eyes.

'Ruby, it's not a quote, it's true. It's strangers who pick me up from the floor of bars and get me a doctor when I've blacked out from being punched. And they're the ones who go for a smoke with me in crap airports when I think I'm dying and, well, you're not really a stranger anymore, but they're the ones who get me out of jail, it seems. And I won't forget Ruby. I owe you. I really do.'

I shrugged, put my hand on his bony shoulder, wondered why it was strangers who always helped him

131

out. What did his family know that we didn't? Outside at the taxi rank, we'd kept a slight distance from each other. I wasn't sure whether this was goodbye. I wanted him with me, but should I really ask him to Vasco? I was having second thoughts about it. Maybe I would have to be on my own after all.

'Where you going?' he said.

'Vasco.'

'Oh shit. Really?' he smiled at me.

'Yeah – I've got to check out this warehouse, where the head was found.'

'I'm going there too. That's where Paulo's offices are. I have to set up a meeting with him. We should share a taxi at least?'

Zim looked strained, anxious I might refuse. We stood with a space between us.

'Yeah, of course. Much cheaper that way,' I said.

He stepped forward and filled the space with relief. He felt the same as me. Neither of us wanted to be alone now.

Our taxi pulled up, not down at the Vasco port, but high above it, at some local viewpoint, looking out over the ocean. Middle-aged men in kurta pyjamas and tracksuits lolled on benches under trees, enjoying the early evening air. A couple jumped a child up above the railing to see the great rusted ships docked ready for whatever long journey they would be making. Mostly to Taiwan, according to our driver. The boats I had seen in Panjim, steaming up and down the Mandovi, they were here too. I had thought them so impressive on the river, but now, in the vast port, bringing their loads to these mother ships, they seemed like nothing more than midges. Like how murder made any other crime, even slashing your girlfriend, seem insignificant.

'What a scene. Wow. It's kind of worth the shit to see this. Industry is beautiful,' said Zim.

He'd cheered up considerably since getting into Vasco, took out his iPhone, started to snap.

Shipping containers stood piled high on the dock, amongst warehouses and cranes. One warehouse was surrounded by police tape, white cars parked outside. Men coming in and out of the building, standing in groups, discussing whatever was in there. A lip of TV cameras and crews stood waiting for news.

'That's where we need to be Zim, down there. Come on, let's go.'

Our driver was leaning against his car, smoking a cigarette and chatting to one of the joggers. He had the gait of a city dweller: relaxed in dirty traffic and people crowded in on one another. Different to the airport drivers, taut, ready to pounce on every naïve arrival, a potential goldmine. Despite the smog and the ugliness things seemed more laid back here than on the ever more precious strips of sand.

We wandered over and asked him to take us right down to the port. He stubbed out his cigarette and wanted to know where exactly. I pointed to the crawling police. He looked at us a little oddly, but shrugged, started the meter and glided down the hill.

'Do you think they're gonna just let us go in and take a look at the head?' said Zim.

'I dunno. I hadn't thought about it.'

'You don't seem to know what you're doing.'

'Fuck off.'

'I mean, you don't seem to have watched the crime shows. If you did you'd know the police fucking hate journalists sticking their noses into their crime scenes. They hate it. It's never a show without a camera getting smacked up in the air. I love those bits.'

'You're the one who messed up a murder scene, not me. Let's just go all right?'

The taxi pulled up to the cordon and I stepped out. I wished I was wearing something a bit more respectable than a tie-dye sundress, but there was nothing I could do about it now. I walked past the sleepy film crews to a small group of men, talking just inside the cordon. Inspector Srinvasen was in a shiny blue suit berating two men in Goan state police uniform. They looked over his shoulder at me. Last time I'd seen this guy I'd been arrested. I didn't want to get in the way of his wrath now. But David wasn't a nice person to fail either. And he wanted an interview with Srinvasen.

'Hi, excuse me, sorry.'

The inspector turned round to look at me. He frowned.

'Who are you?'

'Sorry, I'm Ruby Jones. I'm a journalist . . .'

Inspector Srinvasen turned around, looked at me blankly. He was supposed to have an unbeatable memory. An eye for every detail of a crime scene. He didn't recognise me at all. He was so wrapped up in stolen gods, he'd forgotten completely the one real murder he'd seen since arriving. Real people weren't as important as idols in his world.

'What are you doing here? This is a crime scene,' he said.

'I was wondering, er, could I, possibly get an interview with you?'

The other men surrounding the inspector began to laugh. Even he raised a smile. He patted me on the shoulder. They turned their backs on me and began talking amongst themselves once more. I slunk back to the car. Zim had his hand over his mouth but I could see from his eyes he was laughing.

'Don't say anything.'

'Sorry – but you know, what did you expect?'

'Not this much security. The head isn't there anymore. What are all these police still doing here? They've solved the crime, isn't it time for everyone to go home? What's in that warehouse?' I said.

Zim drew down the sides of his mouth.

'God knows . . . no . . . wait . . . not God, but maybe Paulo Mendes.'

'Your client? What has he got to do with anything?'

'He's in tourism, and shipping. Come on, we're late to meet him already. If he's half the man my dad thinks he is, he'll be able to help,' said Zim.

6

Paulo smiled broadly and raised his arm, gesturing to the vista over which we were looking; high above the grime he apparently loved, on the terrace of his penthouse apartment. I'd just asked him what a man rich enough to buy Pollock paintings on a whim was doing living in such a heaving hole of a city. I'd been more diplomatic of course.

Vasco stretched out in front of us, the blocks of concrete, the regimented streets. The sea. The blue, blue sea; shimmering yellow in the afternoon sun. The ships rusted orange, the smoke and the gravelly port. It wasn't pretty but it was a scene of scale and strength. From up here, you could see life flourishing despite itself. Water and heat engulfed the city. Concrete crumbled and office blocks moaned. Wild orchids grew in rotting gutters, palms sprung from cracks in the road.

'It's my home. I was born here. This is where I'm from. Vasco is my city. You're loyal to your place.

Ram here, he's from the depths of north Goa, the back of beyond, the Hindu heartland. He loves the forests, the rivers, the beaches and the temples. I don't understand him. I don't understand the tourists. I love the smoke. The ships on the sea. I love all of this,' he said.

Paulo's accountant, Ram Kumar, wasn't listening. He was engrossed in a newspaper and barely heard his name mentioned. The two men couldn't have been more different. Paulo was huge, well-kept, with a barrel chest and sloping shoulders. A gold crucifix peered out from his navy shirt. Ram was tiny in comparison, wearing chinos and a pressed white shirt. The way he crossed his legs was a little effeminate. I thought I recognised him, but I couldn't think where from. He clearly didn't know me so I didn't ask him, but I couldn't shake off the feeling that I had seen him before.

'Ram? Isn't that right?' said Paulo.

Ram put the newspaper down.

'Pardon me? They're still not saying what happened to Sister Michael. Just that she was found dead and they are investigating. I just don't understand it,' he said.

I glanced at Zim. Did Ram know her? Should we say something? He shook his head slightly; forget about it, don't mention it.

'Paulo says you hate Vasco. You only like the quiet,' drawled a girl sat by Paulo's bar, smoking. Long black hair scraped back into a ponytail, cheeks rouged. She was popped into a tight blue dress and heels. She was beautiful and she was showing off. I thought I'd met her before too but couldn't work out from where.

137

Maybe my mind was just a little out of place after Sister Michael.

'I don't hate it. Hate is too strong a word. It is what it is. Paulo's attached to the place because he was born here. I understand that. It's a great centre of trade. It always has been. Since the sixth century people have been importing and exporting from Vasco. By the sixteenth century Goa was one of the great trading posts of the world because of Vasco,' he said, folding his hands in his lap.

'Those churches we send all the buses up to. They're only here because of Vasco. You know who we traded with? We traded with Mecca. We traded with Aden. Zanzibar even! People loved to come to Goa even then,' said Paulo.

Zim and I nodded politely.

'This city, it's not like anywhere I've been before,' Zim ventured eventually.

'It's like Russia in the sun,' drawled the girl. That voice, I remembered that too. Russian. Then I knew. I'd seen her just yesterday, in the cell, wearing a green dress and Chanel sunglasses. Galina. She was wearing the same emerald heels now. Her friend, Saskia, said she'd got lucky with men. Paulo, it must be. That would make sense. Rich guy like that, Russian mistress. Head-to-toe Chanel.

'Hey! My God. That is exactly what I said when I got in. Do you remember Ruby? I love Russia. Moscow. What a great city,' said Zim excitedly.

Galina flicked her head and smiled. I didn't say anything. When I'd told Zim I was from Wales he wanted to know whereabouts in England that was. I wasn't jealous. Or if I was, it was purely in the name of Welsh culture. Zim seemed to have forgotten that he'd come here to sell a painting.

'What are you doing in Goa, Galina?'

She closed her eyes slightly. 'I live here now. But I'm a dancer, in Bollywood.'

'Oh wow!' said Zim, putting a hand to his forehead.

'Not many films coming up this year though,' said Ram.

Galina looked over at him. 'I'm shooting one now. You know that. Right here.'

Ram nodded. Galina murmured something in Russian.

'That's so cool. So cool,' said Zim.

Paulo didn't seem to mind him drooling over his girlfriend, just sipped on his rum and pineapple and gazed out at the sea. It didn't look like much could bother him. Paulo Mendes was one of the top twenty businessmen in India. After he had dropped by Blue Moon Gallery, Raoul Moon had done some 'research' on his potential new client and Zim filled me in on the way over here.

Paulo had started out in shipping, bringing down iron ore from central Goa to Vasco, on those rusty little ships. He now owned almost a third of the port, in a country where most of the shipping yards were government controlled. About twenty years ago he'd branched out into tourism and had developed large strips of the Goan coast. He's been the first to bring package holidays to Goa. The busloads of English, German and Russian tourists plying the small roads up and down the coast were his. And now his new plan for the Arambol tourist complex. No wonder he needed his accountant so close.

It was Ram who finally broke up the tête-à-tête between Galina and Zim.

'Ah, Zim. I know you're here because we said a while ago we were interested in buying more paintings. Do you have any prints to show us? Paulo's wife will be here very soon,' he said.

'Shruti just loves the Pomfret.'

'Pollock,' Ram corrected.

'Pollock,' Paulo continued unperturbed. 'You know my wife, she's not from here. She's from Bombay, studied in New York, used to live near MoMA. She's a doctor you know. She doesn't like it here so much. I have to keep her happy. Make her feel like she's living somewhere with culture.'

His wife? Coming here in a moment? So Galina wasn't his mistress. Unless his wife was really, really, relaxed. Ram? They didn't look like a likely couple.

'Oh, yeah. The catalogue? I was gonna bring it with me. But, actually, I, well I'll be honest. I left it with a client in Thailand. It was a kind of crazy rush. But have you got the internet? We can look at the gallery collection online,' said Zim.

Ram frowned slightly. 'We don't have a computer up here in the apartment. We'll have to go down to the offices.'

Paulo waved his hand.

'No, no. Don't worry. I bought Shruti an iPad. She'll bring it with her. We've got wireless.'

Paulo seemed incredibly affable for someone so powerful, even if he was destroying the whole of the

140

Goan ecosystem. Ram's mobile went off. Shruti perhaps. But no. Ram grimaced at the screen.

'Inspector Srinvasen,' he said.

Paulo rubbed his eyes, groaned. Galina smirked.

'I'm going to answer it. He's just going to keep calling if I don't,' said Ram. 'Inspector. What can I do for you?' he said in a tone of impressive neutrality. 'Today? Mr Mendes has told you everything he knows. He's been happy to cooperate with you but you really are making things difficult for him . . . Well, I'll ask him. Yes, yes. If you must. SIX PM. OK.'

Ram put the phone away carefully in his pocket before looking up. 'He wants to come round and inspect the accounts again. See the logs of everything going in and out on your ships.'

Paulo growled again.

'It's in order?'

'Paulo, I've worked with you for twenty years.'

There was no painting sold that day. Ram took us down in the elevator. It was a long way to the ground. No one spoke. The accountant inspected his perfect nails. Once in the lobby he gestured for us to sit down. Worn leather chairs in navy blue. Scuffed carpet.

'I'm going to have to ask you not to repeat the conversation you just heard. The head of Saint Francis has been found in one of Paulo's warehouses and he's become the main suspect in the theft. Of course, it's got nothing to do with him. He owns half the port. He can't, I can't, keep a track on everything that's coming in and out of Vasco. He rents to over fifty businesses. But this policeman, he likes big fish and they don't get much bigger in Goa then Paulo. He likes the glory,' said Ram.

141

'Can we come back tomorrow? I can print out some pictures,' said Zim.

Ram pursed his lips and put his hands together.

'Paulo's wife loves the painting your father sold them. And Paulo adores his wife, would do anything to make her smile. He'd buy the whole of the gallery for her if I gave him the go-ahead. But I'm afraid I'm going to have to put a stop on extra investments right now. If Paulo gets arrested, all his business dealings here in Goa will be frozen. I don't want anything outstanding around to complicate matters.'

Zim flushed red. 'But, my dad, he talked to Paulo. He said he was really interested. Not just one but maybe two or three.'

'He was. We were, but things are difficult, as I said.'

Zim went redder. 'You can't do that man. I've come all the way over to this shithole for nothing. This is just so fucked up. What am I gonna say to my dad?'

Zim was starting to shout. His body grew, expanding with fast growing frustration. The receptionist looked over. Ram glanced to the side. I put my hand on Zim's knee.

'I completely understand how you feel. But as I said, this is a difficult time for everyone. It looks like the Arambol project up in the north will be stopped until Paulo is cleared of involvement with the head. And we've already poured in huge amounts to secure planning permission. Paulo might seem relaxed but things aren't what they appear. This is a very stressful time for all of us,' he said.

Zim stamped the floor. 'Damn,' he shouted.

He stood up, walked away with his hands on his

head. All eyes followed him. Was this a show? To try and win a sale? Ram looked at me. I shook my head, shrugged. The accountant stood up.

'I have to go back up. The inspector will be arriving shortly. Look, I am sorry about this. It's a long way to come to be turned away. Will you get Zim to call me? Here's my card. Paulo will be up in his Anjuna complex from next week. Maybe things will have changed by then. We can set up another meeting. Tell him not to lose hope. We might get cleared.'

'All this trouble for an old saint,' I said.

Ram shook his head. 'I would never have believed it. That saint, he's said to protect Goa but you just have to read a bit of history to see what a devil he really was. Iconoclast. Vandalised, destroyed Hindu culture here. Is that any way to show people God? He was a violent bigot and a racist and is worshipped round the world for it. Is that Divine Justice? You can keep your God if it is.'

7

It was an easy target. Half bald and flea-ridden, the dog had his nose in a pile of rubbish when Zim kicked him in the side. There was a strangled howl of shock before he limped away into the night. I grabbed Zim's arm.

'That's enough. Stop it. What's happened to you? Fucking hell. Calm down. You're acting like a monster,' I said.

Zim turned around. His eyes were all red. He scrunched them shut. Breathed slowly. Opened them again.

'I'm sorry. I'm sorry. I just thought, I was so close to getting something done. It just made me mad.'

I gave him Ram's card. 'He said to call him. He feels bad you've come all this way. You might still get the deal.'

Zim seemed to calm down as quickly as he'd got mad. We wandered off down Vasco's gridded blocks, pulled towards the sea somehow. Night dropped as we found the port once more, lined with omelette shacks and barber stalls. A flower stand lit by buzzing lamps glistened in the oily blackness. Zim bought me a white rose before I knew what he was doing or could protest.

'Zim. What am I going to do with this?'

'Put it your hair, it'll go nicely with that red,' he said, taking the flower from my hands and placing it carefully in my hair. I hadn't had a haircut in a while, it was long and scruffy and tied up in a band. The rose stayed and petals dropped a trail in the grimy alleys as we tried to find a place to eat. It was the closest I'd come to romance in a while.

We ended up in a low den, filled with men and the occasional woman, bent in close over their food. Dim bulbs encased in baskets hung from the ceiling. The bar was stacked, glinting with different bottles standing ready to attention. Everyone was drinking.

'Rum? Since we're in a port?' said Zim.

The waiter handed us a plastic menu spattered with food stains. Neither of us had appetites. Zim threaded his glass through his fingers, inspected the shiny liquid.

'I see her lying on the floor every time I close my eyes,' he said. 'It's horrible.'

'So do I. And I have no idea why or who did it. I'm scared. I keep thinking whoever did it could be following us. That we're next.'

'I wish it could all go away. I wish we could start again. Things aren't going well. First the nun. Now this. Paulo won't even buy a painting.'

'Why did you get so angry? You scared me.'

'You don't understand. That was massive for me. I

really needed that sale. I really needed to show my dad I could do that. I have to prove myself.'

'But you didn't need to get so mad. It was weird.'

Zim rubbed his forehead. 'I know, Ruby. I know. I just see red and I can't help it. Sometimes I wonder if I really did get Melissa's face. Maybe it was me. But I go over what happened and I don't remember ever going for her face. I couldn't have done that to her. I don't have it in me. I'm not a bad person. Just . . . angry. I just get really angry. I don't know where it comes from. You know I don't remember anything before the age of six? My first memory is watching flamingo's fucking on the Discovery Channel. There's got to be something that makes me act this way right?'

He concentrated on his glass; the rum glinted in his eyes, orange globes. I could understand why Melissa would have stayed, despite her best intentions. All his emotions hung off his face. I wanted to look after him, to make him feel better. This time it was me that took his wrist. He looked up instantly. Had he felt that touch too?

'Hey come on. OK, I understand. Let's get out of here. We need to find somewhere to sleep. It's getting late,' I said.

It had rained outside, washed everything clean. The street glistened as we walked along a row of cheap hotels, flashing vacancies. In Kamashi Guesthouse, we found the receptionist watching a preacher wail on a small TV, resting on top of two larger, broken televisions. I didn't like the look of it; it wasn't a holiday place. I wondered who stayed there. Zim spotted a larger, plusher looking hotel opposite and headed straight for it. Citadel was more expensive and there were white towels on the beds.

'Should we go for this one?' said Zim to me.

'I dunno. The other is cheaper.'

'Don't worry about that. I'll get it. Blue Moon,' he said. 'This is one expense I can explain easily. Do you want a room by yourself?'

I didn't want to be on my own. I didn't want to wake up petrified in the middle of the night. It was OK now, with Zim here, with people around, with the rum warming me up. But my veins were still bubbling with the fear that I was next to die; that whoever had got Sister Michael was close at hand, watching me. I knew any sound, any noise would destroy me alone in the dark.

'There's two separate beds here. I mean, it's cheaper to get one room than two,' I said.

'Ruby. I've told you. Blue Moon expenses. This is the price of a milkshake in LA. And besides I owe you. If you want a room on your own, I'm happy to pay for it. I can get you a master suite if you like? Do you have any rooms with jacuzzis? Minibars?' he asked the porter.

The porter looked at him nervously. He didn't understand. I needed to rescue him from this barrage.

'I'm fine. Let's just have one room. We're grown-ups, kind of. You're not going to attack me in the middle of the night are you?'

Zim shrugged and smirked.

'Zim?'

'No, no, of course not. Of course, I won't *attack* you.'

We got some fried crab in the hotel's huge empty bar. In honour of the meal the manager turned on a little electric lamp resting on our table, a weak spot of light amidst the darkness. We ate in near silence. I hadn't realised how hungry I was and sucked on the poor animal to get out all the meat I could.

'Kind of romantic, eating almost blind isn't it?' said Zim.

'Where is everyone? That Kamashi place was practically full. All the keys were off the hooks,' I said.

It seemed weird but I put my jumpiness down to tiredness and felt better after a wash. I showered and used the white towels and felt better than I had done in ages. I bought a toothbrush in a small shop outside and removed the days old sludge from my teeth. Zim lent me a T-shirt. It had a picture of Imelda Marcos on it and a banner saying '30 second blow-job'. I didn't understand it and didn't really like it, but it was clean. I climbed into my bed, under the sheets. I thought I'd taken my time in the bathroom but Zim took three times longer. Steam and perfume clouded around him as he came out the bathroom; washed red, a towel wrapped round his waist. His ribs poked through his skin. He was skinny as hell. That was why he refused to take off his outsized sweatshirts. He turned the light off and got into bed, put one arm behind his head and stared at the ceiling. A streetlight outside threw a slant of light into the room. I shut my eyes.

'Are you tired?' he said.

'Very.'

'Do you think you're gonna be able to sleep?'

'I hope so.'

'You scared still?'

'Yeah. Terrified. Think everyone I meet is in on the murder. Stupid.'

'How did your friend die in Delhi?'

'He fell in a river. Everyone thought it was murder but it wasn't. It was just an accident. About six months ago.'

'That's awful.'

'I know. I know. It's why I came here. I needed to get away. I thought it would be good for me to go and see this saint. But all that happened was I lost my bag with everything in it, my passport, my wallet and my iPod. Stephen had given it to me as a present.'

'I'll give you an iPod.'

I smiled, still with my eyes shut. 'Thanks Zim. But it was the music. That was what was important. He'd made all these playlists for me, I'm never gonna get those back.'

'I'll make you some playlists.'

'Zim, don't worry about it. Go to sleep.'

'Ruby?'

'What?' I opened my eyes this time.

'You don't mind sharing a room with me do you?'

'No, its fine.'

'I didn't want to be on my own.'

'It's fine Zim.'

'I'm not going to attack you.'

'All right.'

'Unless you want me to.'

'Go to sleep.'

I slept another deep, dreamless sleep until I felt a

hand on my shoulder. I opened my eyes. It was still night, the streetlight was still slanting through the room. Zim's bed was empty. It was Zim holding my shoulder. I had a jerk of fear and jumped up and around.

'Hey, Get off me.'

Zim smacked his hand hard on my left shoulder. Fucking hell, he was mad. How could I have been so stupid to trust him? He was violent, he was angry. I had no idea who this guy was. I screamed.

'No, wait.'

Zim turned the main light on. He was covered in welts. His sheet was splattered with small red marks. I threw off my sheet and looked down at my bed to see three or four small brown insects scuttling over my body. There were bites on my legs and little blotches of blood.

I jumped up. 'What are they?' I cried.

'Bed Bugs. I've seen them before. Hotels downtown are full of them. It's the first thing you got to check before you book a room. Even if it's just for an hour, you check.'

I started crying. These little insects, sucking my blood, coming out and crawling over my body in my sleep was too much. Waiting for me, under this mattress, which had seemed so clean and presentable, with a matching towel and a lamp beside the bed. I could hear myself moaning. One part of me registered the fact that I was really losing it, but another part, the more powerful, didn't care. I'd really had enough of Goa, of India. Zim took my shoulders.

'Hey, Ruby. Hey stop. Don't worry. It's fine. They're not going to give you anything. Sweetheart, stop crying. Come on. We'll get out of here; find another hotel. It's not a problem.'

'But what time is it?'

'Three-thirty in the morning. It's not late.'

'But I don't want to go out. I'm scared. What if someone is waiting for us? What if someone has followed us here? We just don't know.'

'Ruby don't be stupid. It's not going to be like that. Don't worry. Just pack up your things, make sure you don't get any of the little fuckers on any of your clothes or anything and we'll get out of here. In the morning we'll head to the beaches. Screw your article. I'll talk to my dad, I'll tell him what's happened. I'll get him to wire you the bail money. We don't need to stay here in this hell hole. Fuck knows why Paulo does.'

I wiped my eyes and nodded. We packed away our stuff gingerly and made our way down to reception in the cranky lift. We woke up the night guard, who had the buggers crawling all over his T-shirt. He was obviously used to them, he barely woke up to open the door.

The street was dark apart from the light that looked into our bedroom. The hotels were closed, the signs turned off. A couple of stray dogs, roaming the streets, sidled up to us, growling, and just added to my hysteria.

'Oh God. They're worse at night, dogs in India. Something happens to them. They go crazy. And there is nowhere to go. We'll be eaten alive,' I said.

'Ruby don't worry. There must be somewhere open. This is a port for God's sake. Sailors don't go to bed early. Let's just walk towards the dock.'

I couldn't quite believe Zim was so in control. I

would have assumed it would be him flipping out and me calm and controlled. I was shaken up more than was reasonable. I wasn't my usual self. I needed to get a grip.

'There's a light over there; come on, let's follow it,' he said.

We walked towards a glinting, red spark, right at the end of the street. It was hole of a bar, with a small entrance and no windows.

'Hey, look. This is fate. It's called Ruby's. Come on.'

One single red bulb made the wall of bottles in this tiny bar dance. A black guy with very white eyes stood cleaning glasses behind a makeshift bar of beer crates. Small groups of men sat squashed together, bottles of spirits between them, smoking and eating pieces of fish with cocktail sticks. The barman stared at us with his bright eyes. We weren't locals, clearly.

'Let's just go, Zim,' I said.

'No, don't be a pussy, wait.'

Zim began to talk in a loud, annoying LA accent to the barman, who stood, mutely polishing, still staring.

'Hey, Hi! We're, we're looking for a HOTEL. Do you KNOW any HOTELS near here? HOTELS?'

The man lined up his last glass.

'You want to drink something?' he said. He sounded Caribbean. Zim hadn't needed to shout.

We got some more rum. The guy brandished his bottle like some soho cocktail maestro, throwing it up in the air and banging two shots down in glasses for us. I gulped mine and felt it steady my nerves.

'There ain't many hotels open at this time,' he said. 'Things close early in the centre here. But you could try down by the dock. There's a place called Maria's Motel.'

'Is it clean? We've just left a hotel because of bedbugs.'

The guy gave a half-smile. 'You were at Citadel right?'

'Yeah.'

'That place. It's almost falling down with those devils. Maria's is clean. The whores wouldn't work there if it wasn't. You want another for road?'

We gulped down another and got on the way. Zim put his arm around me and I leant in.

'Don't worry Ruby. Come on, think of all the things that have happened so far. This is certainly not the worst thing. We're going to Maria's. They'll think you're my whore.' Zim cackled.

'You'd be lucky,' I said.

'I know,' he smiled to himself. It was a pretty dirty smile.

It was easy to find our way to the dock, the Vasco streets lying in straight lines leading down to the sea. The glint of hole-in-the-wall bars along the way – of life and people – took the edge off my continuing fear. Two double rums helped too. We soon found ourselves at the entrance to the port, where the taxi had dropped us. The warehouse where the head was found was no longer a hub of activity but a lonely black silhouette against the blue night, the police tape flapping ghostly in the ocean breeze.

'How the hell did that head end up there? I wonder what else they've got in there?'

'What about it?' said Zim.

'What about what?'

'Going to have a look? The police aren't going to be around there now are they?'

'Zim, what's got into you?'

'I dunno. Once you've tripped up over a dead body, got arrested by Indian police, held in a cell, force-fed curry and been bitten to high heaven by bed bugs . . . I mean . . . why stop?'

I didn't want to be the pussy and back out. But my fear came raging back. I'd been broken by the last few days. All my bravery had vanished. I didn't want to cross this shipyard, with looming shadows, great canyons of black between containers, rats scuttling back and forth, sniffing and whining. The dock was bracing during the day, in the damp night it was suffocatingly frightening.

'I dunno Zim. It looks dangerous.'

'Why would it be any more dangerous in the night than in the day? No one's working now. They're all getting fucked in those bars.'

'You don't know who's around, though, who might be waiting for us.'

'Ruby – did you not see the second series of *The Wire*? The guys who get killed in places like this are the sneaks, the ones who blow the whistle on their bosses. The gang leaders take them down here to the port *because* there's no one else around. They can kill horribly, in peace. No one is just waiting around for some girl to turn up so they can rape and murder them. That happens in city parks. You got to be a pretty dumb rapist to hang around out here. You'd be waiting years.'

'Till today . . .'

'Oh come on.'

'OK, OK, let's have a walk up there, but if there's police around we go. I don't want to be arrested a second time, OK? I haven't got the money for two sets of bail.'

Our steps echoed around us as we crossed the barren concrete between containers and cranes.

Two policemen were asleep on fold-out beds in the shadow of the warehouse. An empty bottle of Old Monk Rum lay on the floor beside the remains of rice and fish. I could see rifles poking out of the rugs that covered them, awkward comforters.

'They're not going to wake up. They've knocked themselves out with the Monk,' said Zim.

'Yeah but if they do, they'll shoot us.'

'Let's just see if the place is locked. There isn't any more security than these two. We can just walk under the police rope.'

Every step seemed to echo agonisingly as we made our way towards the sliding doors. Once there, I pulled limply at the handle.

'It's locked,' I said with some relief.

'You're just being a wimp. Come on, let's both pull it. It's heavy,' said Zim.

I put my back into this time and we managed to haul the door open a fraction. A rat leapt out and ran across my foot. I let out a scream which echoed loudly and continuously.

'Ruby! What the fuck!' hissed Zim.

'It was a rat!' I whispered back.

We looked at the policeman. One of them stirred, moved to his other side, nestled into his gun.

'I don't want to go in. Let's just go back,' I said.

'We have to go in now – get in. Those police will fuck us if they find us hanging around.'

Zim put his hand on my neck and pushed me in between the doors with a force that shocked me.

It was black in there. Musty air choked me. I backed towards the door, away from the darkness.

'Zim, I can't stay in here, it's too dark. I can't stay in here. I'm too scared.'

'Wait, wait. I've got my iPhone. That will give us some light.'

Zim flicked it out of his pocket and shone the digital glow into the blackness. A flying demon swooped out of the air and I screamed loudly once again. Zim pushed his hand over my mouth.

'Ruby! Please. Fucking hell, if I had known you were gonna be like this I wouldn't have suggested it. Shut up.'

'What was that? My God . . . Oh my God . . . where are we? It was some kind of demon.'

'Ruby it wasn't. Look again.'

Zim shone the light at my demon and I saw it was an angel. A flying angel. Rotten and holed from termites and damp, but still an angel, with its hands in prayer and its wings branched out.

'It's a statue, can you see? It must have been carved for one of those big empty churches,' he said.

'What's it doing here?'

Zim shrugged and shone his phone to the right. A large silver cross, embellished with animals and plants, reflected off the weak, greenish light.

'Come on – let's go further in. This place is massive,' said Zim.

The gaping darkness petrified me but I didn't want to lose the one bit of light, so I followed him down a narrow pathway, between tall shelves, filled with statues, crosses, goblets, even a couple of altars. Penitent eyes, hands gripped in prayer, the dour faces of saints materialized in the roaming spotlight of Zim's iPhone, melting away once more as he moved deeper into this strange trove.

'What is this place?' he whispered.

'It some kind of store house for Christian art. Look, all the objects have labels on them, descriptions. They're being sent somewhere.'

Zim shone his torch across the shadowy sculpture of a child, his right hand open in a blessing, his left holding an orb, balancing delicately on a silver globe. We had to get up close to read the label.

Infant Jesus Saviour of the world: This image of the infant Jesus is silver-plated and partially painted. The gown is of gold embroidered velvet made in Goa, where the art of embroidering velvet is practised to perfection by the nuns of the convent of Saint Monica. The combination of image and globe is an excellent example of Indo-European art of the eighteenth century. The Goan goldsmith engraves the globe with secondary gods of the Hindu pantheon as well as nagas with human faces and arms that turn into coils.

Two wooden pillars, tall and elegant. Our weak spotlight showed tranquil faces with carved locks of hair. As we moved slowly down, the sculpture turned from human to serpent.

'God. Why do they like snakes so much? I thought the snake was the devil? It's kind of weird isn't it?' said Zim.

'Snakes are holy in Hinduism. They've just mixed up snakes and angels. Look at the label.'

Altar ornaments: Nagas and Naginas: Nagas (male snakes) and Naginas (female snakes) came to figure in Indo-Portuguese art when Christianity came to India. Carving work on altars, furniture, textiles and silverware sometimes carried nagas which are sacred symbols used in Hinduism. This exquisite eighteenth century pair are carved and gilded wood. The face of the naga and nagina in this set have been given treatment very similar to that of Indo-Portuguese angels.

'The devil was an angel before he was a devil anyway. Is that right?' said Zim.

A tarnished gold crucifix, embellished ornately with tarnished stones, rubies, emeralds, diamonds.

This unique historic piece is said to be an exact copy of the crucifix that the Portuguese explorer and military genius Afonso de Albuquerque held in his hand after he defeated the Bijapuri army. Holding the crucifix up to the sky he sailed up the Mandovi River to plant the Portuguese standard and declare the state Portuguese territory. The crucifix is one of the few surviving local pieces by the famous Goan goldsmith Raulu Chatim. Albuquerque sent Chatim to work in the Royal Court at Lisbon. His work

became famous throughout Europe and was the
foundation for the unparalled reputation of Goan
goldsmiths and jewellery.

'Do you think anyone would find out if I took this? Melissa would love it. She might forgive me if I gave her something like this. She's very into religious jewellery,' said Zim.

Why did he want to get back with her? Why did he want her to forgive him? An unreasonable jealously rose up in me. He didn't really understand people, if he thought giving her an old cross would work.

'How can you be that naïve Zim? Just leave it alone OK? Let's try not to get in any more trouble than we need to Zim . . . and honestly? I don't think the girl would forgive you if you gave her the Ring of the Fisherman,' I said, holding his hand away from the cross.

'The what?'

'The Ring of the Fisherman. It's the pope's ring. You're supposed to kneel down and kiss it when you meet him.'

Zim wrinkled his face. 'She wouldn't like that. She's completely OCD about germs, cleanliness. Like me with smells. We're similar like that.'

I rolled my eyes. 'Whatever, just get away from the cross.'

We arrived at more police tape wound tightly round one shelf; where the head must have been sitting amongst all these other relics. This wasn't just some empty warehouse, like Ram had said. No wonder the Idol Squad were hanging around. They'd hit gold. This must be the centre of a smuggling ring, the kind they were always trying to break. What else were these objects all doing, stored secretly in the port? Was Paulo a secret big-time temple thief? David was going to go crazy for all this.

'Well, I'm sure he felt at home here, old Xavier,' said Zim.

I giggled nervously. A window in the far side of building showed a grey, pink sky. I heard a gull. The deep black in which we had entered had lightened and I could see my hand in front of me.

'Come on, Zim, it's nearly dawn.'

We made our way slowly through the many objects. There must have been hundreds, dusty and sleepy, waiting for delivery. Then, by the entrance, I saw something, or someone, I recognised. I dropped to my knees to take a better look. A saint, with his wings spread and scales in his hands.

'It's Saint Michael.'

'How do you know?'

'He saves souls at the hour of death. He weighs their deeds and gives them a chance to repent. He protects us in times of battle against evil.'

'Well let's hope he's protecting us . . . Sister Ruby.'

My omelette was oily and hot and filled with chillies and onion. I forked it quickly into my mouth, trying to replace my lack of sleep with food. Zim played around with his, pushing it around his plate, lifting it up, inspecting it, letting it drop down with a heavy splat. No wonder he was so thin if that was how he ate. I could see the cook, his white T-shirt splattered with years of grease, watching him with wonder, I'm sure he'd never had one of his creations treated that way. I smiled and took a slurp of insanely sweet tea to make up for his behaviour.

'Don't they have coffee?' said Zim, holding up his glass to the light.

'Just drink it Zim. It'll make you feel better. We've had no sleep. '

'I guess I can't complain about the location anyhow.'

We'd found the omelette stall off a spit of the dock, frying food twenty-four hours a day, surrounded almost entirely by the ocean. Sliding past the two slumbering guards, we'd walked quickly in any direction, getting as far away as we could. We got right to the end of the port, where we dropped down on our cook's red plastic stools and sat stunned in the pink air, watching the red sun and the gulls meet the morning.

Zim left his omelette and flicked out a cigarette. I took one off him too. The smoke, the grease, the chilli and the sugar mixed in my mouth. It felt disgusting and totally appropriate. I sucked on it and squinted my eyes at the sea. A smuggling ring. Taking out Christian artefacts from Goa to God knows where. But why would you steal the head of Saint Francis? Sister Michael said herself it had no market value, that no one would be interested in buying a crumbling, papery head of a corpse, even if he was a saint. I'd get in touch with David Dryden. Maybe he could do some research at his end.

Zim stubbed his cigarette out in his omelette.

'That's disgusting Zim.'

'What? I wasn't going to eat it.'

'It shows a lack of respect for food. People are starving in this country.'

'Anyone would think you were, the way you wolfed that down.'

'Are you saying I'm fat?'

'I'm just not used to girls who are so fond of their food that's all. It's not normal where I come from.'

'I just can't believe you just said that. You think I'm fat?'

'I didn't say that. You're not fat. I mean maybe you could lose a couple of pounds –'

'*Lose a couple of pounds?*'

'What? I'm just being honest.'

'Fuck you Zim. Just 'cause you're anorexic doesn't mean everyone else has to be. Those baggy jeans aren't fooling anyone, you must weigh less than a seven-year-old.'

'I have half my weight in my cock. It's fucking huge.'

I looked at him in disgust. I couldn't quite believe this was the same person who had been so good and kind last night, who'd bought me a rose and looked after me when I needed it. Perhaps he was bipolar. Or maybe it was me; maybe I just didn't like the idea that he thought I was fat, that he preferred girls like Galina or Melissa.

'You really are a horrible human being Zim. Really I have never met anyone like you. I don't know how your girlfriend put up with you as long as she did.'

Zim shrugged. 'I don't know why you're getting so offended about a couple of pounds. I didn't say you weren't attractive. You are, you're very attractive. Very attractive.'

'Look – should we forget about this? I've got more important things to think about. How am I going to write an article about the head of Saint Francis and a warehouse full of Christian statues without the police knowing I broke in and entered?'

'God knows.'

8

I was back at the old mansion, standing in the door, waiting for Father Jonathan to open up. He fiddled with the keys in his pocket, sniffing heavily as he did so. He didn't want to let me in.

'Have you asked Inspector Ferreira? Isn't it a crime scene still?'

Of course I hadn't. But I took the chance that Father Jonathan wouldn't check.

'I've spoken to him, of course.'

The priest sniffed and wiped his nose. 'I'm very, very busy you know. The cardinals are still here. It's been a terrible time, terrible. I don't have time to let you go roaming through poor Sister Michael's home.'

'I'm sorry. I just really need to see if the Bombay consulate has sent my passport. You understand don't you? Couldn't Maria let me in?' I said.

'The police are still looking for her. She's nowhere to be found. Her family are so worried. They are looking everywhere for her. They say she is very fragile. It's really just a dreadful situation. Dreadful. I miss Sister Michael terribly. I just, I wish she was here now.'

Father Jonathan continued his whining lament as he clunked the key into the keyhole.

'I just, I just, I never thought she would die. I didn't. I never thought she could die. She was so strong. She was stronger than me. Really, much stronger than me. That's what I'd always believed. I've known her for years and years. I knew her husband very well. We studied together. I never thought she would die.'

The door opened with a heavy swing and Father Jonathan stopped talking. Not a sound. She'd kept it well-oiled. The air inside was very still. Torn bits of police tape hung from the door of the conversation room. I hesitated and turned around, waiting for Father Jonathan, before going any further into the house. He had moved a few steps back and was wringing his hands in the shade of a drooping mango tree. He opened and closed his mouth a couple of times before speaking.

'I, I, would prefer to stay outside.'

'Are you sure Father? Didn't you say you needed to check the mail yourself?'

'I don't want to go in,' he whined. 'I'll just stay out here.'

I turned back to the room.

'Don't be long,' he called out after me.

A pile of mail was littered over the floor. I picked it up myself and went through it. No passport. It was mostly bills, junk, a few Christmas cards and a bank statement from Coutts. That surprised me; Coutts was where all the Old European barons and English dukes held accounts. It was an unusual place for a poor ex-nun from Goa to be banking. I stopped myself from opening it.

I turned the door handle of the conversation room. I could feel my hands were sweating. It was early but the sun was fierce. The windows were all closed now and heat was building up in here. There was no Maria to clean and air and keep the place alive. Where was she? I hoped she was all right. Had she been murdered too?

Nothing had changed since the afternoon we'd found Sister Michael. The decorations were still all over the floor, the tangle of tinsel was in the same place, forensic markers scattered about. The string of Christmas cards threaded across the room. It was only a week to Christmas now. Only a week. I wandered through the room, my footsteps echoing around me. My eyes roamed over each corner, remembering standing here, just a few days ago, with Sister Michael, as she proudly explained how she'd renovated her house. Everything was the same, the velvet love chairs set out at even spaces along the long room, the Indonesian ship wood still hard and solid under foot. But her beloved statue had gone. The statue was missing. It had been the same statue, the same Saint Michael in that warehouse, looking after his namesake once more I guess.

I sat down on the love chair. What was going on? Did Sister Michael get killed for that statue? Was it robbers? Did it mean that whoever killed Sister Michael was involved, in some way, with the stealing of the head? Was Paulo involved? Could I tell the police? Could I risk getting involved again? Who killed Sister Michael? Who stole the head? Who was in charge of all those objects, sitting there in the dark of that dusty warehouse, with the rats and the mice? Where were they going and where had they come from?

I flicked through her mail till I came to open the thick cream statement from Coutts and ripped it open. If I could wolf-whistle I would have done.

'Fucking hell,' I said myself.

The woman was rich. She'd got just over one million pounds in a savings account and ten grand had been paid into her current account last month. Where the hell was the money from? And who got it now she's dead?

I stood up, looked around me once more. There was a bright white dot on the wall in front of me. It was a reflection from one of Sister Michael's Christmas cards, a silvered star dropping light in the night. I opened it up. It was from the Church society of Chandor, thanking Sister Michael for her generous contribution to their fund this year. There were about fifteen cards strung out along the line. I picked them all off. I could see Father Jonathan from the window of the conversation room, still standing in the shade of the mango tree, his hands clasped around what looked like a chocolate bar. He took a bite, wiped his brow and looked anxiously up at the house. It was early but it was fierce out there. I waved to him but he didn't see me. The sun must have been reflecting off the glass.

I dumped the bills and began going through cards, flicking through images of Jesus, three kings, snowflakes and the holy family. Most murders were committed by someone the victim knows, I think I'd heard that somewhere before. There was one from her sister, another

167

from an old nun in Italy, another from a novice here in Santa Monica Convent, her old home. I could just imagine Sister Michael assiduously sending tasteful cards throughout the year; thank you notes, get well soon, congratulations, consolations. And at Christmas time, she reaped the rewards.

I stopped at one particularly fine card; heavy, embossed with a drawing of an ornate gold filigree crucifix. The words 'Edward Jones Antiquities' were written in a tasteful Times New Roman font on the back of the card and inside was a handwritten note.

Dear Dorothea, Thank you for all your hard work this year. It hasn't been an easy time for us, but I think we've cracked the problem. Much love, Edward.

I flicked through a few more until I came to a card of the baby Jesus coloured all blue, just like Krishna. The woman holding him, Mary I imagined, was wearing a pale blue sari and white shawl. Inside was another note addressing Sister Michael by her old name.

Dorothea, You've gone too far. We must talk.
Ram x

Ram? A common Hindu name, but pretty unusual in Christian Goa. The accountant had been engrossed in an article on the death when we met him. He'd been so involved in his newspaper he hadn't heard his boss talk to him. I peered out the window once more. Father Jonathan had become tired. He was sitting under the tree now, still wringing his hands. He could sit there a little longer while I used Sister Michael's computer. It took time to load up but eventually it cranked into life with zips and buzzes and whirs. The thieves should have taken the computer as well as the statue of Saint Michael. It was almost as old, definitely antique. I tried not to get too impatient as it slowly pieced together the Facebook home page. Finally I logged on and found David Dryden. He was online.

David?

Ruby. How was Vasco? Did you get my interview?

No, but I know what's in the warehouse.

What?

We're not supposed to know. So don't say anything to anybody yet, OK?

Of course. What's in the warehouse?

It's some storehouse for antiquities. There's hundreds of statues in there, altars and gold too. The police are linking it to smuggling. They've got their eye on this big business man. If they charge him it'll stop this huge tourist complex he's planning in the North.

God, Bukowski will love this. He's got a thing against mass tourism.

The privilege of the rich.

Of course. He's never been to Butlins. He doesn't understand. He'll see this as divine retribution. He won't think of all those Liverpool kids who won't now see a palm tree will he?

Liverpool?

They're poor there aren't they?

Don't pretend ignorance David. I know where you're from. They're poorer in Rhyl.

169

Touché. Well, anyway keep going. Have you got an interview with Srinvasen?

Not yet no. He's not an easy man to catch. Can you do some research for me down that end? I think I've found something that might get me an interview with the guy. But I want some more facts before I do anything.

I've got an intern . . .

OK cool – can you get them to check out Sotheby's and Christie's Antiquities sales over the last say, ten years? Indian art – specifically Indian Christian art.

OK . . .

Also – find out which dealers specialise is this kind of antiquity in London.

Anyone in particular you're thinking of?

I won't bias you. And just, I dunno, is there anyone you can talk about the process of getting art/antiquities out of India into the UK?

There is actually – friend from New College – did classics, he's works for Sotheby's. Our office is close by. I'll take him out for a bottle of claret. Heavy French wines always get him talking.

Sounds wonderful. Speak soon.

Ciao . . .

A surprisingly strong wail came through the house. It was Father Jonathan at the front door, still unable to go any further into this haunted house but getting impatient.

'Ruby? What are you doing?'

I shut off the computer without logging out. The old dinosaur could handle it.

'Coming, Father Jonathan, sorry, I was just using the bathroom.'

It was as weak an excuse as the limp pile of post that I handed him. Just a few circulars and bills, the rest was in my rucksack.

'The post must be delayed. The week before Christmas,' I said.

He nodded, took them with his large hands and found a place for them somewhere in the folds of his black gown. He didn't register any lack of post. He didn't seem all there.

'Ah, there was just one thing Father Jonathan. I think it's a matter for the police, perhaps you could tell them. There's a statue missing in the house. A statue of Saint Michael. It was there the night before she died.'

Father Jonathan shook his head.

'We are all under a tremendous amount of pressure. A tremendous amount of pressure. Tremendous,' he said.

'I really think this is important. It might have something to do with Sister Michael's death. I think you should tell Inspector Ferreira.'

'I don't want to talk to that man again,' he burst out shrilly.

I didn't know what to say. Father Jonathan and I both looked at one another in silence.

'I don't like that inspector,' trailed off the priest, to fill the air.

'OK. I can go and talk to him myself then,' I said.

Father Jonathan, wrung his hands. 'He'll only come back here with more questions.'

'But I am positive the statue is missing.'

'You know she may have put it in the old chapel up the top of the hill. She sometimes stores pieces there before she sends them away.'

'Before she sends them away? But why would she be sending this away? She loved it. It was of Saint Michael.'

Father Jonathan shook his head in frustration, his voice rose into a treble.

'I don't know. I just don't know! I'm sure it's in the chapel. It will probably be there. We don't need more police around here, just when things are almost back to normal.'

'Have the police checked it already though? Wouldn't they have asked you if they found something in there?'

'It's part of the Idol Squad's crime scene. The local police are not to disturb any parts of their crime scene.'

'Well should we have a look? Do you have the keys?'

'No,' moaned Father Jonathan. 'Sister Michael kept the keys. She kept them on hooks above the dresser in the kitchen.'

'I'll go and have a look. How do I know which one it is?'

'It's large, iron. Very heavy.'

The keys weren't there. Father Jonathan wanted to give up. I said I'd go on my own. I knew the chapel he was talking about. It was where I had been sitting when Sister Michael's dogs had bounded up and found me. The old priest didn't like that. He hitched his robes up and followed me up the hill through the long grass, swatting flies away with his free hand, breathing heavily.

I tried to peer through the window of the old place, but the curtains were still pulled over with black cloth.

'Look, I think the door is ajar,' he said. 'The statue must be in here.'

I heard Father Jonathan jolt the door. It creaked open. There was then a wailing gargle. I followed him in and was hit by a deep rich smell of rotting flowers. He'd found Maria. We'd found Maria. Bloated and bruised and covered with flies. Hung from the eaves of the chapel. She must have jumped off the dilapidated altar. She must have been there a few days already.

9

I was back in the police station. This time, out front, staring at my hands, holding a scalding cup of sweet tea. I waved away a fly. I wasn't a suspect in this death. It was clear Maria had done it herself. That's what Inspector Ferreira said. There had been a prayer of forgiveness written out over and over again in her pocket.

'Ruby, you have to make that statement. Please,' Zim said.

He was crouched down beside me, on his knees, beseeching me something I had just refused Inspector Ferreira.

In the aftermath of finding Maria, in the rush and the haze, the police acted more as rescuers than investigators. Cups of tea for me and the old priest, as many calls as I wanted. I'd just used one; to Zim, waiting for me in Panjim.

Father Jonathan took it worse than I did, his huge gnarly hands shaking too much to even place his cigarette in his mouth, mumbling over and over again that she had never gone to confession. I couldn't stop talking about Maria's wedding bangles, the wedding bangles Sister Michael had told her not to wear. The inspector wanted to hear about this, about their argument. He quickly formed new theories about the suicide. Maria had been angry at Sister Michael, hit her with the vase without meaning to kill her and then couldn't handle the guilt when her boss had died.

But I didn't agree. It seemed as desperate as pinning the thing on Zim and me. Ferreira hadn't even checked if the handwriting on the note was her own. Or if she could write at all.

'Ferreira wants to palm this murder off on an old woman, because they had an argument the night before. Why should I help him do that? Why doesn't he investigate this properly? Find out who made that call about the murder in the first place?'

Zim looked at with me, black rings around blue desperate eyes.

'Ruby. Please. I don't want to get the rap for this murder. Please . . .'

Zim rested his head on my knee. He didn't say anything. After a while he lifted himself up, walked off, leant against the wall, his hands in his pockets. He was still wearing an outsize hoody despite the heat. I knew what a rake he was underneath; there was nothing to him. He was so frail.

I snapped. Why was I defending a dead woman? Why was I so sure that Maria hadn't done it? Maybe she had. What was worse, that a killer could be walking around free – or that this boy got blamed?

And so I was back in that interview room again, in the same sticky plastic chair. Ferreira's hand hovered over the recorder then rested back down on the table. I gave him a look.

'I wanted to apologise before we begin,' he said.

I wasn't expecting that. David Dryden really had helped us out. It seemed he'd somehow managed to convince this policeman I was practically best mates with the British Ambassador.

'Don't worry. Really, I don't know the Embassy . . . that well,' I said.

Ferreira reddened slightly, leant back.

'No, no. It's not that. I want to explain. I made up my mind on you two too fast. But you have to understand that we're up against it here. We're a local police force trying to deal with international crime. Goa is the main transit point for drugs coming from Afghanistan now. Not Mumbai. Goa. Not the fourth biggest city in the world; but a small port. And there's been mafia wars between gangs to control the trade and the beaches going on for years. Not between locals – between Israelis, Russians, French even. It's an invasion, of the worse kind. We can't cope. We're being taken over. Its painful to watch. And then it's us, Goans, that get the blame when things go wrong. Is it any wonder I assume it's foreigners involved in a crime like this? For all I knew you were both high as kites, and then when I found out about Simon's previous offence. It fell into place.'

'But now it's falling out of place.'

'Your story stands up and you've given Simon an alibi. Maria's prints are on the vase. Then there was the note in her pocket. This makes more sense. We can keep it out the papers. For the sake of her family. Suicide is a sin you see. Editors here, they understand the shame to the family. We're still a community, despite everything. We try and look after one another.'

He looked me in the eye. He didn't see anything shameful in this neat tying up of the two dead women's lives.

'She's already going to hell. Why not pin a murder on her as well?' I said.

'You don't have to put it like that. Look, all I want you to do is make a statement explaining the argument the two had the night before Dorothea died. That's all. It's enough with the prints and the notes to close the case. The bail hasn't been transferred to court yet. We could finish this all up with the statement. Charges against you both completely dropped and your money back.'

It was very tempting. Put it all behind you. Enjoy Goa. Enjoy the beaches. But could we? Could I? Wouldn't I just be haunted by what had happened and the horrible sense that whoever had killed Sister Michael was close by. Was watching me? I couldn't shake off that feeling. And what about the statue of Saint Michael? Why was it in the Vasco warehouse, along with the head of the dead saint?

'But what if Maria really didn't do it? What if the killer is still out there and getting away with it? What if they're watching this whole thing now? What if we're in danger? Don't you think this might have something to do with the missing head? You know, her statue of Saint Michael is missing.'

Ferreira rubbed his forehead. He was losing patience.

'I don't think so Ruby. And I can't get involved with Inspector Srinvasen. He's . . . very . . . careful about how he works.'

'He's an egomaniac and won't let you anywhere near the case because he doesn't trust anyone who isn't Tamil, especially not a Goan.'

Ferreira almost smiled. The side of his mouth twitched, at least. 'I don't think Saint Francis and Sister Michael are connected. At all. Will you make this statement or not? I don't have all day. We have so many other problems Ruby. Christmas, New Year is coming up. They'll be three or four foreign deaths a week over the holidays. There's already been a drowning reported up at Baga Beach today. And we have to investigate. We have to. Though I can tell you now there was a party there last night and we'll find mind-boggling levels of alcohol and ecstasy in the corpse.'

I shrugged, nodded. 'OK. Let's do it.'

He pressed down the record button.

Zim was waiting for me, squinting, on the steps of the station. It was another blastingly hot day and he was getting burnt, that convict skinhead of his naked to the sun.

'Hey,' he said.

'Hey. Do you have sun cream on?'

'Sun cream?'

'Let's just get in the shade . . .'

'Wait . . . I've got to give you something,'

'Zim it's hot here – you've hardly got any hair. You'll get sunstroke and I'll be looking after you.'

'Here.'

Zim pulled an 8GB iPod out of his pocket and put it in my hand.

'What's this?'

'I bought it before you made the statement. I bought it while you were up at that house. It's for you.'

'Zim, you didn't need to. I can't accept this –.'

'Yeah you can. I made up some playlists too. Dunno if it's your kind of music . . .'

He was getting red. I didn't know if he was blushing or burning or both.

'Thanks Zim. It's really lovely of you. Thank you. I'll listen to them. I bet they're good.'

'And, something else. We should get out of this city. You've been through shit, so have I. We're free now. I'm not a suspect. You have the bail money back. Forget about all this, the article, work, Delhi. I can help you forget Stephen. Come with me up to the north, to the beaches. I've got somewhere to take you. Somewhere that hasn't changed. That's still a paradise.'

'I dunno Zim. I've got work to do. David Dryden's relying on me for his next issue.'

'Please. I want to do something nice for you. I want to show you how good I can be,' he said.

I put my hand over my eyes to see him better. The sun was so strong; all the colours were doused in white. The tarmac was sticky and petrol fumes were waving in the road. We were squinting at each other as if we were mirages. It was Christmas in a couple of days. I'd like to spend it with Zim. And what else was I going to do? Go back to Fernando's? To the cricket?

'OK, all right. No one will be working over the holiday. A few days won't hurt.

PART 3

1

There was nothing paradisal about the road to paradise. Highway 17. Heat and dust. Traffic. Heat and dust. Traffic. Buses, jeeps, four-by-fours, innumerable scooters and swarms of Maruti cars. Gone-off coconuts at four times the price. Dusty snacks and roadside bars filled with tourists. Topless thickened tattooed men and their ageing wives, drinking warm cocktails in the smog and spew of fumes. The scooter Zim had hired didn't help. It was a good deal according to the man he had got it from in the market. Once on the road it was clear it was falling apart. The exhaust scraped the ground and let out black clouds in random belches. Zim was determined to make the two-hour journey up the coast on this bone-cruncher.

The first place we hit was Nerul, a scrubby looking village just before the town of Candolim. It was where Maria's family were from. That's what the newspaper said. I hit Zim, told him to stop and he came to a coughing halt. Nerul was a dusty place on a beautiful blue river, though the village had turned its back to the view. Instead it gathered around the main road, where a huge white church and a small plastic looking temple stood, along with a vegetarian restaurant, a phone shop and a shady looking beauty parlour.

I told Zim I wanted to visit Maria's family. Ask them some questions. He shot me a look of horror.

'Why the hell do you want to do that? Can't you just forget about it? I don't want to.'

'Just wait here then. Get a beer or something. I won't be long.'

A skinny guy with stubble and a sub-woofer playing out Hindi pop ran the phone shop. I asked him about Maria, if he knew where she had lived. He called someone on his mobile phone. An even skinnier, rattier looking boy turned up, his cousin. The cousin led me through a maze of dirt paths, past concrete houses, set back in forest that couldn't help but grow. Dogs barked aggressively as we walked by. The owners, sat on their steps, didn't bother to shut them up.

We reached a small bungalow, painted yellow and pink. A white tourist taxi stood outside. This was the house, the newspaper had said Maria's husband was a taxi driver. The cousin came to the gate, there was no dog. He yelled out. No answer. He yelled again. A mumbled shout came back and soon after the door opened.

A grey-haired man with a long face and sloping shoulders appeared. He looked as if he had liver trouble, there was a yellow tinge to his face and black circles around his eyes. He looked as if he had been punched. Maria's husband, Victor. The cousin lowered his voice, depressed by the appearance of the widower and the air of death that hung around him. The man stood, holding the front door, listening to the boy with a frown. He nodded, gestured for me to follow him into the house.

It was dark inside. The curtains half-closed. The stale, heavy smell of cigarettes hung in the air. Holy Pictures were hung all over the walls. Old faded posters of the Virgin Mary. A statue of Jesus, his arms opened, waiting to comfort, stood on a side table by the old chair Maria's husband slumped himself down in. He lit a cigarette, the smoke wafted around the statue. Strange kind of cloudy heaven.

'Sit down,' he said.

I sat on the sofa opposite.

'What do you want?'

'I'm really sorry about Maria. I found her,'

He looked up from watching smoke float from the red tip in front of him. 'You're that girl. You found Maria. You and that priest. That mad old priest.'

'You know about what happened.'

'Of course. Inspector Ferreira. He told us himself. He told my sons for me. I couldn't do it. He's keeping it out the newspapers.'

He stared into the space in front of him. His lips began to move up and down. After some time he turned to me.

'What do you want?'

'Can I talk to you about Maria?'

'Why?'

'Do you think she killed Sister Michael?'

The man shrugged.

'I'm not sure. She could have done,'

That wasn't the answer I was expecting.

'What do you mean? Surely you can't think that,'

'Maria, she was depressed. She'd been in and out of it for years and years,'

'Why?'

He took an inhale of breath.

'It runs in her family. Her grandmother killed herself. I didn't think Maria would do that though. She was never so bad. She would pray if she got too bad. If she had hit Sister Michael, if she had killed her then it would have tipped her over the edge. She would have done it because God couldn't help her anymore.'

'But was she violent?'

'No, no. Not violent. Not before. Just, just black. But she would take against things, with no explanation.'

'Like what?'

'Soon after she started working for Sister Michael, she banned us all from the exposition of Saint Francis. And she had loved that. We had so many statues, relics, charms from the festival. One day she just took them all away. Threw them out.'

'Why?'

The cigarette had burned to the end.

'I told you. She took against things.'

'But how could she hold down a job like she had if she was so unstable?'

'She enjoyed working, it took her mind off herself. It stopped her mind over-working,'

'Did she come home the day that Sister Michael died?'

'She didn't come home during the week much, once or twice. And every weekend.'

'I'm sorry. Your wife, I would never have thought there was anything wrong with her. She had seemed so, capable. I had dinner with Sister Michael, the night before she died. Maria cooked. It was delicious. The house was spotless.' I said.

'She was very good at her job. She loved to cook, to eat too . . .'

He laughed and the laugh turned into a gargle and then a sob. His hand shook as he reached his cigarette to his mouth. I took his other hand. It was very soft, thin skin.

'I'm very sorry. You must miss her.'

'Yes. Yes I do. This is all my fault.'

'No, no you shouldn't say that.'

'If she had just come home, just come home then I could have helped her. We have medicine here for her. I should have stopped her staying there so often, with just the priests and Sister Michael. It wasn't a good atmosphere. She didn't need to stay there so much. Those two women, they got on each other's nerves. If Maria, if she had been ill, feeling very bad and Sister Michael had done something to upset her. Then I don't know. Maybe her mind was out of control. They are all mad up there. That Father Jonathan too.'

'He does seem it, a little bit strange.'

'He doesn't just seem it. He is. He had a breakdown last year. Couldn't handle the pressure of the exposition. He shouldn't have still been hearing confessions. It didn't help Maria, going to see him. Didn't help her at all. Two of them, locked up with their wild thoughts in those little boxes. It's all a mess up there.'

'Maria went to confession a lot?'

Father Jonathan said she'd never gone to confession. Why had he said that?

'Yes, of course. She was found with her prayer book, the one she used for confessions.'

'Would you mind if I looked at it?'

'At the prayer book?'

'Yes.'

'Why?'

'I'm sorry. I don't want to intrude on you. Father Jonathan said that Maria hadn't gone to confession. That seems strange that he said that now. I'm a journalist. I don't think things are as simple as they seem. Could I just look at it?'

Victor went to push himself up but failed, wheezing back into his chair.

'You can get it yourself. It's in our bedroom. On her dressing table.'

'It's OK for me to go in there?'

He rubbed his face in defeat. 'I can't get up. I can't.'

The bedroom was dark too and smelt of old sweat. It was incredibly neat apart from the unmade bed, the sheets writhed and knotted and dirty. The old seventies dresser was empty except for an old pot of Pond's Cold Cream, a bible, a box of Depakote valproic acid and a battered confession prayer book. The leaves splayed out and furred at the edges. I opened it up. Printed by the Saint Francis Xavier trust, Old Goa, 1971. She'd kept it all that time. Her name and address were scrawled at the top in spindly writing. The first prayer in the inside of this book was to Saint Francis Xavier, Patron of Missions. It had been scratched out, seven or eight times with a hard biro. I flicked through the book, let it come to the place it naturally stopped.

It stopped on a prayer to Saint Michael the Archangel for protection against evil.

Saint Michael the Archangel, defend us in battle, be our protection against the wickedness and snares of the devil; may God rebuke him, we humbly pray and do thou, O Prince of the heavenly host, by the power of God, thrust into hell Satan and all evil spirits who wander through the world for the ruin of souls. Amen.

The page was greasy from being held so many times. Maria had read this prayer more than any others. What did she need protecting from? Who were the evil spirits? Why was she so against Saint Francis Xavier? What had Father Jonathan done to her? What had made her, delicate-minded, but with a family and a husband, take her own life? Maybe she had really killed Sister Michael. You just never knew what was going on in people's lives, in people's heads.

Victor was smoking another cigarette in the same chair. I sat opposite, took his hand again.

'I'm really so sorry about your wife. Are your sons nearby?'

'They live close by. They have families. They are very upset. They work very hard,'

'Are you working now? Maybe it would help you.'

189

His eyes were hooded, losing their presence. He looked like he wanted to sleep.

'I'm sorry. Look, I don't know if it would help. Would you like my email address? Do you use email?' I continued.

He nodded. 'I use it at my son's house.'

'You can contact me if you feel like talking? Maybe you'd remember something Maria said about Saint Francis. Or Sister Michael or even Father Jonathan?'

He nodded. I wrote my name and my email address and Zim's mobile number down.

'This isn't my number. I've lost my phone. But you can call me if you would like to. The guy, he's my friend, he'll put you in touch,'

I found Zim on his second pint of Kingfisher. He had finally succumbed to the heat and taken off his jumper. His white T-shirt was so thin it was transparent. Sticking to him in parts. He looked like a turtle who'd lost his shell. I wondered about his ability to drive after so much beer but it seemed like everyone else on the road was drinking too. One man flew past with one hand on his bike and the other curled round a bottle of Chivas.

'You ready to go?' he said.

'Kind of. It was weird. What he said. Victor said she always went to confession, but Father Jonathan kept saying she hadn't been. I don't know whether I should go back and tell Ferreira about it. She was doped up, it sounds like. She only just had it in her to do her job, not to smash someone over the head. I don't think it was her.'

Zim groaned. 'Ruby, please don't make us go back.

Please. Come on. I've got somewhere to show you. Two, three days. It isn't going to make a difference is it? No one is going to come back to life. You can come back to Panjim after Christmas.'

'OK, OK. We're going. I wish the police could trace the delivery Sister Michael was talking about. Didn't Father Jonathan know anything about it? That's a clue. She was getting a delivery exactly around the time she died. Why can't they find out who it was?'

Candolim was the next town up the coast from Nerul. An ancient Portuguese fort settlement, now a sprawling mess, awash with trinket shops and off-licences and travel companies baking in the sun. Brash restaurants announced fish and beer and mojitos and pleasure. Girls strode down the dusty street in crop-tops and hot-pants. Men stared and no one cared. We stopped at the beach very briefly. It was dirty and full of guys trying to get you to ride their dodgy jet-skis. Whole Indian families were happily bumping off into the ocean at high speed, their legs and their arses flailing, coming dangerously close to some kind of sea-motor pile-up.

I stared at the scene in disbelief. Is this what people came to Goa for? Is this what people in Delhi raved about? Why all the rich kids were buying apartments down here? I couldn't believe it. We were in the wrong place.

'This is what we're escaping. It's completely different up north,' Zim assured me as we got back on the road.

'How do you know?'

'Ah – you know I have my sources,' he said.

We were headed to Arambol, up past Anjuna beach.

191

It was where the old hippies were apparently. The ones who come in the sixties and the seventies, who'd slept under coconut trees and got naked in the sun and smoked charis and had fun. They'd travelled further and further north, trying to escape the tide of package tours and chicken tikka, to find a small patch of the place they remembered.

The hotels made way for green paddy fields as we moved out of Candolim, but the road didn't get any quieter. Our scooter wove in and out of taxis and cars and scooters and bellowing Yamahas. Men and women, tanned and not so tanned, sunglasses on, biking from beach to beach, from patch to patch of supposed heaven. Booze shops lined the way, selling spirits, beer and orange petrol filled up in old water bottles. Massive tropical churches, white-washed and crumbling, watched the show without comment.

It was so crowded. It was supposed to be remote. Was everywhere like this now? We were supposed to be escaping but we'd brought the world with us. Where were all these people from? I wanted to enjoy the landscape alone. Just like Peter Bukowski did.

We stopped to get some petrol at a cafe. Three young kids drinking coke and the mother breastfeeding. The dad smoking and drinking a beer. One of the kids, he wouldn't stop talking about how warm the sea was. He couldn't get over it.

'You can swim in it without your balls freezing off. That's right isn't it dad?'

The father laughed. The mum told him not to say things like that in front of his brothers. But she was smiling too. They were having a good time, they were on holiday. That made me feel bad. Not everyone was a billionaire. Or even free and single. Most people had families, work. Why shouldn't they see a bit of paradise too?

We got back on our way. The sign pointed to Arambol. The wind flapped around us and Zim sped up.

'This road – it used to have one bus a day – Ram told me that,' Zim yelled back to me, turning his head.

'Watch out – we're coming to a bridge!' I yelled back.

I held on tight to the bike and looked out over the long blue river. Smoke rose through the banks of jungle. Two old wooden houseboats moved slowly along in the pink sun. The traffic had thinned out. It seemed we were the only ones headed so far. Maybe Arambol would be a paradise. Maybe we could forget about everything, even if just for a couple of days. But Arambol was more like St. Tropez; India's Côte d'Azur. We found the beach as the sun was going down. Restaurants lined the shore, candlelit tables spreading out towards the sea. Suited waiters invited us to sit down for the catch of the day, holding up freshly caught lobster, snapper and octopus for us to inspect.

'You hungry?' said Zim.

'Well, yeah, I guess I am.'

We sat down in a stylish place, advertising a Danish chef. Zim ordered oriental noodles with catch of the day, roasted beetroot salad and white wine. He surprised me, how in control he seemed. I guessed he'd been to a lot of restaurants.

'Sound OK to you?'

'Sounds amazing. Where the hell are we? Where are all the hippies?'

We sipped our cold wine and looked around the room. A posh English couple with two young kids looked incredibly bored by our side. The mother drank her Piña Colada quickly and kept threatening Felix with going home and cancelling their order.

'You want kids?' said Zim.

'With you?'

He laughed. 'Well, it could be with me. I meant in general, but I wouldn't mind. I want children. I'd love to look after a kid.'

'Really?'

'Wouldn't you?'

'God. I hadn't thought about it much. I always thought it was for when I was older.'

'My mum had me when she was twenty-three. I'm twenty-eight. I'm worried I won't ever find someone to be with and marry and do all these things with. I think about it a lot. It's hard to find anyone who gets me, who even likes me, let alone loves me. No one ever laughs at my jokes,' said Zim.

'I don't want to be on my own either, like Sister Michael. That doesn't look fun. But I don't know. I can't see where my life is going, let alone another life,' I said.

On our opposite side was a loud bunch of young Delhiites discussing Goan house prices. These guys were worried the prices were going up too quickly, they wanted to close deals on new places before their holiday was up.

'Would you buy a place here?' I asked Zim.

'I think I prefer Vasco. It's more honest. I don't know. Maybe the place we're going. Maybe that's the place to be . . . Are those hippies?'

Zim peered across the subtly lit restaurant at a group of dreadlocked kids in baggy pants, drinking rum cocktails and talking about yoga. One of them was explaining how he had thrown up green bile after his Pranayama lesson this morning. He seemed incredibly pleased with himself.

'No, they're students. They look kind of similar but it's definitely not the same thing. I don't know where the hippies are. They're not here,' I said.

'Then let's leave. Let's go,' said Zim.

'But it's getting dark. Why don't we just stay here tonight?'

'We'll be fine. I'll look after you.'

We drove in the night and the wind got cold. My skin prickled and I pushed myself into Zim for warmth. The only sign of life and light now were Christmas stars, lighting the eaves of houses dotted sparsely around, set back in the trees. I shouted at Zim, I asked him where we were going. He didn't answer; he just kept on riding. I was scared again. All day we had been searching for solitude, for a quiet piece of country and now we were in the middle of nowhere and I wanted light and people and cocktails. Suddenly Zim veered to the left, a road through a patch of low forest. A rough path, rocks and sand. We skidded. I fell off the bike, grazed my knee. Mud and blood mixed together. It hurt.

'Ah fuck,' said Zim.

The bike was on its side, still growling, wheezing, the back light shining red on us.

'What now?'

Zim pulled out his phone, the white screen lighting up his face ghost green.

'It's just over there – through those trees.'

'Where?'

'Just some place I thought of.'

Some fear inside me gripped me round the throat. It wasn't the lurking fear that the killer was nearby. It was a new, quicker kind. The fear you get when you realise you don't know the guy whose taking you home from the party and suddenly drives really slowly. Or you just got in a unlicensed minicab drunk and this isn't the way home. Maybe it's going to be OK. Maybe the guy is just a careful driver. Maybe this is a detour. But you don't know, really. And there's no one around and no one to help you if he isn't completely trustworthy. It's a sinking feeling of stupidity and panic. Who was this guy, really? Where was he taking me? Why were we in a deserted forest in the middle of the night? Fuck. Did he slash his girlfriend? Did he murder Sister Michael? My stomach dropped.

'Zim fuck off. Where are we going? I don't trust you.'

'Just come on – through those trees.'

'No.'

He tried to pull my hand. 'Just trust me. Please.'

'No. I'm sorry. I'm scared.'

I heard my voice raise to a high pitch wail. That pissed him off. He took my hand again. I took it away. He wrapped his hand round my neck and yanked me towards him so hard. I screamed, tripped and threw myself down. My knee hurt. I could feel it bleeding into the ground. I pressed myself into the ground and I began to cry. The earth smelt cool and damp. I could feel Zim behind me. He was going to grab me again. I screamed. He shouted.

'Ruby I'm not going to touch you. What's wrong with you? Why are you so scared?'

I turned around. He was standing away from me, grey-red in the light of the scooter, wheel still spinning, still growling. He was as scared as I was.

'What do you think I'm going to do with you? Why can no one just trust me?'

He put his hand on his head, pulled down hard. Turned around and yelled. Curled himself up and yelled again.

'Zim,' I could only whimper between sobs.

He turned around. 'You made me fuck up something nice by losing my temper. And it was supposed to be a surprise. Do you think I'd take you anywhere dangerous? Do you think I wouldn't look after you? Haven't I been looking out for you since we met?'

He was crying. He was as upset as I was scared. He was right. I hadn't any reason to fear him. I was losing it for no reason. Overwrought. I needed to calm down. Hadn't he proven himself in Vasco? Looked after me in the middle of the night? Saved me from being eaten alive in my bed? What could I do but go with him? And it was Christmas tomorrow.

'Just . . . just take me to where ever it is.'

We stumbled and searched. I could hear the sea crashing some way away. Zim began sniffing.

'Can you smell that? Honeysuckle.'

197

He was right. There was something heavy and sweet hanging in the air.

'Ram said there was honeysuckle growing around the house.'

'Ram?'

'Just come on.'

We saw a thin light and then an old plaster house. It stood at the mouth of a river, looking out over dark waves crashing on to a small black beach.

'This place? Someone's house?' I said.

'Ram's. But it's our house for a while. He felt bad about me coming all the way here from the US and then there being no deal. Offered me his holiday home for Christmas. I'm more a Full Moon partier, but I thought you'd like it up here,' he said.

There was a boy sleeping on a charpoy outside the house. Zim woke him up. He was expecting us, led us through a creaky corridor to a room at the front of the house. The floor was red concrete. The night was getting lighter, a lilac shade. Thick honeysuckle air. It was very calm. You could hear the waves crashing on the shore.

The boy flicked the light switch on and off. The bulb was dead. He came back with a buzzing storm lamp which he set on the floor. It cast a dim orange circle across us and the room.

Zim screwed up his mouth into a smile, leant his arm on the wall. He was frowning, smiling, embarrassed, awkward, pleased with himself, unsure of himself.

'I'm sorry I didn't explain. I just wanted it to be a surprise. I'm sorry.'

198

'I'm sorry too. I don't know why I lost it so much. I suddenly thought you were taking me to a shallow grave or something. Too many horror movies . . . or I don't know. Too much horror, in general, recently.'

I had a go at laughing, though it really wasn't that funny. He tried to laugh too.

'Let's just forget about it all. About everything. It's Christmas. Happy Christmas.'

'Happy Christmas Zim.'

'Do you trust me now?'

'Yeah, yeah I do I guess.'

'Are you tired?'

'Exhausted.'

'Me too.'

There was one large bed. We changed on separate sides, turned to the wall. I watched his shadow pull off his shirt and throw it on the floor. I wondered if he was watching me too. I undid my bra and pulled on the T-shirt Zim had given me in Vasco.

The sheets smelt of washing powder. We lay on the edges with a space between us, watching the oversized shadows stretched grey across the walls, listening to the sea. I pulled my hand into a fist, bought up my index finger and my middle finger.

'Hey, it's a rabbit. You've made a rabbit on the wall,' said Zim.

'You never did that when you were a kid? We did it all the time.'

Zim shook his head. 'No. At least if I did I can't remember. Let me have a go.'

He made his own and was delighted. I showed him a dog. Put your hands in prayer position and turn sideways. Separate your little finger from the rest to make a jaw. Bend your left ring finger to make an eye. I showed him a bird too. Hold your hands up, palms facing the wall. Point your thumbs up. Make the bird fly by flapping your fingers.

Zim flew his dark, looming vulture around the room and into mine. Our birds flapped together and I got that touch again. That poker heat, spreading down to my stomach. But this time we weren't in a church, or in prison. We were in bed together. I glanced at him. He was staring at our fingers, frowning.

'Zim,' I said.

He carried on looking at our fingers, then across at me, then back at our fingers. Clenched them hard together so it hurt, like his scratches had hurt, like he was angry.

'Hey,' I said, pulling them back. But he grabbed my arm and pulled me into him and then we were kissing and it wasn't a mistake, that touch, that heat. It was all over me and it was all over him.

2

I woke up early, in a grey-pink cave of a sheet and Zim, sleeping soundly beside me. I slid out the bed and into my dress, left behind in a jilted heap last night. I padded out of our room to a quiet morning. There was a chilled thickness to the air, the sheen of the night not yet evaporated.

The old house was backed by palm trees, coconuts and forests. It looked out over a strip of blonde sand, about a kilometre wide, curved slightly like a lip. A river ran from the beach and swooped in a wide 'S' behind the house. There was a canoe tied to the bank and hammocks tied between the palms. These were the only signs of habitation I could see around. The silhouette of a dog gambolled and played on the beach.

I walked towards the sea. It was calm with a mirrored sheen across the water. I felt the break of the tide with my toes. It was warm, warmer than the air. Far out, towards the horizon was a fishing boat. I could only just see the small shadowy figure throwing a net. He couldn't see me. I took off my dress and dived into the water. I broke the glassy surface with my hands and swam towards the sunrise, towards the black palms, frilled and waving in the orange sky. Flying fish jumped over me and into me but it didn't scare me. I didn't feel scared. I swam back towards the house. Zim was there, he'd woken up early too. He waved to me. I worried about my dress – about a towel – but then realised it didn't matter much anymore. He stripped down to his shorts and swam out towards me. We didn't talk, just swam and dived and floated in the warm water with the sun coming up. I felt happy and forgetful.

'What happened last night?' I asked Zim, drying off with my dress.

'You know what happened.'

'OK, let me ask you another question. Why did it happen?'

'We like each other.'

'Do we?'

'I like you. A lot. You can't admit it but you like me too. We're alone on a far-off beach. Why not?'

'I guess so.'

I did like him. He was right. He scared me but he excited me too. He was strange. I didn't quite understand him. I wanted to look after him. I wanted to calm him down and make him happy. I wanted his company. I wanted to stop being so lonely. And he was the only one around. That too. Why fight it? He was right. Why not? And today was Christmas.

We spent the day swimming, lying in the hammocks and sleeping, sometimes with our arms entwined. We walked to a small chapel nearby. It was open but there was nothing inside. Just a small plaque explaining the origins of the Angel Gabriel statue. It had been bought from Portugal by one of the first explorers to Goa, Fernando Collor, a captain of Vasco de Gama. Someone must have taken it back to Portugal. Gabriel wasn't there anymore.

There was one other couple, living in a house on the far side of the beach, back into the trees. Sita Mahadevi and her American husband, Abe. Ram had let them know we were there, asked if their cook could make extra for us, for a small payment. We ate with them, outside their house, sitting on plastic tables and chairs. They were in their fifties, didn't talk much. Abe preferred whittling a stick or playing his guitar sitting on the stump of a palm, to much else it seemed. He was from Texas, Zim said, from his accent. He wore a cowboy hat when he walked along the beach in the evening. He was a solitary, strange figure; a black silhouette outlined by the fancy pink sky, his dogs gambolling around him. He didn't even seem to look his wife in the eye, just a nod of thanks when she lay down his fish and rice in the evenings. She seemed devoted. I told Zim that Abe was probably good in bed and he got upset. I was surprised how pleased that made me. He was jealous.

It seemed this is what beach life was about, something very simple, watching the sea, being close to nature. The sun, unhampered by buildings and living, carried its changing lights across the sky. The sounds of the local temple sounded far, bells marking morning and afternoon prayers, the only indicator of time going by.

'Should we go and see it?' I said to Zim, on the

third morning. He was sleeping, burying his face in the crook of his elbow to make the dark last a bit longer.

'What?'

'The temple.'

Zim buried his head further into his elbows.

'And?'

I shook him.

'The temple, it's not far away. It's Hindu.'

'I don't care.'

'Come on. I want to go. I've been up for ages. You've been sleeping. It's 11 AM already.'

Zim sighed. Turned his head to the side without opening his eyes.

'OK, OK, Give me five will you? God.'

I gave him five and he didn't get up so I asked Abe to call me a rickshaw. I was pissed off, upset he couldn't get up to come. Zim and I, we seemed to be turning into some kind of couple after only a few days. It prickled my skin. It scared me.

3

The way to the temple was lined with thick forest and quiet. The light flickered in and out of the trees. It was hard to believe Candolim, with its massive tour buses, top restaurants and beer-lined, trinket-lined, tourist-lined streets was only a couple of hours away. Occasionally the woods cleared for low houses, made of wood and thatch. Fires of straw burnt and smoked. Buffalo chilled and chewed in mud yards, their oily skin reflecting the setting sun. There were more butter-flies than people. Red and primrose-yellow, they flitted from the forest across the road. I did see one woman hacking at a tree aggressively. Her husband was prob-ably still in bed.

At regular sections along the road were metal signs advertising 'The Arambol Tourist Complex'. A happy Indian family splashed in a swimming pool against a backdrop of large, yellow towers. This was the area to be transformed by Paulo Mendes into a massive concrete holiday park. I could see why the NGOs were upset.

The wheezing rickshaw arrived at a clearing. Two dark, stone pillars marked the entrance of the temple. A couple of touts offered sagging lotus flowers, cheap incense to Shiva, cold drinks. They eyed me up but when I waved my hand they leaned drowsily back against trees. They weren't too bothered about making a sale.

A pool, gathered in a passing river, ran by, mossy steps led down for bathing, washing. Another woman had hitched up her sari and was smacking the life out of her husband's shirts. There were people living here, in a village, hidden in the forest.

The temple itself was tiny, squat and black and slightly lopsided, like some old witch's gingerbread hut. It had a shiny patina to it, polished by time. Beside it were three or four druidic stones, bedded in the grass. Proof this was a holy site as old as they come.

I took my rucksack off my back and sat down, enjoying the light, soft and old and golden. Small butterflies, red and yellow and brown, flitted around. I wished Zim had come with me. He'd like it much more here than around those crumbling churches in Old Goa. I leant my head back against the cool stone and closed my eyes feeling the warmth of the sun. A sound rang out. I looked up to see a man ring a bell and enter the temple. I waited a while before following inside.

The sanctuary was oily black and ancient. In the centre of the room sat a Shiva Lingam, a brass lamp lit directly above. Fresh lotus flowers have been placed carefully around. A woman entered behind me. She was young, in her twenties, dressed in shiny pink. She lit incense from the lamp and knelt down, waving smoke around the Lingam. She began to cry. She prayed, looked overwhelmed and incredibly sad. I didn't feel right, staying there with her so upset. I moved on.

The second room was lighter, cool and clean, the stone here worn and smooth. Niches were spaced evenly around the room. Some contained crumbling statues of Hindu Gods; others were empty. In the centre of the room was a Nandi, the bull, Shiva's carriage, facing back into the inner sanctum.

He had no head. Sharp, light splinters stuck out from the neck. This was the Tambdi Surla bull. The bull Inspector Srinvasen was supposed to be putting back together, before he was made to look for the head of Saint Francis instead.

There the man I'd seen, all in white, was kneeling and pressing his face to ground. I stood silent and watched for some time. Tears trailed down his face as he lit his own incense, waved it around the empty nooks and then came back again to the bull, placing the smoking perfume beside the hooves of the animal, before wiping his eyes and leaving the temple.

I followed him out, into the flickering light and the butterflies. I sat on the grass and pulled one of Sister Michael's cards out of my bag, the one with the blue Jesus, from someone called Ram. It was a Hindu Christmas card. I remembered now where I recognised Ram, the accountant, from. From the airport in Delhi, from the TV. The news report on the bull. He was the man in the front, angry about the head of this animal going missing, vowing revenge on anyone who had done this.

Back at Casa Bonita I kept my return quiet, stepping softly through the house. Most of the doors were open, the living room, the kitchen, our bedroom. One was closed. I tried the door. Locked. There were keys, hung in the hall. I flicked through them. Two were outdoor keys; another, smaller, silver. I picked up that one. I turned it and it worked. I was in the room. A bedroom. Ram's. A double bed with a neat checked spread. Large wooden wardrobe containing Chinos, shirts, kurta pyjamas and a selection of expensive dresses.

The dressing table was heaving with make-up and beauty products. Bronzers, fake-tan, old mascaras, facial peels, youth serums, deep-sea-mud face masks, a pot of moisturiser I knew cost over 200 pounds a bottle. Signs of a woman wanting to stay beautiful. A woman who knew she was ageing. Galina? Ram and Galina. God. What a strange couple. I opened up the moisturiser. There was only a small bit left but I couldn't resist trying some. I dabbed it on my face, rich and thick. It sunk in quickly. It felt good. I looked in the mirror. No difference. It wasn't worth it. It was all a myth.

There was a drawer to the dresser. I opened it. Not much. A pad of thick paper. A photograph in a frame, face down. A much younger Ram, dressed in Indian clothes, on this same beach. A friend draped his arms around Ram and they grinned for the camera, squinting their eyes up against the light. Why did he have it here? I groped further into the drawer, pulled out a pair of handcuffs and some champagne flavoured lube. God. You really could never tell what people were like in private. I pushed them back, closed the drawer gently, scanned the room for anything else. Any clues to a relationship between Sister Michael and Ram. Any clues to anything. But it was bare. This was a place for holidays, relaxing from work; not a real home, filled with clutter and secrets.

I found Zim lying on our bed, streaks of sunlight slanting over him, knees up, playing some game on his iPhone.

'Hey, how was the temple?' he said, without moving his eyes off the game.

'Yeah, beautiful, interesting. The head of the bull there has been stolen though, you know.'

'Yeah, yeah I know that. I saw it on the news when we were at the airport . . . Seems a long time ago now . . . Everyone losing their heads around here.'

'Listen, are you done playing that game? I'd like to check my emails.'

'Yeah, just give me a minute OK.'

'I don't know why you want to play that thing here in the room when you're surrounded by all this nature.'

'The light reflects off the screen, I can't play out there.'

'I don't know why you need to play the game anyway. Don't you want to get away from all that? Don't you like the quiet? I do.'

'Yeah? Is that why you haven't listened the iPod I gave you yet?'

Zim didn't move or take his eyes off the game but there was a catch in his voice.

'What do you mean?'

'You haven't listened to it once. And the way you talked about that music you lost, you'd have thought it was the most precious thing to you. Like a fucking work of art or a statue. Something you needed. But you haven't even looked at mine.'

'It wasn't the iPod that was the important thing, it was that Stephen gave it to me.'

'So me giving you one doesn't mean so much does it?'

'What are you getting at Zim?'

'I'm just saying. It's not the same is it? You don't care about it like you cared about the other one you had.'

'I'd known Stephen for a long time. I lived with Stephen. I've known you about two weeks.'

Zim got up, threw the iPhone down on the bed, pulled off his hoodie.

'I'm done. Use it.'

'Where you going?'

'Walk,' he said, not looking back behind him.

I shouted after him. I could have followed; maybe I should have. But it had come out of nowhere, this, well I guess it was jealousy, but it was stupid, I couldn't take it seriously. Besides, I needed to see what David had found out. I grabbed the iPhone, lay on the bed myself and logged on to my email. There was one from David Dryden entitled 'Information'.

Ruby,

I hope you're being as productive as we have been in London. I love interns. It amazes me how products of the best schools and universities in the country, people whose education must have cost hundreds of thousands of pounds, are quite happy to trot into a shabby office, stay long hours for little or no pay and do menial tasks, such as buy sandwiches, make coffee and do dog-work research in the name of journalism. But they do and I, for one, love it. This particular bushy-tailed, long-legged delight has turned up some faintly interesting facts, as did the bottle of claret with my Sotheby's friend. Forget drugs, Ruby, you can find just as much vice in antiques.

So to start with, my friend, who shall remain anonymous at his request (he doesn't want late night calls by the Sotheby heavies – yes they exist) says that everyone in antiquities is well aware of the amount of smuggling that goes on from India.

India takes her idols very, very seriously. Laws relating to smuggling are incredibly severe. No object more than one hundred-years-old is allowed out of the country except temporarily for exhibitions. It's illegal to even possess antiquities in India without a government licence. This doesn't stop Sotheby's holding an annual Indian sale, however. Perhaps not as plush as the Russian sales are at the moment, but still a high-class event – champagne, samosas and very sweet tea apparently. Chocked full with rich ex-pat Indians wanting a piece of home for their mantelpiece. Annual profit from these sales is reported to be between 3 and 4.5 million pounds.

But things are changing. In the last few years there's been a huge crackdown on smuggling antiquities out of India and the Government have created what they call the 'Idol Squad' especially to target the gangs of thieves and the dealers. There's a ready-meal millionaire from Birmingham who bought two pink sandstone temple pillars and a six-foot statue of Parvati, *remarkable for her large, swinging breasts, the year before last. The Archaeological Society of India got hold of a copy of the Sotheby's catalogue and matched the Parvati to a picture in the encyclopaedia of Yogini: Cults and Temples. All hell broke loose. The Idol Squad were sent over here, demanding a search warrant for the Sotheby's offices saying they were dealing in illegal goods from India. They didn't manage to get it and the pillars are still holding up the door of this man's Birmingham mansion. Sotheby's of course strongly denied any knowledge of wrong-doing, saying all their pieces came from credited dealers bought and sold outside of India. It's difficult to dispute this because, of course, there are lots of artefacts around that were taken out pre-Independence. In the end all the Idol Squad did was issue a press statement, which was circulated around all the auction houses and the main trade publications. Pretty ineffective but powerful nonetheless; our delightful intern managed to get hold of one from* Antiques Trade Gazette. *I've scanned it and attached it to this email FYI.*

I opened up the attachment before reading any further. A creased and shadowed copy of a heavy stamped A4 letter entitled 'TEMPLE THEFT CRACKDOWN IN INDIA'. It revealed slowly on the phone and I had to read it in sections. It began by saying that the Archaeological Society of India in conjunction with Interpol were making a serious effort to crackdown on the illegal trade in antiquities. It was a serious crime and any individual, or institutions, that were found to be involved would be pursued with the greatest international effort. After explaining the insanely tight regulations regarding the dealing of Indian antiquities there was a final emotional paragraph. Indian idols were not the same as Christian statues. Hindus believed the spirits of their gods lived in the images. Shrines all over India had suffered horrendous damage with vandals carting away temple doors, pillars and gods and goddesses. Villages which had worshipped at the same site for thousands of years were the devastated victims of this temple 'rape' and were forced to worship stone rubble and at empty platforms. 'How can you sell a god?' ended the letter.

Now, from what the lovely intern has found out (I'm taking her out for a bottle of something cheap for her hard work) Goa and Goan antiques are in a slightly different position to those in the rest of India. Frankly, the Indian Government don't really care what happens in Goa. They've assumed all the old bits and pieces there are Christian and therefore anyone's game. Possibly because of this leniency – and definitely because of the Vasco Port – there's been a steady supply of Goan crucifixes, altar-pieces, statues, communion chalices through Sotheby's for the last twenty years. The main dealer for all these Christian Goan pieces has been Edward Jones Antiquities. I talked to my unnamed friend about this and he says It's pretty likely that for someone to have such a steady stream of pieces from a country such as India means they have a serious, steady smuggler there.

These Goan pieces are treated differently to the Hindu antiquities. They sometimes go in the Indian

*sale but more often than not they go into a sale called
'Catholic Art'. The ex-pat Indians aren't so interested,
it's usually Portuguese and Spanish collectors that
hoover it up. But since Lisbon announced bankruptcy
and Spain isn't far behind, sales have stalled.*

*One other interesting thing my intern found. Over
the last couple of years there have been three Hindu
statues from Goa sold in auction by an 'Anonymous'.
While the price of these Christian pieces has fallen and
aren't moving, the Hindu pieces are far rarer and much,
much more expensive. And as Goa isn't an Idol Squad
'hot-spot' and has easy access to the shipping route to
Taiwan – where Sotheby's Asian office is – getting the
few Hindu pieces out of Goa would be far easier than
getting them out of the rest of the country. Is
'Anonymous' actually Edward Jones? It's merely conjec-
ture of course.*

*Can you connect all this to the warehouse? And
better still, the devil of tourism, Mendes? Bukowski
would be in heaven.*

Best,

David

I lay back on the bed. Sister Michael. The card from
Edward Jones. Her account at Coutts. I'd thought that
whoever had stolen the head of Saint Francis, whoever
was in charge of all those statues and crucifixes had
killed her. Maybe she was in charge of all those dusty
old relics. She was the smuggler. But why would she
steal the head of Saint Francis? She said herself it had
no value. Did she steal the head of the bull? Is that

what Ram meant when he had said she was going too far? Did he kill her? How were they connected? By the warehouse, but what else? Was he trying to protect Paulo? Were they all in it together? 'The police aren't saying how she died, just that they're investigating the case'. That's what Ram had said to Paulo, about Sister Michael. Did the two of them kill her?

4

The lobster glistened a disconcertingly healthy pink colour and lay patiently waiting to be devoured, surrounded by garnishes of lemon, salad and prawns. But Paulo had hardly touched the lunch he'd ordered. He didn't look like a man who lost his appetite easily.

We were sat once again in the penthouse suite, this time of his Anjuna Tourist Complex. He gazed vaguely out of his tinted windows, the hot Goan sky a weirdly cold grey colour.

'They're charging me with smuggling. Apparently that old warehouse is loaded with antiques. That man from the Idol Squad, Inspector whatever-his-name is, he's delighted. Damn Tamils. They hate Goans. No one in this damn country really respects us. They just think we're running some kind of playground, where anything goes, where they can bring their mistresses and gamble and get drunk. Because we're not Hindus, we're unclean, they think. And they can be as unclean as they want here. It's not like that,' he said.

Zim gulped his champagne awkwardly. I picked at a claw and kept quiet. I had wanted to go back down to Panjim, to open up Sister Michael's old computer again, try and find some more about the smuggling, some connection between her and the accountant sat opposite me. But Ram had called Zim that afternoon, said that Paulo wanted to meet. Zim said he needed me there too, for support. I was happy to come. I wanted to see these two men again. Were they murderers? Were they all in it together? There was someone else I wanted to find down in Anjuna too.

Ram pressed a napkin to his lips before clearing his throat and explaining.

'We invited you here today, Zim, because we thought you might be able to help us. Mr Mendes is going through a difficult time at the moment. The police have found a hoard of antiquities in his warehouse at the port. Because Mr Mendes also runs a shipping line, taking iron ore out to Taiwan, the police believe that he is running a smuggling ring, taking antiquities out of Goa to sell in Europe and America. The special police force, the Idol Squad, have been looking for someone connecting shipping with antiquities for a while now. They're trying to prove a link between Indian antiques coming out of India and through Taiwan dealers before going on to Europe. They think they have found this in Mr Mendes.'

Paulo growled.

'Of course, it's completely false. Mr Mendes has no idea whatsoever about the antiquities trade. His only interests are in Goan tourism and Goan shipping. But the charges are very serious and it looks like this business will completely put a stop to his Arambol development until further notice. The Goan Government are under immense pressure from the central Government, from the Vatican, from many places, since the head of Saint Francis has disappeared. Officials are starting to ask questions, there seems to be a lot of empty churches and not all of the missing treasures are in the Museum of Christian Art. They want a scapegoat. I've advised Mr Mendes to invest in foreign business as soon as possible. Once taken in for questioning his business dealings here in Goa will be frozen, and if charged, which of course will not happen, all his national savings and investments will go over to the Goan Government. This is obviously of great concern.'

Ram spoke calmly and carefully, unhurried by his heaving, disturbed boss. He was a man of little movement, poised and almost birdlike. Would he have been able to lift that Ming Vase above his head and crash it down on Sister Michael's head? Was he definitely the Ram who had sent the card?

What would a man like him have to do with a woman like Sister Michael? But then what would a woman like Sister Michael be doing working a smuggling ring? Were they all in cahoots? Were Paulo, Ram and Sister Michael working together. Had Paulo killed her? Or had they employed heavies? There had to be a link between the warehouse and her business. Her favourite statue had been sat there.

'But what's all this got to do with me?' said Zim. 'I don't understand.'

'Fine art is obviously of interest to Paulo and his wife – it's also a very quick and easy way to move large

218

amounts of money out of the country. We're interested in buying several paintings from your father, asking him to keep them on display at his gallery until a time when Mr Mendes is in a position to collect them or sell them on at auction,' said Ram.

Zim gulped another glug of champagne. It was real stuff, Mumm, but it could have been diet coke for all Zim cared. He was thinking of the deal. His eyes were wide.

'Wow, sure. Amazing. I need to talk to my dad of course but I think he'd like that a lot.'

'Excellent. Would it be possible to get together a list of possible purchases by tomorrow perhaps? We could have another meeting here. It's not too far from Casa Bonita?'

'No, no. It's not.'

'Thanks for letting us stay there. It's beautiful.'

Ram nodded. 'It is. It is. It's very close to the village where I was born. I love it there. Have many good memories. Unfortunately I don't go up there as often as I would like,' he said.

'Terrible what happened to the bull there. Did they ever find the head? It wasn't in the warehouse?'

Ram shook his head.

'No. We're still desperately looking for the head. My father is the temple priest actually. It's had a terrible effect on his health. It's very, very upsetting to everyone concerned. I've lost hope we'll get it back. I thought we were getting close to finding the culprit but it looks like our trail has gone cold,' he said.

5

Zim grabbed me and pulled my face towards his. I felt his lips hard on mine, pushing into me. I shook him off me. The doorman outside the tourist complex was staring at us.

'Zim. We're in public. This isn't LA. It's India.'

'It's Goa. Anything goes. Come on? What do you expect? I've just got the deal of my life. I'm gonna go home a hero. You don't understand how good this. Man, when I tell my dad,' he said.

'It's great. But you've got to close it first. Try not to get to excited.'

Zim's face darkened. 'Why do you have to piss all over it?'

'I'm not. I'm just saying, it's not a done deal yet. You don't know those guys. You don't know. They could be criminals. Just 'cause they say they're not, doesn't mean they're not going to prison.'

'Whatever. Let's celebrate anyway – let's get some champagne.'

'I've got to go and find someone. In Anjuna. For the article.'

'What. You're starting that again? I thought we were having a break. For each other?'

I winced at this. I didn't know if it grated on me so much because it was so over-emotional or because I didn't want him to need me so much, so quickly.

'We had one. Christmas is over. Now you're working and so am I. Come on, we can celebrate at the flea market. Have you heard of it? I think you'll like it.'

Anjuna Flea Market. An infamous hippy landmark, where the first travellers to Goa had arrived, got naked in the sand, got stoned and played guitars under palm trees. When they needed to go home they sold their belongings in a cool little Wednesday sale. For years I'd been hearing about the place. First at university, where tanned, spaced students airily mentioned buying their scarf, jacket, sarong at Anjuna. Then from Delhi friends, who always raved about the market after jaunts to Goa.

I was excited. But Zim was quiet on the journey there, just stared out the window as we wound through Anjuna guesthouses, German bakeries, pranic healing centres. He was upset I was working again. He'd wanted to prolong our holiday idyll indefinitely.

All at once, the market appeared. There was nothing flea-like about it; it was more of an elephantine bazaar. Stretching out as far as the eye could see; a massive camp of ragged polystyrene sheets on open, barren sand. Like some God-awful refugee camp, apart from the huge white tourist buses parked at the entrance.

I sat in our taxi and suddenly realised that wherever

221

I went in the world I was destined to be disappointed. Nothing was ever how I imagined it to be. Everything had been ruined before I got there and I only added to the destruction by turning up as well.

I was too late, too young, too old, too foreign, too local to appreciate anywhere I was. I missed my flat in Delhi, close to an old Muslim shrine, surrounded by dirt and kebabs and the wail of minarets. There was no natural beauty around there. The place hadn't changed for centuries and probably wouldn't and that was what was comforting. But I'd given it up. I couldn't live there any longer; memories had lingered painfully. Pungent smells, Stephen's shadow floating through the rooms. I'd needed to get away from it. And now I was here, followed around by yet more death, yet more pain and mystery that needed resolving. There was no point running away from anything, pushing things down inside you, they'd just leap up some place else. I could have just hung around with Stephen's ghost, someone I loved. Instead, I was now haunted by two strange unhappy women who shouldn't have died, and a frail, needy guy I was starting to care for.

'Ruby? Come on!' yelled Zim.

Zim was already out the car and surrounded by touts, grinning and waving for me to join him. His moods changed so fast. I hauled myself out the car to join him. Straight away I was bombarded with sales pitches and special offers and waving hands. One man with a small wooden duck stuck it in my face and made it quack repeatedly and very loudly. In between the grating squeaks he shouted 'only 250 rupees.' I wasn't sure if that was the price of the toy or the price for him to leave me alone. A woman dressed in old desert costume lit fistfuls of joss sticks and waved them madly in my face.

Kashmir shawls, fake Birkenstocks, Christmas stars, plastic-wrapped spices; it was all here, sold to the sound of dull throbbing trance music. But I wasn't looking for souvenirs. I needed to find someone. I was pretty sure Anjuna Flea Market was the right place to find them. Whether they would want to help me or not – that was the question. They hadn't been too friendly last time we had spoken.

I scanned the shoppers. There were a number of English tourists. Middle-aged couples, greying and fat around the middle, cheap vest-tops, tattoos, orthopaedic sandals. Some burly Russians, naked but for tiny trunks, their chests waxed and bare, gawping at bongs. Zim was engrossed in some charis pipes. I wandered further off, telling him to catch me up.

I found a group I thought could help me smoking a spliff at a makeshift tea stall. Dreadlocked and loose-eyed, ragged T-shirts and plastic sandals, these guys were here for the long haul. Did they know a Russian girl, Saskia? I thought she lived around here. They did. Sometimes she sold brownies. One guy saw her trying to sell a bag of clothes today, I should check the stalls round the front of the beach, the ones that sold second-hand stuff.

I wandered through the clothes market, stopped in one of the larger places, run by a local guy, dressed all in black with a fake diamond in his ear. I needed to pick up some more clothes myself, I'd been wearing my dress for the last few days straight. But flicking

223

through the racks of musty cloth disturbed me. All these little, worn-out vest-tops. Who's had they been? For all I knew they could be from one of the poor girls who'd died of a drug overdose here. It happened a lot apparently. Foreigners were always dying in Goa. I bought a pair of new fake Levis and an over-priced green polo-shirt.

'How much for this Mukesh? There's some new stuff in there too. It's too big for me now,' I heard a voice I recognised and turned round to see a girl in cut-off denim shorts and a crochet poncho hand over a bag of clothes to the guy. It was Saskia. The girl from Panjim prison. The friend of Galina. Just who I was looking for. The guy sniffed.

'Seventy rupees.'

Saskia curled her lip up in disgust and frowned with worry. 'Seventy rupees? I can hardly get a cup of tea for that here now. You have to be kidding.'

'Seventy-five.'

'Mukesh, you're selling hairbands for more than that. There's a lot in here. Look.'

Mukesh shrugged. 'Take it or leave it.'

'But I'm starving.'

'Stop spending all your money on coke then,' he said, turning round to serve a German girl who wanted to buy a sombrero. Saskia rubbed her hand across her brow and took out a cigarette. She lit it then pulled her hair back in an elastic band, before walking off. I went after her. I put my hand on her shoulder, it was all bone. She whipped round quickly, frowning.

'What do you want?'

'Sorry, do you remember me?'

She pulled her lips down and shook her head.

'From Panjim, the police station? I was in the cell with you.'

Recognition began to dawn and some kind of respect. 'You were in for murder.'

'It wasn't us. Thank God they realised that. They think the maid did it.'

Saskia nodded, rubbed her brow, turned back around.

'Hey can I talk to you for a minute?' I called after her.

'I haven't got time. I've got to sell these clothes. I need to get lunch. I'm starving.'

'I'll buy you lunch.'

She turned round once more. 'I have a large appetite.'

'That's fine. So do I, apparently.' Saskia turned on her heels and led me through the smoky crowds towards the back of the market, where the beach met the forest, to the German bakery. A Banyan tree sat in the centre of a large courtyard, cotton flags entwined in its branches. Dusty wicker chairs, cushions and ashtrays were scattered around. Pictures of Hindu gods hung on the walls.

Saskia nodded to the few grey-haired hippies hanging about, men with long moustaches sitting beneath Tibetan prayer flags, lighting their spliffs and drinking chai. A few richer looking Indians, in baseball caps and shorts, drinking beer, guts hanging out, eyed her up as she walked past. One woman sat at a MacBook, writing earnestly. She looked like she hadn't had sex for a while.

Saskia sat down in one of the booths and called over one the waiters.

'I want a banana-karma lassi, triple Shiva sandwich with masala houmous on the side and three honey oat yoga cookies,' she said, without bothering to look at the menu.

I asked for a tea.

'You're hungry,' I said.

'I don't eat often. When I eat, I eat.'

'What's a triple Shiva sandwich?'

'It's a three layer sandwich, paneer, humus, grated carrot, salad and yoghurt sauce.'

'Wow.'

'I could murder a burger but that isn't going to happen. It's easier to get crack cocaine than beef in this cafe. It's run by some insane old Dane who thinks he's a reincarnation of Krishna. The Shiva sandwich is the closest thing you get to protein here.'

The food came quickly, they seemed to know Saskia here and she didn't seem the patient type. She squeezed the sandwich down and forced it into her small mouth. Houmous and yogurt dripped down the sides. I blew on my tea and tried not to stare. When she'd cleaned her plate, she sat back, lit a cigarette and took a slurp of her banana-karma lassi.

'So what did you want to talk to me about?'

'Your friend, Galina.'

'I told you. She's not exactly a friend, anymore.'

'She got you out of jail.'

'We go back a long way. We came over from Moscow together. I looked after her. She was just a kid, seventeen. I was only a year older but that was something. Ten years ago. Ten years changes you.'

Saskia looked younger than she was, so small and

so petulant, more like a teenager. Galina, with her make-up and her ennui and her designer clothes, she could be any age, she could have been much older.

'Why did you come over here? Two Russian teenagers coming over to Mumbai, seems strange.'

'Work, that's all. To dance. We're trained ballerinas but where could we find work in the nineties? We had hyperinflation, we could hardly buy bread.'

'So you came to work in Bollywood? Doesn't seem the most obvious choice of work.'

'There's plenty of Russian dancers in Bollywood now. Film agents started recruiting in Moscow, around two thousand. We didn't know what was going to happen to the country. Yeltsin resigned. We had this new guy, Putin. We didn't know what he was going to be like. We took a risk and left. Galina and I were some of the first to go. And they like us here, at least the producers do. Russians work as many hours as we're told, we don't stop for lunch and we'll wear whatever the directors give us. The Indian girls scream blue murder if they show so much as a shoulder – and need at least an hour to digest their curries. They really don't like us. Think we're all whores. They don't realise how much we've trained.'

'It doesn't sound easy.'

'It was hell. The smells, the heat, the food. We couldn't understand anything. There were four of us from our dance school. The studio put us in a tiny flat, near to film city. No windows, forty degrees, even at night, sometimes. It flooded in the monsoon. Six days a week they would pick us up, six-thirty in the morning and we'd work for ten hours straight. For nothing.'

'God. Why didn't you go home?'

'It got better. More girls came over. We had company. Men were interested in us, we got, I don't know, fashionable. Invited to parties, paid to go to parties. Paid much more than the films paid. Galina and I got an apartment together in Juhu. It was fun.'

'So what happened?'

'Ram.'

'Go on.'

'We all had boyfriends, they took us out, bought us clothes, drinks, other things we wanted. But that was it. They all had wives they went home to in the morning. They didn't see us anything more than jumped up whores, white girls to dance with and do drugs with and fuck. And we let them. We accepted it, took what we could. We had each other still.'

'And Ram was one of these guys?'

'No, no. He wasn't, that was the thing. He wasn't married for a start. He was quiet, polite. Not the usual kind of guy we got at parties. All the girls liked him, liked him a lot. He turned up at first at the Taj Palace, a twenty-first for some son of one of the big hotel families. Paid attention to us Russians, said he was interested in our country. Asked Galina out for breakfast after the party ended. Took her for pancakes at an American diner she told me, real maple syrup.'

'So what happened? Why aren't you friends anymore?'

'That's our business.'

'So what happened with Ram and Galina? Can you tell me about that?'

'Why do you want to know?'

'I'm just interested in him. Is that OK?'

'I guess, you bought me lunch . . . I don't owe those two anything. I don't know him well though. Ram was only was ever in Mumbai for business, never for a long time. He had a client who was getting into shipping. He had to come up to Mumbai to talk to the port authorities, working out tax or something like that. Galina would drop everything when he arrived. Whatever we had planned, whatever work we were doing. Left me to sort things out. I tried not to mind, I could see she was mad about him. She liked the way he treated her and him, well, he wasn't married. Galina is beautiful. Why not? He asked her to move down to Goa. To help him with some business. She did, she left me in Mumbai on my own. Things happened. I was lonely. I got in with the wrong crowd, partying too much. I met a guy but he wasn't right. I had to have an operation and it didn't go well. I stopped dancing. If she hadn't left it wouldn't have happened. I came down here to see her, to ask her for some help. She put me up for a week or so, but she didn't want me around, I could see that. We had an argument. I left and I never managed to get back up to Mumbai. We don't see each other much anymore. Sometimes. I call her if I'm in trouble. I'm an embarrassment to her.'

'How do you know she didn't want you around? Why didn't she?'

'She didn't want me to see that she was miserable. She's so proud. She thought he was going to marry her but he didn't. I heard them arguing about some other woman one night. She's ashamed. She dumped me for a man who doesn't love her. He doesn't love her. She

229

knows that but she's trapped. She can't help loving him and she can't go back to the life she had. She's too scared, she needs his money too. She's dancing again, she's got her first film for the last few years. But only because it's shot in Goa and no one wants to dance in it. She can't afford her lifestyle. She's too fond of Chanel now.'

'Is he violent? Does he hit her?'

Saskia shook his head. 'He wouldn't show that much emotion.'

'What business are they involved in? Why did he need Galina? I thought he was just an accountant. Is it something to do with smuggling.'

'I don't know. Galina says he's an accountant. But I don't know. I've no idea what he could be up to, how much she's involved, why he needed her down here.'

'I need to talk to her.'

'Well go down to the beach. That's where they're shooting today. Don't tell her I talked to you OK? I don't want Alexander coming after me.' she said.

6

I made my way back through the stalls, through the hasty, edgy trance, through the smoke and the sellers packing up now, until I was spewed up out the market on to Anjuna beach. Who was Alexander? Saskia hadn't wanted to talk about him. She'd told me where Galina was at least, that was the main thing. I didn't need any more people to worry about.

The sun hung heavy in the sky, dark-yellow, like a marigold. Its deadliness had waned and now emitted a motherly sort of warmth. The sand and headland were orange. It must have been a good place to end up after the hippy trail. A deserted beach; get naked, live with nature, the reward for the months of hard, dirty 1960s travel.

Goa was just eight hours direct from Heathrow now. The beach was packed. I made my way past beach huts and nightclubs, rickety sunbeds and restaurants. Past chicken tikka, fish and chips, mojitos and white wine spritzers towards a great silver light at the end of the beach. A film light board, reflecting swathes of evening sun.

Film equipment lay all set out on the sand, small groups were chatting, sitting down, smoking. The tech guys, managing the cameras, the lights and the sound booms were mostly young Indian dudes leant back on their equipment. Further away was a large Indian guy in a black polo-neck T-shirt and slicked-back curly grey hair. I recognised him as a movie director often on page three of the newspaper, Vivendra Khanna, known for high-living, controversial films and six wives. A kind of Bollywood Henry VIII. I remembered reading about this film. It was supposed to be his most contentious yet, about the young English girl who was supposed to have been murdered right here, on this beach.

A lot of people said it wasn't going to make it to the screen. All the big stars had turned it down; not even the B-listers had wanted to touch it. Khanna was having to scrape the barrel to find the cast. He was battling against government and a growing sense in the media and in Bollywood that it wasn't right to make a movie out of the death of a young girl in Goa.

Galina wasn't the only one who was risking dancing for him though. There was a group of about twenty girls, all dressed in blue wigs and sequinned mini-dresses. They looked like they were in the Jetsons, not a Goa movie, but lovely nonetheless. Their dresses glittered in the sun and sparkled off the sand. Most of them were Indian but there were a significant white minority. The Russians I assumed. All smoking. Galina was there, standing a little apart, sucking on her cigarette, eyes screwed up to the sun, like she was daring it to burn her or something. The director bawled out directions for a take with his loudspeaker. The girls languidly put out their cigarettes and arranged themselves into lines. They weren't the best-looking dance troupe I'd ever seen. Some of the Indian girls were rather on the weighty side. The Russians were bone thin and kind of worn-looking. I settled down on the sand to watch the scene. I couldn't imagine what exactly the dance was about. Was it a going to be a pre-rape fandago? Or some cocaine fuelled party anthem? It didn't become clear, the girls just flicked their legs and arms, a little slower than most, and wiggled their bums and then it was over. Khanna called a wrap and the dancers scattered. Wandering in twos and threes over to a big trailer set up on the sand, surrounded by black boxes and spotlights.

I followed over at a distance, waited a little, then knocked on the door of the trailer. A chubby Indian girl with bright red lipstick opened it with a large smile which abruptly turned into a frown when she saw me. I asked her for Galina. Her mouth turned down at the corners and she shrugged, turning back into the trailer and yelling loudly.

A few moments later Galina came to the door in a thin green negligee, make-up half-wiped from her face. She held the door open with a sinewy arm and stared at me with open blankness.

'Hi Galina, do you remember me? Ruby Jones?'

She shook her head.

'I met you in Vasco de Gama, with Zim Moon? You were with Paulo Mendes and Ram Kumar, at Paulo's apartment. It was just a couple of days ago.'

She frowned. 'The art dealer guy? From America? What do you want? What are you doing here?'

'I just wondered if I could talk to you for a minute.'

'How did you find me? How did you know I was here?'

'Ah – I remembered you saying you were doing a shoot in Goa and er . . . I met a friend of yours, Saskia?'

'What do you want?'

'I just wanted to talk to you about Sister Michael . . . and Ram Kumar.'

'I don't know anything about it. Sorry. I'm tired. I want to leave.'

The door was shut firmly in my face. A large man in T-shirt and jeans was sitting close by on an upturned camera case, drinking a coke. He looked up at the sound of the door slamming, eyed me up. I hadn't had any trouble on the set yet, but he looked like he could cause a mess. I smiled at him.

'My sister. We're talking about mother.'

He nodded slowly, but carried on watching. I knocked on the door again. It swung open and Galina stood there, lined and bare of make-up.

'I'm not telling you again.'

'Could you just listen for a second? I'm a journalist. I'm investigating the head of Saint Francis. Your boyfriend—.'

'Boyfriend?' Galina raised brows.

'Ram Kumar?'

'I think I'm too old to have a "boyfriend".'

'What do you want me to call him then? Your partner? Your husband?'

'We're not married. Just carry on.'

'Ram and his boss are getting the blame for a huge smuggling ring. They could be going to prison.'

Galina shrugged. 'So?'

'So. I've heard that you're involved too.'

Galina frowned. 'Who did you hear that from? It's got nothing to do with me. I'm a dancer.'

I shook my head. 'Will you talk to me? I won't quote you. I just want to find out a few things.'

Galina glanced back behind her. There was a scream of laughter.

'OK, come in. You haven't got long. Ram's coming to collect me and I don't want you around then. Don't think he hasn't noticed you're a journalist.'

The trailer was a garish mess of costumes and underwear and make-up. It smelt of hot bodies and sweating lipstick, cheap perfume and hairspray. A strange jabber of Russian and Hindi and shrieks hung in the air. Galina rubbed her hand across her face.

'The last film I did, I got my own trailer. I didn't think I'd finish up here. I trained at the ballet,' she said.

'We could stay outside?'

'OK. I want a coffee first. Do you want one? I have tokens for the machine.'

She rummaged through a case on the floor. Tights, bras, a strange foreign brand of cigarettes, face-pack, eye-mask, tinted foundation, another pot of that insanely expensive face cream. Ram couldn't treat her that badly; she could never have afforded it on a bit-part dancer's wage.

We walked away from the trailer with plastic cups of instant black. She lit a cigarette. The big guy in the jeans had finished his coke and was crushing the can in his hands.

'What do you want to know?' she said.

'About Ram. About Sister Michael. What was their relationship?'

'Why do you want to know about her? She's dead. The maid did it.'

'I don't think she did it.'

'That's what Ram says. Says she didn't have the energy,' said Galina.

'Did he kill her?'

Galina laughed a short, sharp laugh. 'God. No. No I don't think so. Why would you think that?'

'He knew her didn't he?'

'He did. A lot of people knew her. Goa isn't a big place. One Christmas party at Government House is all it takes. And we've all been here long enough for several.'

'Was she running a smuggling business – with Ram and Paulo?'

'Where on earth did you get that idea? Paulo wouldn't hurt a fly. He's a complete innocent. He has no idea what's going on.'

'Why did Ram get you to come down to Goa?'

Galina turned round to look at me. She was beautiful, no doubt, but it seemed a hard-won kind of beauty. She was popping herself into dresses that no longer fitted her, tanning herself with tea and dying her hair with brash black Indian hair-dye. She looked tired and she had lines around her eyes.

'If I knew that, my life would be clearer.'

Galina turned away from me. Took a drag on her cigarette and threw it in the sand.

'Look – Ram isn't someone to mess with. There's nothing I can tell you now. I've got my own problems.

I don't want to stay here. You'd better go, before he gets here. I'll think about talking to you another time.'

'So you've got stuff to tell me?'

'I didn't say that. Don't push me,'

'OK. OK. Would you mind if I just used your phone? I need to get in touch Zim. He's going back up north and I need to go down to Panjim.'

Galina thought for a moment. She slitted her eyes thinking of a reason why she shouldn't give me the phone but couldn't think of one, it seemed. She shrugged.

'Why not? Here. Be quick.'

I got out my notepad to find Zim's number. Before I typed it in I scrolled through Galina contacts. It didn't take long. She couldn't have many friends around here. Ram, Saskia, Shruti, Vivendra, Alexander. Alexander. The guy Saskia mentioned, the guy Saskia didn't want coming after her. Another Russian?

'Is it a local number? Or international?' Galina asked.

'It's international. I'll just text. I won't call. I know it costs.'

'Call him if you want. I have international minutes. Just don't be too long.'

But I didn't want to call him. I knew already he would be upset – or angry. He would want me to go back with him, or he would want to go with me. He would ask me questions, try and find out where I was. I was just going to text him, telling him I was going to Panjim, that I would stay the night there. I needed to go digging in that old computer.

PART 4

1

'But why? I just don't see why you keep coming back here?' whined Father Jonathan.

I'd taken a motorbike-taxi from Anjuna with a bearded guy called Guru. He was chilled out and he was fast, weaving in and out of the traffic easily. I was at the door of the Basilica residence in an hour or so. The sun had dropped and it looked like I'd interrupted the old priest's tea time. I could see a housekeeper beyond, bustling about, in and out of the kitchen and the dining room with biscuits, cakes and a teapot. One of the Italian cardinals followed her into the room eagerly. Father Jonathan kept glancing behind while talking to me.

'It's my passport. It hadn't arrived last time. It must have by now. I'm sorry to keep bothering you.'

'Why did you have to have it sent to Sister Michael's? I don't understand at all. I don't. Really, I don't understand.'

Sister Michael had died the day I sent the Embassy

her details. I hadn't corrected them. I needed my passport. Thankfully there didn't seem to be much coordination between departments. No one had got in touch to say my passport witness was actually dead.

'Would you like to come with me? If you're worried about me in the house on my own?'

Father Jonathan looked behind again, just as the contented maid carried through a large pineapple upside down cake, layered with cream.

'No, no. I haven't got time for that. I really haven't. I need to have my tea. I'll get the keys for you but please be quick. It's all very difficult still here. It's all very difficult.'

It was dark by the time I let myself into the house once more. I clicked on the light in the hall and heard it burn out. I had to make my way to Sister Michael's library quietly in the dark.

I stumbled around until I found a side-lamp perched on top of her bookshelf and switched that on. I hit the computer's power and while I waited for it to load, I tried the drawers of the old oak desk. Locked. Where would she keep the key? Somewhere private. In her bedroom? It was the room next to the spare room, where I had stayed.

I turned the handle and switched on the dim light. It was a surprisingly feminine room, a four-poster bed with a pink cotton cover, embossed with gold hummingbirds. A large bevelled mirror stood on a long dresser at the side of the room. Photos, all of the same man, surrounded it. Like a shrine. He was dark, a Goan, eyes spaced evenly apart, a fine chin.

The largest picture, framed in dark wood, was of

the man dressed as a priest. A small shelf below held candles. He had an open face, confident, his eyes looking at the camera with defiance almost. I recognised the same look in photos of the man as a lanky boy, his arms round a friend, dressed in football kit, looking proud. They'd either just won or he knew they were about to.

Then photos of his wedding day, with Sister Michael, Dorothea. Of course, her husband. The priest she had fallen in love with, Francis da Silva, from the great political family. She was wearing a simple white veil, more like a nun's habit than a bride's. He had his arm gently around her shoulders, outside a small chapel. Was it the one up above the house? It could have been. The door was the same, but polished, not rotting, not yet a place for suicide and bats, but a place for celebration. Francis gazed a little off to the distance, less sure of himself as a newlywed, less defiantly confident. Sister Michael had her eyes down to the floor, leaning into her husband, the corners of her mouth rising just slightly. Then just a few more, of Francis, outside this house, but dilapidated, the garden overgrown. And another photo, of them together, holding hands, in what Sister Michael had called the conversation room, the eaves falling in, the windows broken. They weren't looking at the camera this time, but absorbed in the house, pointing up to the roof. Who'd taken this photo?

The dresser top was sparse but expensive. Nothing like Galina's heaving mass. One French cleanser, an old bottle of Chanel No.5, Dior mascara. A black lattice box held Sister Michael's jewellery: amber necklaces, gold chains, hair-pins and brooches. Beside this was a patterned ring box. But she'd said she'd had wedding bangles. I opened it up. There was a small tarnished key. I turned it in the desk lock and the drawer slid out, heavy and smooth. A bible lay on top of a stack of files – accounts. I opened up the first one, headed with a neat Ram Kumar Accountants logo. So he was her accountant? I began at the beginning and flicked through the first couple easily. There was nothing going in and nothing going out. And then a big sum of money into her bank account in 1983 – from E.J. Bond Street – fifty thousand pounds. Edward Jones Antiquities.

A big sum of money out too, to a company based in Bali – for the Indonesian floor probably. She'd said it had cost her. Over the 1980s there was a regular flow of money in, not as large as the first amount, but steady and good. And there was a steady flow of money out; presumably as she renovated her husband's house the way they had dreamed of together. Over the last ten years she had simply been saving all her income. She was a rich woman. And Ram knew that. There had been a dip in the amount two years back but this had spiked again over the last year. Ram knew all about the money coming in, where it came from and he knew exactly what she spent it on. I took the account from 2006–2007 and stuck it in my pocket.

Had Ram murdered her? What did he mean when he said she was going too far? Had she stolen the head of the Tambdi Surla bull? It was supposed to be worth millions. The head of Saint Francis? But why would she do that? She'd said herself she couldn't understand why anyone would want it, it had no market value, she had said.

I dug further down into her drawer, to a small steel box. Nothing ornate or beautiful about it. Very simple, the kind you find in markets all over India, alongside plastic kitchenware and hammered aluminium chests. I opened it up. Newspaper cutouts. A small announcement of Dorothea and Francis's marriage, then several articles on her husband's death, of a heart attack at the age of thirty-four. Grainy photos of people packing out the cathedral in Panjim; eulogies on the talent and promise he had shown and accounts of the vital role his family had played in gaining Independence in Goa. Very little on why he had abandoned the priesthood or the young wife he had left behind. Letters. A letter from her husband, in an old-fashioned scrawl. I read through, careful with the paper, worn soft from age. Dirt had gathered in the folds and the edges were feathery. It was dated 14 February 1985.

Dorothea,

I shouldn't be writing this letter to you. It's been forty-eight hours and forty minutes since I last saw you. I am making mistakes. My numbers don't add up. My mind is clouded and I can't calculate. Because of you.

I know you will find writing this confession on Valentine's Day too obvious, unstylish. I can't help it. There's red hearts in all the shops. I can't get on with anything until I at least try.

You're determined never to love another man. You're determined that your life is over now. Every day a slow plodding towards the grave that Francis is lying in. It doesn't have to be like that. Why do you refuse to see that I'm prepared to die for you?

Who do you see me as? You confide in me, you say you need my help. But I'm not your lover, I'm not your friend, I'm something else to you. I don't know what. I want to be your husband. I want to save you. I want to make you happy, stop you being so terribly sad. I would die for you.

Why do you pretend like an aged widow? You are so young and beautiful. You want to ruin it, settling that cigarette smoke all over your skin. Why all this pretence? Why do you feel the need to return to the convent? To pretend you're still a nun? You left. You can't go back. You don't have any more faith than I do. All you believe in are beautiful things. You are ruthless in pursuit of beauty and when God got in the way you threw him to one side. You're a fallen angel. You aren't innocent. You are not a nun. You're of the world. I love that about you. I love that. I love you.

You say all you have is that old house. All you want to do is make it new again. All I want to do is make *you* new again. All I want is to see you standing in the sea, up north at Tambdi Surla. I want you to be free, swimming in the waves, laughing in the twilight, with the birds flying all around you.

We have money now. We have freedom. I don't want to take the place of your husband. I know you could never really love another. I know that feeling too. But live in the world a little Dorothea, stop seeing it as a work of art, be a little human and kind to yourself. Let me look after you.

I am a fussy man, I know, but I'm not hard to live with. I'm tidy, quiet. I would like to take you out to restaurants and eat seafood with you. I have a good business now and Paulo wants me to begin working for him as his exclusive accountant. That means good money, not too much work either. Trips to Bombay every so often. You'd like Bombay, if you'd let yourself relax. I could take you to some of the parties there. In a few years we could give it up, retire to Tambdi Surla, live on the beach. Maybe, I don't know, we could have children. You're still young enough Dorothea. We could have a family. We could stop the business. We could be normal, honest people with a home and a family. We wouldn't have to give up your house either. We wouldn't forget Francis. I loved him too, you know.

I never thought of you when you were

married to Francis. He was an old friend, my oldest friend. I was happy for him. It was only when you turned up, thin and unhappy in my office, asking for my help, to carry out your plans, that this began. At first, I just wanted to help you. It was terrible to see you so helpless and scared. It makes me happy to see you get stronger, more independent. But don't change too much.

I remember that first day as being very hot. The sun blaring. You were wearing a slim, blue dress with buttons along one side. I remember thinking how incredibly slim you were and how you really shouldn't smoke cigarettes. It's raining outside my office today, the sky is so dark, it's blue and purple. It's making me feel very oppressed, very sad. I wonder what you're wearing today.

I don't know what will come of this letter. Maybe it will persuade you to open yourself to me, to persuade you we can make each other happy. Maybe you will put it away and we will pretend you never received it and we will go on as before. Maybe we will continue for twenty years or more. Maybe I will get a wife. I won't love her like I love you. But at least I know, today, I tried.

All my love,
Ram

Ram? Poor man. Reading the letter made me feel terribly sad. What doomed passion. She had put it away, she had never given him a chance. He was one of those few lucky people who know clearly who it is in life they were meant to love. But more unlucky because it had been unrequited. And Galina. Did she know? Had she any idea that she would always be second? It would explain that bitter, trapped manner of hers.

More than twenty years ago. A long time. Their relationship had faded away to nothing more than business perhaps. Or perhaps not. Maybe Ram killed Sister Michael in some last fit of jealously? Why now, though? What had his card to her meant? We need to talk. They were still in touch, that was clear.

The computer was whirring quietly now. Sister Michael had been worried about me using her account. I clicked on it straight away. A password. Easy. Francis. It worked.

Her homepage was Catholicnews.com, the headline: 'The Miracle of St. Francis – head proves God still blesses saint and Goa.'

Forensic analysis of recently found head suggests a corpse of only thirty-years-old. This proves the saint is still protected and blessed by the Lord. Vatican and Church in Goa rejoice in the return of the head and the continuing miracle of the founder of the Jesuits. Pope gives mass of thanks.

Dead but eternally youthful. I wondered what the old saint's secret was. It couldn't just be good acts.

History painted him as a bigotted racist. Whatever it was, if the church could bottle it, they'd make millions. Galina would be a customer.

I clicked on Sister Michael's Outlook and her email inbox sprang up. It was empty. Completely empty. I couldn't quite believe it, that even this old fashioned nun wouldn't send a few emails, especially with all her business interests so far away. I searched the screen. I clicked on folders. Bingo. A series of correspondence folders popped up. She was so incredibly organised she saved all her email like letters. A folder for miscellaneous, a folder for Museum of Christian Art, a folder for someone called Vanessa, perhaps her sister. A folder for Edward Jones and a folder for Father Jonathan. No folder for Ram. I began with Father Jonathan, more out of curiosity than anything else, to see what the grumpy old priest would sound like in cyberspace.

I didn't get further than clicking open. I felt something hard smack me on the head and I fell to the floor. I lay there for a few minutes before trying to lift my head. Another smack and I fell back down. I could taste blood in my mouth. My eyes were blurring. I could feel myself being lifted up under the armpits and heard a groan of effort. Then I passed out.

2

There was a sharp pain running through my eyes and forehead, down through my body. My mouth was very, very dry. I tried to lick my lips but something was gagging my mouth. I tried to move, but my hands and legs were restrained. My legs were together and my hands tied beside me with a large piece of purple cloth. The knots weren't well done, but I was too weak to try and struggle. I could hear birds calling outside and see a slip of red light cracking into wherever I was. It smelt musty and old. It was dark. I tried to crane my neck around but the effort exhausted me and I lay back down again, closing my eyes.

After some time it got hotter. I began to sweat. My thirst was growing, moving down my mouth into my throat. My eyes were caked with sleep, or pus, or something. The sun baked through the coverings on the windows and passed a grey sheen over the place. I noticed through my crusty eyes a police forensic number on the opposite wall. I knew where I was. I was in the chapel. Where Maria had killed herself. I began to cry. The tears stung my eyes and I tried to stop.

A slant of light was hitting my face and burning me. I tried to shuffle out of the way. My whole body ached but I managed it. As I did so, I felt something in my pocket move. It was the iPod Zim gave me. I curled my body up and used my arms to move the earphones closer to me. After several attempts I caught them with my chin and pulled myself back to a lying position. It took me time, I don't know how long, to shufffle headphones into my ears with my shoulder and my chin. They were scratchy with the dried blood. Silence. No sound. No music. I used the right heel of my hand to press into the pocket of my new trousers. I hoped there was something good on this machine. 'Gracelands'. Paul Simon. God, I needed some grace. I lay my head back and let the music wash over my painful body, my throbbing head, my dry, dry throat and my cracked lips. And my fear, my incredible fear.

Who had done this? Who had followed me down to the house? Who didn't want me looking into Sister Michael's accounts and her computer? Who knew I was coming here? Galina. Had she told Ram? Had it been Ram? Had Ram followed me? How? The only other person who knew I was coming down here was Zim. It hadn't been him. It couldn't have been him. I texted him at least.

Half way through my second listening to the album, the door of the chapel began to open. I expected to see the pressed chinos of the accountant staring me in the face, but no. What I saw was a sea of black robe.

'Oh dear. What a mess,' whined a familiar voice. Father Jonathan.

He moved closer towards me and I craned my neck up to see him. He bent down and removed the tie around my mouth.

'Oh dear. Oh dear,' he said again.

'What's going on?' I said.

'I just don't know. I just don't really know anymore. It's all gone so horribly wrong.'

'Can I have some water? I'm really thirsty.'

'Oh dear. I should have thought of that. I just, I don't think I have time. I have mass at one and then we have a large lunch, for the cardinals, they're on their way back to the Vatican.'

'Was it you who hit me last night?'

My voice was croaky. My head was in a fever and pounded when I tried to think and talk at the same time.

'I didn't have any choice. Why were you looking in her desk Ruby? Why did you need to keep coming back? Why did you make me do this? I didn't want to do this. Don't you think its been hard enough already? Don't you think I feel bad enough? Do you know how hard it is? Being the curate of the shrine, protecting Saint Francis?'

I wanted to ask him what the hell he was talking about, or spit in his face or tell him to fuck off, but I didn't have the energy. I lay back down on the floor with my eyes closed.

'What are you doing with me?'

'I just don't know. What should I do? What do you know? I have to leave. I need to prepare for mass.

Please don't make a fuss. Don't cause me more problems please.'

His large hands fumbled the cloth over my mouth and then he left, closing the door behind him.

What the hell was going on? The old priest was mad. He'd hit me over the head with something last night, tied me up and brought me here, just as I was about to look at his emails with Sister Michael. What the hell was he doing? Had he killed Sister Michael? Had I got it completely wrong? Was he involved in the smuggling too? Was he involved in stealing the head of Saint Francis? But why would he do that? No wonder he had been so nervous going into Sister Michael's house. What was he going to do with me? I'd never liked him. He hadn't even given me water when I'd asked. And he was supposed to be a priest. There was no way he would ever incite Stockholm Syndrome in me. I would have preferred Ram to kidnap me. He was at least quite attractive.

My head still hurt. I lay back down and tried to shuffle the iPod around with the heel of my hand. Pot luck with Zim's musical taste. I hit Faure's 'Requiem'. Lying there, listening to the harps and soaring voices, I was almost as surprised with Zim as I was with the old priest. I never thought he would have it in him to listen to this. The songs vibrated around my aching brain and around this dank, seedy little chapel. Religion. God. Saint Francis and Father Jonathan, Maria, Sister Michael and her poor weak-hearted husband, all supposedly working for God. Amazing what you could get away with under that banner.

I wondered if I would ever see Zim again. I wondered

if he was getting worried. He would be. Perhaps not this morning, but later in the afternoon. He'd tell the police. They'd come looking for me. I hoped. Would they look up here? Would anyone ask Father Jonathan? I thought of Stephen, dead and buried. Sister Michael, Maria. What was it like to die? Did it hurt? Were they scared? Of course they were. I started crying. I was still very, very thirsty.

It was getting dark once more by the time Father Jonathan returned. He seemed calmer, satiated after a grand Goodbye Vatican dinner probably, relieved he'd managed to get rid of his cardinals. He'd brought me some water and he'd brought me some wafer biscuits imprinted with the head of Saint Francis, baked for the special occasion he told me. I took them from his hand, like communion, and ate them gratefully.

'What are you listening to?' he asked.

At least he didn't mind about the music. That was quite nice of him. He could have taken it off me.

'Faure's "Requiem".'

'Ah, I like that. Sister Michael liked that too. We would sit and listen to music sometimes, in her study.'

He smiled and sat down in the corner of the room, remembering. He didn't seem to really know what he was doing. He'd hit me on the head and now he couldn't decide what to do. He was protecting some secret. Something that Sister Michael knew. That could have been on her computer.

'Why have you done this? Please let me go, if this is about the smuggling, then don't worry. I'll keep quiet. I haven't told anyone,'

Father Jonathan looked at me oddly.

255

'What are you talking about?'

'The smuggling,'

Father Jonathan smiled blandly. 'I don't know anything about that.'

He seemed relieved.

'What's this about?'

'It's about protecting the church. About protecting Goa and Saint Francis. I tried to talk to Sister Michael about it, but she was losing her reason. She wasn't thinking clearly.'

'It was you who killed her? You who knocked her over the head?'

'No, I didn't kill her. Of course not. We had an argument, while she was putting out the decorations. I left. I feel bad about that. I wish I had been there.'

'You smashed her skull in. You hit her hard, at least twice over the head.'

'I didn't. I just warned her not to disturb the visit. The cardinals were arriving, I couldn't have the visit disturbed by Sister Michael.'

'Why would she disturb them?'

'You don't know?'

'Tell me.'

Father Jonathan shook his head. 'I don't know what to do with you. Maria, she did what she needed to do. Of course, it is a sin to take your own life, of course. But in these circumstances I know she'll be in heaven now.'

The man was completely off his rocker. What was he talking about? Had he killed Maria too?

'Why did she need to commit suicide?'

'She came to confession. She said she couldn't stand

it any longer. I said that as long as she walked the earth she would have to stand it. Death was the only way out.'

'You told her to kill herself? Is that why you kept telling the police she hadn't come to confession?'

He'd gone on and on about it at the police station. I thought it had been weird at the time. But I never would have thought he could be so devious. Poor woman. Her husband had been right.

'I didn't tell her that. She came to confession, she sought out my advice. I gave her solace. That with death would come relief. But she took it too far. I didn't know she would kill herself.'

'She had serious depression. You must have known that. Why was she so against Saint Francis? I went to see her husband. She wouldn't allow anything about him in the house. Why did she need protecting from evil. Her prayer book, all she did was pray to Saint Michael.'

'I just heard her confessions. Only that. I just heard her confessions. We all bore these crosses. Not just Maria. We all had to live with this. But I don't know what to do now. We're all in trouble here. What do I do with you? I don't know what to do. I'm going to have to pray. Why couldn't you just go away? You're not going to kill yourself too are you? That would make things easier. Would they believe it though?' he said.

I didn't sleep much that night. My bones hurt. I was very scared. He seemed such an ineffectual old man, but he could have killed two women already and he didn't seem to have any perspective on this. Waves of guilt made me want to vomit. Guilt at my irresponsibility, at my thoughtlessness, at my lack of caution. Guilt at the thought of my family. I heeled round Zim's iPod and tried to block out what was happening with some more music. Ryan Adams. I'd been listening to him the day after I met Zim. One song was called 'The Rescue Blues' and that made me laugh and then cry more.

I must have slept a little while as I woke to the sound of the door opening. It was Father Jonathan. He was holding a silk chord in his hand. He had some water and some croissants with him. He fed them to me. I didn't refuse. Once I had finished, I lay back down. I was getting even weaker. My head still hurt. It had stopped bleeding. He hadn't hit me as hard as he had hit Sister Michael. That was a good sign. If he had wanted to kill me he could have done it then, like he did her.

He looked around the room and found a dusty stool and pulled it opposite me, sitting heavily down on it. He fondled his rope through his fingers.

'What is that for?' I asked.

He shook his head. 'The problem, the problem always was Francis. Has always been Francis. Why couldn't she just leave him alone? She seduced him. That was obvious. He would never have left the church without being seduced. She pretended she was so full of the holy spirit. She never was, she was always a whore. She had a problem with passion. She was extreme. Why do you think she became a nun in the first place? Francis, Francis was a true servant. He was truly blessed with the spirit. We all had such high hopes for him. Such high hopes. He was a beauty. It was a wonderful thing to take communion from Francis. Such gentle hands.

His touch was so soft. But then she had to ruin it. She had to ruin him with her passion and her obsession, her need to own what was most beautiful. Jesus wasn't enough for Sister Michael. No, she had to have Francis.'

Father Jonathan had wound the chord tightly around his hand and was unwinding it once more. Was he going to hang me? Pretend I'd killed myself like Maria had? I didn't know what to do, what to say, whether to respond or just to lie there. I guessed I should keep him talking, at least when he was talking he wasn't wrapping that thing around my neck.

'Francis? Sister Michael's husband?'

'He should never have left us. If he hadn't have left us he would still be here. He would still be here with me. It was the devil's work. His heart broke you know? He missed us so much, he missed the church so much, his heart just broke one day. He couldn't live with that devilish woman one second more. She killed him. She killed him and then we all had to pretend, to pretend it wasn't her fault, that she was innocent. She's lived in that house up there for twenty years, just on Francis's memory, on his reputation, on his money. They say his family had lost it all, but she found the money somewhere. She did. Where did all the money come from if not from poor Francis?'

I nodded my head slightly. He didn't know about the smuggling or the money it had yielded over the years. Then what was the big secret? Father Jonathan came over to me, sat creakily down beside me. He looked carefully over me and began threading the rope through his hands again.

'It's women. Women ruin it. Ruin it all. I tried to save

him. I tried to bring him back. She agreed. She agreed and then suddenly she doesn't like it anymore. She wants him back in the grave she said. But you can't just do that. You can't do that. She would ruin us all. Just like she ruined him. She would ruin us. She would ruin Saint Francis. There would be no more Saint Francis. I had to do something. Do you see? I needed to protect them both from her. She was a devil. A devil's whore.'

The old priest was rambling with hatred. He had unwound his rope once again and was now threading it through his hands, clutching at it morbidly.

'What are you going to do with that rope?' I asked him.

He sighed.

'What should I do with it? I'm just so tired. Of trying to protect everyone here, of trying to protect what they believe in. I'm tired of women. So tired of women. I'm just tired and I don't know what to do. What should I do?'

'Maybe you just need to have a good sleep. Have you been sleeping?' I croaked.

'No, no not at all. I haven't been sleeping at all.'

'Perhaps a cup of tea? That calms me down,' I whispered.

'Yes, yes it would. It's Thursday today too. Monica will have made coconut cake.'

'Sounds nice.'

All I really wanted was more water.

'It is, it's lovely.'

'Perhaps you could get some extra biscuits as a treat, just to calm your nerves. You like sweet things don't you?'

Father Jonathan looked up. 'I do, I do. They make me feel better,' he whined.

'Maybe you should go and eat something nice before you make any decisions,' I said.

He nodded, and went off with a hang-dog lope and his hang-man rope.

I had to get out of here before he came back. Father Jonathan had left the cloth off my mouth. I could shout but what if only he heard me? How would he react to that? I struggled against the ties at my hands and feet. They weren't bound together too well but I was feeling weaker and weaker. The back of my head was still hurting. The cut throbbed painfully and it was probably infected. I couldn't remember if I'd had my tetanus. I hadn't bothered getting my injections renewed before I came out to India, like I hadn't bothered taking out insurance. It all cost money and I'd assumed luck would get me by. Born lucky was what my father said, and I believed him. So dumb. If I had insurance I wouldn't have needed to wait around to replace my passport. I could have got a flight. I would never have got myself messed up here, tied up in ropes, bleeding.

How could I be so naïve? To think nothing could ever happen to me? After Stephen, I thought I'd learnt. But not really. There was still some part of me that thought I was invincible. If I got out of here I would change. I would work harder. I would stop feeling sorry for myself. I'd stop leaving things to some strange, home-made idea of fate. I would make a new start. I would write a fucking great report on this head and this crazy priest.

I made another effort at getting out of the ties. If I

had been well, they wouldn't have been a problem. Father Jonathan had locked the door but I could have smashed a window and got out with a few cuts. But I just didn't have the strength. The adrenalin I should have been feeling seemed to be weakly ebbing away into my wounds. I could feel my eyes caking up too. I lay my head back. Just to have a sleep for a few minutes to get my strength back.

I woke up with the door handle being turned. A shot of fear ran through me. He was back, sugared up and ready to go. What the fuck was going to happen to me? But the door went slack. He wasn't coming in. The door clanked again and then went quiet. Whoever was at the door, they didn't have keys. It wasn't Father Jonathan. I tried to shout out. But all that came out was a croak, my throat was too dry. I screamed but hardly anything came out. I yanked my head in frustration. I would have been crying but I didn't have the moisture inside of me.

I heard voices outside. A low Indian muttering and then a louder, higher, indignant, American voice. Zim. My limbs flooded with some emotion, relief partly, frustration, even a slight amount of irritation with him. I tried my hardest to call his name. But it did no good. My voice wouldn't carry beyond my sad little space. Their voices died out and with them what seemed to be my only chance of getting out of here. The tingling in my legs and arms was replaced by a deadened, weighty depression. What the hell was going to happen to me? God, how had that poor woman felt when she lifted her head, hardly alive, to see the vase smash one more time down on her. Did she feel it? Or were her nerve endings dead already? God, even seeing the blood and the gore and the stained pink figures, you don't think, you don't feel the horror, the fear. And Maria? What happened with her? Did she do it to herself? Or did he do it to her? What did he say to her to make her so deeply distressed? So petrified that she would kill herself, when she had a family? Sons. A husband. She would never have wanted to hurt them, she would have cared for them more than herself. I thought of my own family again. He must have said something to her about her family, he must have got to her that way. She must have thought she was helping them, sacrificing herself for them. He'd had years of practice at manipulating people in confession boxes. I let out a groan. He wouldn't manipulate me but he could do anything he wanted. I couldn't fight. And he was a big man. His eyes were sunken but his hands, his body were large, strong. He didn't ever go hungry. He could easily lift me up on to that broken-down altar and drop me down with a rope round my neck.

The old iron door handle creaked up once more. Oh God. Oh God. My breathing was shallow and quick, I began to hyperventilate. The handle went flat once more. Who was it? A pause. And then a crack. A smash and splintered glass over me. The window cracked open with a small statue of the virgin Mary, now lying at my feet, her arms up in serene prayer.

'Yeah, hey. She's in here. She's in here. I told you she was missing. I told you something had happened,' yelled Zim.

3

They kept me in hospital on a saline drip for almost forty-eight hours, journalists and police outside at the door. Inspector Ferreira was allowed a very brief visit to verify it was Father Jonathan who had held me hostage. I told him I thought it was Father Jonathan who had hit Sister Michael over the head. He had talked about her a lot, he had hated her.

Ferreira didn't like that idea. It was very difficult for him to think that a priest had done anything so criminal. He didn't want to believe me, I could see. He kept asking me why. I said they seemed to be keeping some secret together. Something to do with Saint Francis. Ferreira asked the doctor if I'd been checked for concussion, if my head was OK.

I said it was fine. But he had seemed a lot more enthusiastic about Zim or Maria killing Sister Michael. He said he would have to investigate further and couldn't make any quick conclusions.

'As soon as we have that Idol Squad off our hands,

things are going to get back to normal. We're going to be able to investigate this properly,' he said.

As for me, there was nothing too badly wrong. Concussion and deep dehydration. The doctor admonished me for not drinking more. Told me I should be drinking coconut water in this heat, that it was full of electrolytes. I didn't explain the relative difficulty of this over the past couple of days. I called my parents from the hospital payphone.

The long bleep of an overseas call. My throat hurt at the thought of the hall at home and our old phone blaring out its bell.

'Hello?'

The wavering pre-occupied voice of my mother, sounding older than before; in the midst of another poem, probably.

'It's me,' I said. The tears were already welling up into my voice.

'Ruby!'

A delighted warble. 'We've been worried about you. You never called over Christmas! We were waiting for your call. Your father was upset.'

'I'm sorry,' I began. A sob ballooned up in my throat and stopped me saying more.

'Ruby. What is it? Are you OK? Are you pregnant? Oh God. Is he Indian?' wailed my mother. That at least made me laugh. Why was that always the first thing she thought?

'I don't think so. No. No don't worry.'

'Well what is it then?'

She sounded disappointed. She was disappointed.

'Oh, look. It's nothing. You know I had some trouble.

265

But I'm OK now. I just wanted you to know I was OK.'

'You don't sound OK darling.'

'I'll be fine. Just a bit emotional that's all.'

'Are you on your own? We worry about you, you know. We wish you would come home.'

'I'm with someone. Don't worry.'

'A friend? Indian?'

There was tangible, desperate, hope in her voice. All she really wanted was for me to meet someone and have a baby. Preferably Indian. She'd got that into her head somehow, it was the one way she could reconcile herself to me being out here. I wished I could make her happy, make both of them happy. I wished I could be around more. But I couldn't. Not now. Not yet. I needed to know leaving had been worth it. That I'd achieved something, or at least learnt something other than loneliness.

'Just a friend mum.'

'Oh . . . Ruby. Why don't you come home? We miss you,' she said. I bit back more tears. I was homesick; but it wasn't going to do any good to start crying about it on the phone.

'Mum . . . I'm sorry. I'm thinking about what I'm doing. I might come home. Just . . . mum. I'm going to call you and dad again soon. On Skype, OK? I miss you too.'

Zim cheered me up. He bought me a coconut from the Majestic Panijm, complete with an umbrella, straw and rum. He got me the newspapers too, the *Goan Chronicle* and the *Times of India* as well as the *Telegraph* and the *Guardian*. I ignored the stamp across the front page, asking for the newspapers to stay in the hotel coffee shop. He'd already got in trouble for using a statue of the Virgin Mary to smash the window of the old chapel I'd been kept in. He pulled up a chair and sat by my bed as I drank.

'Mmm. Better than a drip in your arm, it's good, thanks Zim.'

'No problem.'

'I don't think I'll ever be able to thank you enough, for everything. I tried to shout, but I just couldn't. I don't know how you managed to find me.'

'I went round with Inspector Ferreira when he was checking out the house. Father Jonathan was acting so weird. We tried the door of the chapel, but he just kept on going on about how there was no key. The key was lost. But it didn't make sense to me. It had been open when you found Maria right? So someone must have locked it. Ferreira, he just arse licks those priests. He really believes in all that shit, like everyone here. He just swallowed everything the guy said. So I went off and found the statue. Smashed the window. I didn't care.'

I don't know what would have happened if you hadn't.'

He shrugged. 'I was so worried. I knew something was wrong. Why did you just text me like that? I didn't know where you were. No one knows where you are, Ruby. Have you spoken to your parents?'

'I spoke to my mum.'

'They must be concerned about you.'

'They want me to come home.'

'Are you going to?'

'Still haven't finished this article for Touchstone. I need to make some money before I leave.'

'You got the story – Crazed priest kills ex-nun and kidnaps investigating journalist.'

I shook my head. 'Inspector Ferreira doesn't think Father Jonathan killed Sister Michael. He's not going to stick his nose into the church. They're all so religious here.'

'What? Of course he killed her. Of course he did. He's mad. He would have killed you too.' Zim stood up, raised his voice. The nurse on duty looked at him.

'David won't be interested in that story anyway. He's being paid by a devout Catholic. He's just interested in the head. The warehouse. He wants to know about that. Smuggling, money, power, that's all, I'm just going to put it all down to experience. Maybe I'll write it up one day. For now, I've got to get on with what I have to write. I still got to get an interview with Srinvasen.'

'Ruby, you should just go home. Your parents want to see you. Why did you stay after Stephen died? Alone? You're not happy. You should leave. Don't hang around here if you don't want to.'

I shrugged, sucked the last of the coconut. Breathed out heavily to stop my voice waving. I didn't have anything to go back to. I'd been away three years. How was I going to get a job? All the stories from back home were about unemployment, cuts at the BBC, cuts at all the newspapers. It would be *Baker's Weekly* or back at the *Cardiff Echo*, living with my parents. I didn't want that. But I didn't want to stay either. I didn't want to end up like Sister Michael or Father Jonathan or Galina or that girl Saskia, away for so many years, apart from the normal world. Lost in India.

'I can't go home. There's no work. I'll just have to think of something else.'

'Do you want to come back to LA with me?'

'What?'

'I've got to close this deal with Paulo. That's gonna take a few more days. And then I'm heading back. Why don't you come with me?'

'In what capacity?'

Zim shook his head. 'It doesn't have to be a big deal. Just come out, see what it's like out there.'

'What the hell would I do?'

'I've been thinking about it. My dad needs someone to write up his annual catalogue, research the artists, interview the ones that are alive. A few articles on the general art market. The woman who's done it for the last few years, who's written all my dad's press releases and that shit too, she got together with the dog-walker who takes my mum's Afghan hound out for his morning constitution. They're moving to San Francisco, to set up some dog beauty parlour or something. I was thinking, you know, you could do her job, at least for a bit. You can write, and he pays well. And he owes me one. There's a major, major investment going on here. My dad is palming off every piece of art he couldn't shift over the last ten years on Paulo and calling it a portfolio. For once in my life I am the golden boy, I'm returning to the US in a shower of glory. He cannot fucking believe it. Neither can I. It feels fucking great. I'm on a roll.'

'I can see that, you're happy. But you don't know I can write. You haven't read any of my stuff.'

269

'Yeah but I know you're clever, and you're kind of funny. My dad will like you. He likes weird people. He'll think Wales is exotic.'

'Weird? You're saying I'm weird?'

'Yeah, come on, you can't take offence at that. I mean, its clear that anyone who goes on holiday to Goa and then ends up chasing round after a dead man's head is pretty fucking bonkers.'

Zim got a call, his dad. They needed to go through the final collection that they were going to offer Paulo. He went back to the hotel to Skype and left me with the papers.

'Just think about it Ruby. Please?' he said.

I sat there for a while, chewing on the straw of my coconut. Zim wasn't Indian, but at least he was male. That would appease my mother just a little. I began to read the papers.

Father Jonathan's kidnap attempt was front-page news in the Indian papers and made the first page of the international foreign news. But it didn't look like the police had investigated or questioned Father Jonathan at all. It was assumed he had just gone insane after the head was stolen. He'd been taken not to Panjim Police Station, as Zim and I had been, but to the Institute of Psychiatry and Human Behaviour, on the outskirts of the city. The chief psychiatrist there, Joseph Palma, explained that the curate of the Basilica, had suffered an episode of acute psychosis, caused by the deep trauma of losing the head of Saint Francis.

'The body of Saint Francis and his shrine had been under the direct charge of Father Jonathan Gibson for over twenty years. The devotion and faith with which

270

he has carried out his duty was of such fervour that the loss of the head of the saint pitched him over the edge of sanity. This is just another example of why the perpetrators of this terrible crime should face the direst consequences,' he said.

The doctor was quoted in all the papers and Father Jonathan received varying amounts of sympathy.

My own theory, that the priest was a repressed homosexual, in love with Sister Michael's dead husband, whose death had sent him mad years ago wasn't discussed.

It still didn't make complete sense to me though. Did Father Jonathan kill Sister Michael? Why? Out of hatred and jealously? Why did he wait so long to do it? And why would he convince poor Maria that she had to go too? And me? Was he just an insane misogynist? Or was there something else?

Was it the smuggling racket of Sister Michael's? Was he involved in it too? Had she stolen the head herself? But when I'd mentioned the smuggling he'd looked at me blankly. It seemed he really didn't know anything about it. He'd thought all Sister Michael's money had come from Francis. Hated her the more for using up his inheritance.

Father Jonathan wasn't the biggest story in the papers. It was the smuggling.

'TAMIL NADU IDOL SQUAD UNCOVERS BIGGEST STORE OF EASTERN CHRISTIAN ART IN ASIA,' said *Times of India*. 'HEAD OF GOAN SAINT LEADS TO MASSIVE TROVE OF STOLEN ANTIQUITIES,' said the *FT*. The Goan papers were more shocked at Paulo Mendes being arrested. 'PAULO

MENDES ARRESTED!' was the front page news in the *Goa Chronicle*. There was a Q&A with his lawyer, a Mr Antonio Aurelio, who claimed the arrest was false, there was no evidence to connect Mr Mendes with the warehouse or the smuggling. Inspector Srivansen rejoined by saying that ignorance was not an excuse.

'There are no police reports on Warehouse 10 in the shipping yard records. Where are they? Where are the usual checks in place to ensure against illegal activity? Is Mendes Shipping above the law? It is clear that major theft and smuggling has been going on through this company and in this case, Mr Mendes is guilty until proven innocent. It's his company, he must take the brunt of the consequences for what looks to be one of the biggest smuggling rings in the history of Independent India. This is a crime on par with the sacking of the pyramids.'

The doctor on my ward wouldn't let me get up to use the internet. He seemed to think it would somehow affect my recovery. Zim lent me his iPhone overnight and found me the password for a nearby café's wireless network. It was a weak signal, but it would do. When everyone was asleep and the lights were off, I logged on to Facebook and found David Dryden online.

Hey
Ruby. Is it a habit of yours, to always feature in your stories? Rather egotistical.
Thanks for the sympathy.
How are you feeling?
Fine. Just dehydrated.
Good. We haven't long before we go to print. I've

looked at all the news. Sounds like the old priest was a mad old queen to me.

You've got it.

Takes one to know one. Though of course he has a good few years on me.

Lol.

I think you should just forget about him, concentrate on finishing off this smuggling piece. Bukowski wouldn't be keen on Father Jonathan popping up in Touchstone. And it doesn't make for a smooth story if we start bringing in the suicide and this whole kidnapping thing. They've made an announcement about the warehouse now, but we've got a very good head start. Sister Michael's accounts. Edward Jones Antiquities. Ram Kumar. I'll deal with Edward Jones. You need to get an interview with Srinvasen and an interview with Ram and then start putting it together.

I thought I could try for an interview with Ram first. Trade whatever I learn – if I learn anything – with Srinvasen for an interview with him.

Ruby, that's why I have so much faith in you as a writer. Is it going to be hard to find the man?

He's retired to his holiday home, unavailable for comment. But I know where it is. Easy.

4

Peaceful as ever round Casa Bonita. The air clean and quiet. Sea crashing. I didn't like sneaking in here, causing mischief. It would have been better to see Ram in his office, in Vasco or in Panjim, places where vice hung in the air. But he was here, staying on his beautiful, uncorrupted beach. I'd just have to forget his hospitality, letting Zim and me enjoy this place too.

The boy who looked after the house wasn't around. The front door was open slightly. I knocked, not loud. No answer. Nobody home? I could hear the temple bell ringing out over and over again. Evening prayers. Perhaps Ram was there? I pushed open the door and wandered inside.

Ram might have been at the temple, but Galina wasn't. She lying on the sofa right in front of me, groaning. Her arms were above her head and her wrists held by another man's hand. Abe, in the same old jeans he wore walking his dogs. No wonder they hadn't heard me knock; they were into each other fiercely. If I'd come in just a little bit later, Abe wouldn't be wearing those jeans.

Galina had her eyes closed, was concentrating on herself. But Abe, he glanced up and locked his eyes with mine. He didn't stop what he was doing immediately, but slowly. Maybe he was taking his time to digest the scene, maybe he just didn't want to stop. Galina noticed something was wrong and soon we were all locked still together. Just looking at one another.

'I think I should get going. The dogs need a walk. Sita will be getting dinner ready,' said Abe finally. He disentangled himself from his lover and made for the door, nodding a goodbye as he passed by me.

That left Galina. Sitting up on the sofa now, crossed legs, wearing only a large shirt. She was sweating and she had no make-up on. She looked scared, defenceless.

'It's not what it looks like,' she said.

'What does it look like?'

Galina stood up.

'Ruby. Please. Don't say anything to anyone. Please. Not for me. For Sita. For Abe. They love each other. She's devoted to him. They'd both fall apart. They need each other.'

'I feel sorry for Sita. But it's nothing to do with me. I'm not looking to cause trouble. I'm looking for Ram. I need to talk to him.'

'Look please don't tell him. Don't say anything to anyone. You know, things get out so easily.'

'I won't. I need to talk to him about something else. Where is he?'

Galina sat down on the sofa, closed her eyes and

rubbed her head. She didn't trust me. She was thinking.

'Galina, just tell me where he is.'

'Why do you need to see him? What do you want to know?'

'What do you mean?'

'What do you want to know? I can tell you pretty much all of it. He won't. He's very good at making you believe what he says. But it won't be true.'

I took out the account I'd taken from Sister Michael's. After some hesitation I also took out the love-letter Ram had written. It wasn't just Galina and Abe. They were all as bad as one another. Maybe it was the tropical weather. Got you horny.

Galina held the letter in both hands, prayer-like concentration on the yellowed scrawl. When she'd finished, she held it out to me between her fingertips like it was a stinking rag.

'That's Ram. Yes, that's Ram. So romantic. I told you, he can make you believe anything.'

'I need an interview. On the smuggling, on the connection between Ram and Sister Michael. On the missing heads. What has he got to do with them? Are you prepared to give that to me?'

Galina shook her head. 'I can talk to you. But I can't be quoted. Ram would make me pay for that. He doesn't forgive.'

'I thought you were leaving? You told me you were? Are you leaving for Abe?'

'No. No. I could never split those two. He loves her. I'm leaving India. I'm going home. Please don't mess this up for me. I'm nearly . . . I'm almost home.'

She'd started to cry. Were real tears streaking down

her face? Or fake? I wasn't sure. She was going blotchy and swelling. Maybe they were real.

'If you can't talk to me. Find someone who can. Or I'll go and find Ram.'

Galina was mixing up me finding Ram and asking for an interview with me telling him about her and Abe. I wasn't going to do that. But I didn't reassure her. Maybe I took advantage.

'Honestly, there's no point asking him. He's at the temple now anyway. I'll help you. I want him to be found out. He's mad, really. I think he's mad.'

'Who the hell has actually been stealing this stuff in the first place? It wasn't Sister Michael or Ram was it? They weren't doing midnight raids. Who was it? Do you know?'

She wiped her eyes. Stared at her hands, rubbed her finger and thumb together, thinking.

'I have to make a call first,' she said.

She took her time on the phone, speaking fast and quiet Russian, smoking a cigarette. Nodding occasionally. I didn't trust her but I felt sorry for her. By the time she finished, she'd regained her composure. Her face was tight again.

'I've got someone for you to talk to. Alexander. He's a cousin of mine.'

'A cousin? Really?'

'We're not related, but this far away? We're cousins. He's from Moscow. He runs the Diamond Dogs.'

'The Diamond Dogs?'

'A gang. It's just a name. They all give themselves names. These guys, they're into jewellery, diamond. They like to wear black. They're pretty but they like girls. They're mean. They sometimes work for Ram. Alexander knows about what he's been doing. Alexander is in Anjuna. He says we can meet him there tomorrow. He'll talk to you.'

'No. I can't. Zim is signing his contracts. I need to be there. It's New Year's Eve too. The traffic will be crazy. Everything will be crazy. It needs to be today.'

'OK. OK. Maybe we can go and meet him tonight. He's working tonight. I'll need to ask Ram if I can use the car. I can't phone him now. We'll need to wait.'

I sat waiting on the step with Galina. We both smoked. Watched the sun begin to get a little heavy.

'I like this time of day. Before sunset. Sunsets upset me,' she said.

'They're beautiful here.'

'They're painful. As soon as they arrive, this perfect orange light, you know it's over. That night's coming.'

Abe was walking his dogs, just like at Christmas. A quiet silhouette. Galina watched him.

'Do you love him?' I asked.

'No. Yes. I mean, I needed someone to love. I'd been alone so long here, I couldn't stand it anymore. Ram doesn't give me what I need. I was going crazy. I needed someone to touch me and mean it. Abe, he was here, he was the only man around. I fell for him, I led him on. Not because he was wonderful, not because he was my dream man. Because it was just us two on the beach at sunset. He really is as quiet as he seems. He doesn't talk more when you get to know him,' she said.

'Does he love you?'

She shrugged. 'No. He'd never leave Sita. He loves her.'

278

'Why is he doing it then? If he loves her so much? It doesn't make sense.'

'Since when have people made sense? You can never know what makes someone do what they do. He just wanted me. He couldn't help it. He doesn't even like me that much. I can see that. But I'm grateful to him. I'm leaving, because of him.'

'Because of Abe?'

'He made me feel alive again. I'd been dead for so long. I remembered what it felt like to be happy. I wasn't happy, but just remembering what it felt like, that was enough. I'm leaving. I'm going home and I'm going to be happy.'

The sound of a smooth car. Ram. Fresh in a white kurta suit, grey beard trimmed. He nodded at me, didn't seem to notice it was strange that I was here. His brow was knotted.

'How is your father?' asked Galina.

'Not good. More pains in his chest. I've called my doctor in Vasco. It's the bull. It's broken his heart. He won't last. I know it.'

Ram couldn't look at us. He stared out to sea, squinting his eyes at the sun, almost dead now.

'He needs to rest,' said Galina.

'I tried to make him let one of the younger priests take the ceremony. But he wouldn't. He's stubborn. He's angry. He won't be told,' said Ram.

Ram shook his head and the subject was closed. He saw me properly for the first time. Asked me if everything was OK. He'd heard what had happened with Father Jonathan, said the man had been mad for years. He wanted to know what I was doing around here. I

279

said I was just doing some sightseeing in the area, before I left Goa and had called in. Galina said she'd offered to give me a lift back to Panjim. Ram narrowed his eyes at her, probably not used to such shows of altruism from his dancer. She saw this, lit another cigarette and said she'd run out of moisturiser. The boutique at the Panjim Majestic was the only one that stocked her brand, she could feel her face cracking right now. The sea breeze was ageing her, she said. Ram looked more familiar with this talk. He shrugged and told her to give up smoking and turned into the house.

5

The car was a surprise. A silver BMW with red, leather seats. I wouldn't have thought such a fastidious man, devoted to his temple and his quiet home, would have enjoyed a car like that. I would never have thought a man as solitary as Abe would want two women. Or that an ex-nun would be so keen on money and crime. So many different ways to justify ourselves. You could never really tell.

Galina obviously enjoyed driving the car. It was dark by the time we got on the road and the lanes were black, but that didn't stop her speeding along winding corners, air conditioning on full blast, one hand fiddling with the radio. It was all Hindi pop. She scratched it off.

'I'm sick of it all,' she said.

'I've got an iPod if you want to listen to that. You need a jack though.'

'There should be one in the dashboard. This car came with everything.'

I searched around and found one.

'Do you want to choose something?' I said, handing her the machine.

She scrolled through, concentrating. I hoped she found something she liked quickly so she'd start looking at the road again.

'Here, this,' she said, flinging it back to me.

'Tchaikovsky?'

'What? You think I can't appreciate this music? Because I worked in Mumbai? I trained as a ballerina. I'm Russian. Put it on.'

I plugged in the jack and the car was filled with 'The Nutcracker'; tingling strings and cymbals and crashing chords and horns and nineteenth century romance.

'Sorry, I was just surprised that it was even on there, that's all. I don't know the music. It was a present.' I said.

Galina shrugged. We swooped round the lanes, listening to the music.

'My parents would take me to the ballet at Christmas. We lived in the country. I told you, where Alexander grew up too. Going into Moscow was a treat, part of the holiday. They always had "The Nutcracker" on at Christmas. I thought "The Nutcracker" *was* ballet. It was why I wanted to be a ballerina. Presents and magic and princes. How could you not want to be part of that?'

'My parents live outside of Cardiff. They took me to the Rugby. It's all about aggressive men and sweat and broken noses. I never really took to it,' I said.

Galina smirked. 'Sounds more true to life. Sounds very much like life. I never got to play Clara but I know a lot about aggressive men and sweat.'

'Broken noses?'

'My own. It's OK. I've seen them broken. And more. Goa isn't the paradise place it seems, Ruby. You have to be careful. Don't let Ram know you're snooping around about him unless you've got your facts straight. He could make life difficult for you.'

'Tell me then. Let me get my facts straight. Ram and Sister Michael. What's the story?'

'Sister Michael. Dorothea. Ram has, had, been in love with Dorothea for years. He can't stand to see a woman alone and in trouble. He feels he has to rescue them. He falls in love with them. Maybe if he'd met me first he would have fallen for me like he fell for her. But I was always second. And I didn't need that much rescuing. I was happy in Mumbai, I had friends.'

'How did they meet?'

'Ram was friends with Francis, her husband. School friends. That's all I know. He's never told me much. Always denied it. But as soon as I saw them together I knew all those dreams we'd had in Mumbai, they were just dreams. Ram was never going to marry me.'

'How did you know?'

'Ram took me up to her house to meet her. I'd just arrived here. I still remember the journey there. It was like heaven, just to ride with him in the car, look around Goa. I'd never seen a place like this. The colours, the green and the blue and the yellow, we don't have that kind of colour in Russia. And it was quieter then. It was still a special place. My elbow was out the car. The sun made a triangle on it. Ram said he'd never seen skin that golden. My hair was waving all around me and he took a hand off the wheel to push his fingers through it. I felt so warm. Happy. And then . . . we go to see this woman. She couldn't have been very old. Forty, forty-five. But I was only twenty, she seemed old. She was very pale. She asked me if I liked Goa, if I'd like to help Ram and her out with talking to some Russians that were living here. A little business. I nodded. I wasn't really listening. I was watching Ram. Something had come over him. His face had changed. His eyes too. Something lit up inside him. He tried not to lean into her, but he couldn't help it. He was breathless, almost. I knew. Any woman would. I wasn't really the one he loved, it was her. I was, I don't know what I was to him. It was dark by the time we left. It was still hot, I kept the window down. He tried to touch my hair again. I started crying. I wouldn't tell him why. He got annoyed. I stayed, but it wasn't ever the same. It didn't last long; heaven.'

We listened to the music for a while. 'Dance of the Sugar Plum Fairy'.

'But you helped them with the business? Why didn't you just go back to Mumbai? Start dancing again?' I said eventually.

Galina lit a cigarette, didn't bother to open the window.

'I wish I had left then. But I loved Ram. I did. And we were living like we were a couple. He acted like he loved me. He did in his way. Somedays we could just pretend it was all all right. But this jealousy, this anger, it would just flare up inside of me. I couldn't help but hate him then. I acted badly. I hated to work for them but I did it because, because they needed me and it made me part of something. I didn't want to go back. It's hard to go back.'

284

'What were you doing for them?'

'They'd been working for a few years together already. It must have been romantic, driving round Goa, picking up beautiful little pieces, sending them out. But they, Dorothea, I think, wanted to make more money. They couldn't post large items out. They needed people to transport the pieces they had down to the port. To smuggle them. Ram caught a Russian importing drugs through Paulo's ships. He didn't tell Paulo. Just asked the Russian who his boss was. It was Alexander. Alexander didn't speak English. They needed a translator, someone they could trust and who Alexander could trust. Me. And Russians, away from home? Like Indians, they stick together. He wanted to help me. I think he saw I was miserable, didn't tell him why though.

It was me who set the whole structure up. Alexander would import drugs from Pakistan, using a couple of Russians on the port. They'd load the empty containers with statues and put them on ships bound for Taiwan. He'd get the antiques transported from Old Goa for them too. Alexander, he was small then, but Ram helped him. He started his gang, local boys. Got more powerful. After a while Dorothea wanted him to start raids, robberies. People began to worry about their precious things. She couldn't pick up things for nothing anymore.'

'I found a card, at Sister Michael's from Ram. A warning, saying she'd gone too far. What did it mean?'

'Things started to go wrong a few years ago. Ram's father had a stroke. It looked like he was going to die. Ram felt guilty. He'd learnt none of the temple rituals, he knew nothing about his father's work. It was going

285

to die with the old man. An old Sadhu from inland turned up at their doorstep, mumbled some prayers over his father and in a couple of days he was up and walking. With a limp. He needs a stick now, but it was, it looked like a miracle. Ram changed. Got religious. On the outside, he's the same, but he's different. Before, he wanted money, he wanted a good life, fine things. He loved Dorothea. He didn't care about the sea or the land or the temple or Goa. Now he's angry with himself. Angry with everyone, but mostly himself. He's spent his whole life helping Paulo and Dorothea destroy, ransack his home. He's made up his accounts and he's realised that it's time for him to pay back what's he's taken. Whatever way he can.'

'And what way is that?'

'Have you not worked it out?'

'No. What.'

'The head, the head of Saint Francis. It was Ram who stole it. Not Paulo, not Dorothea. Just Ram. For revenge.'

'Revenge?'

'Ram's clever. He'd thought it all out carefully. And it's worked, kind of. He stopped working with Dorothea, a while ago now. When Hindu temples started getting raided for idols he assumed it was her. He warned her. She denied it. Then the bull's head went. He knew it was her. He would have done anything for her. But she should have known he had a breaking point. That was it. She should have realised. He stole the head to get revenge. To show her how it feels, to get the spotlight shone on the church. He knew the dirt they'd find if they started looking.'

'And the warehouse? He put it there himself?'

'Dorothea and he have used that warehouse as a storing place for years and years. Paulo has no idea. He's got so much business going on, what's one warehouse? He trusts Ram to keep everything accounted for. And he has. He's accounted for all the hotels and the pollution he's helped Paulo create over the years and decided it's time to stop him. Paulo should have listened to Ram when he asked him not to develop up around Casa Bonita and his temple. Who do you think gave the Idol Squad their tip off? Ram of course. They trust him. They think he's one of the few decent Hindus in Goa.'

'Did Ram kill Sister Michael?'

Galina grimaced, screwed up her face.

'I would say no. I, I don't know him like I used to. But I don't think so. He's put it down to robbers. But I don't know. Maybe he's just saying that. Maybe he's lying to me. I don't think he is. Why would he? He trusts me, at least,' she said.

The headlights lit up a sign to Anjuna. In the night, Goa was a strange black sea, the paddy fields darkened into great blue pools. There were islands of light, small pockets of activity. Chapels, dressed up in multi-coloured fairy lights and lanterns, dotted about like ships in a harbour. Fluorescent crosses stuck up out of ghostly white churches, just visible in the black. Bars sprung out of nowhere, covered in whisky and beer posters, dusty bottles lined up on display as if to prove they had enough in there to get you really smashed, or even kill you.

The first sign of real life was the pumping trance. A

nasty, epileptic beat with angular, drugged-up edges. Spotlights dancing in the sky. We took a few wrong turns but suddenly the roads had filled up and we followed the crowd to the party. Men by the side of the road flagged down party-goers with glow sticks. Local rickshaw drivers stood at the entrance staring, strobe lights reflected in their eyes.

Girls with glitter and bindis stuck to their faces. Blond, bare-chested men with bongos. Asian girls with cheekbones and boots and lace tights turning up on Enfield motorbikes. Ram's gleaming new BMW looked out of place, but Galina didn't seem bothered. She strode out the car, slamming the door behind her, without thinking about locking it. I followed on.

The party wasn't anywhere near the beach, but set back in wooded clearing. There was a stage covered in black and silver where a DJ dressed up as a spaceman was pumping his hands up in the air. Fire-throwers danced around in similar costumes. It was frantic and hectic.

A few groups of friends, sitting on the grass, were smoking a joint. One or two couples holding hands under the trees. Young Indian men in white shirts and caps were clicking their fingers and grinning wildly. Some European guy was going around shouting out for pills and speed. It was like the cheap bit of Edgware Road on a Saturday night. There just needed to be a fight with some Australians.

Leaning against a tree towards the back of the party was a couple of Indian guys dressed in black with diamond earrings, effeminate but kind of mean looking. Galina walked over. I followed at a short distance. She didn't invite me to join them. She kissed them on the cheeks. She knew them. They talked but I couldn't hear anything. The music was too loud. One of them made a call. Soon afterwards, a blond man in a leather jacket wandered towards the group. He kissed and hugged Galina. She beckoned me over.

'This is Alexander,' she shouted over the music.

The guy nodded. He didn't look the talkative type. He didn't take much notice of me. He couldn't stop looking at Galina. His head followed her every movement. He was in love with her. Galina appeared not to see it, though she flicked her hair a little more, her face was more animated, she seemed happier.

'So can I ask you a few questions?' I yelled.

He nodded and yelled back.

'We go to my car.'

I followed Alexander, Galina and the two Diamond Dogs through the party to a black Mercedes parked slightly further off than the rest of the bashed-up motorbikes at the entrance. Luxury cars were suddenly in abundance.

Alexander held the door open for me. I hesitated. I didn't like the look of his two boys. The more normal looking one had a shiny ponytail, a slight paunch and nasty beady eyes. He was groomed to perfection, with sparkling earrings, but without much taste. His T-shirt was too tight and bulged in the wrong places. The other guy was very skinny and wore heeled boots. He had a high-pitched outrageous laugh that sounded slightly demented.

Should I really get in a car with them? I really didn't want to be kidnapped again. Twice in one holiday was too much. Should I trust Galina? Was she trying to get rid of me? I looked behind. She gave me a half-smile. She didn't look nervous or particularly devious. And Alexander, he didn't look too blood-thirsty. More like a teddy bear, thick-set with a swathe of blond hair, chubby chin and soft crystal-blue eyes. He didn't look the sort to go to the beach. One thing I was learning in Goa was people didn't always appear as they were, but I decided to go for it. I breathed out and jumped in the car.

Alexander sat in the front passenger seat. The pony-tail drove. Galina sat directly behind her 'cousin' and I sat next to the weird skinny one. He smelt. We drove along dark lanes listening to manic techno for some time before coming to stop on a high viewpoint, over-looking a black crashing sea. Galina opened the door and lit up a cigarette. Alexander flicked on the overhead car light and turned round heavily.

'Galina told me to talk to you so I am. You ask any questions. You call me Boris Nekrassov in your story. OK?'

The skinny one let out a short high laugh.

'Did you help Ram Kumar steal the head of Saint Francis?'

'Yes.'

'Why?'

'Because he paid me.'

Another squeal beside me.

'How did you steal it?'

'Easy. I had two of my boys go to the exposition. They had pistols in their trousers under loose shirts. No security, no checking. When they got close to the shrine they started shooting in the air. Panic. They had a knife to cut the head but they didn't need it. It came off very easily. I gave them a box and bag to put it in. They went out shooting. No one stopped them. There was a car waiting outside the festival. It drove north up to Anjuna and then turned and slipped round to Vasco. But we didn't even need this precaution. Everything was chaos. No one followed,' he said.

Alexander smiled at the memory.

'Who told the police the head was in the warehouse?'

Alexander shrugged. 'Nothing to do with me.'

'Did Sister Michael, Dorothea Caperelli, did she steal the bull's head?'

Alexander pulled down his mouth, looked at his guy with the ponytail. Wouldn't look at me.

'I think so. I didn't have anything to do with that.'

'You didn't? But who helped her then?'

He shrugged. Laughed loudly. Craned his neck for a look at Galina. 'There are lots of people in Goa, they all want to make money. They will do anything for a price.'

'You don't know who?'

He shook his head, continued to look at Galina. She didn't seem to be listening to us. She had her back turned and her head up to the moon.

'But you worked for Sister Michael before?'

He turned back to me. 'Many times.'

'Did you talk to her directly?'

'Through Galina. All my jobs with Dorothea and Ram were arranged through Galina. I trust her.'

Galina turned around when her name was mentioned

and smiled at Alexander. His face lit up. God, he was besotted with her. She must realise.

'When was the last time you worked for Sister Michael?'

Alexander's face creased for a moment.

'The day she died. I was picking up a delivery for her.'

'*You're* the delivery?'

'Yes.'

'What were you delivering?'

'I wasn't delivering. I was picking up a delivery, to take down to the warehouse. A statue, a saint.'

'Saint Michael. Her namesake. Did you do it yourself? You know she died around the time of the delivery?'

'I know, I know. I questioned my boys. They didn't see anything. They picked up the statue and left. I trust them. I don't know anything about it. I was upset. I had known her for years.'

'But how did they get into Old Goa? There was a police barrier.'

'We have a van with the Basilica logo painted across it. Sister Michael got it for me. We look like part of the church.'

The delivery. It was nothing to do with her death it seemed. She had sent her own statue down to the warehouse. But why?

'Do you have any idea why she would have sent it to Vasco?'

'No. I don't ask questions. I told you. I just do the jobs. I do them well.'

A tinny version of Shakira vibrated round the car.

Alexander's phone. He looked at the number and took the call.

'I have to go now. You have enough?' he asked politely.

'I guess so, thanks.'

'Remember – Boris Nekrassov,' he said.

6

Highway 17 was a vision of hell on New Year's Eve. It was a shock to see just how bad this paradise could get. The celebration fireworks got out of hand before the clock struck twelve, shooting out into the road, not up in the air, banging and crackling and smoking like weapons of war. Wild fires lined the road.

There was gridlock just after midnight. Traffic screeched and screamed and pulled and pushed. Crowds throbbed and beat their paths round the cars and the buses and the rickshaws and the scooters, through clouds of dust and fumes, shown up in red and white headlights.

People gave up their true destinations and got drunk on cheap whisky in roadside bars. Sunburnt Russians, poor English families, countryside boys and Goan gangs all collided together that night. A mob, all dressed in glitzy black, manicured nails and vicious punches, kicked a man half to death while their new, white, girlfriends looked on peacefully.

'Diamond Dogs,' I said.

'What? What are you talking about?' yelled Zim back at me.

'Don't worry. Just drive. We're late.'

The great, old churches were crowded too, for late-night mass; fans spinning, fairy lights glowing, locals seeing in the New Year with faith, trying to block out the screams and the cries and the drugs and the business around them.

We got lost. No one knew the way to Arambol beach anymore. The crowds, the great surges of people, changed the look of familiar routes. Everyone told us something different. I clung on to Zim, trying desperately to keep our juddering scooter from going under a truck or skidding on sand and killing us both. Smoke rose all around. Cars lit up my legs and knocked my ankles.

Finally we made it out of the ruckus, on to a quiet, dark road lit with white fluorescent strips, dangling vertically, giving little real light. Our eyes were sore from the dust. It was too quiet now and too black. The only sign of life was the dogs, snarling and barking as we drove on through, up to our party on the Marbela Casino ship.

Usually moored in Panjim, the matronly white ship had made a special New Year's Eve journey, ploughing up the coast to Arambol, where the rich had started to congregate among new French restaurants and cocktail bars. A speedboat jogged and dipped by the beach, waiting to take punters to the exclusive party, where Paulo had arranged to finalise his art deal with Zim.

We parked in soft sand. Zim kicked the bike on to

the ground. Once he'd finished taking his aggression out on the bike he collapsed, holding his head in his hands.

'Zim?'

'Why did they have to sail it up here? We're so late. Hours late. It's after midnight. It's the New Year already. How did I know it was going to take so long? That road was hell.'

I crouched down. 'You're making us later by doing this. They'll understand. Come on.'

Zim shrugged my hand off his shoulders. Stood up, clenched down with his hands on his head. He was too nervous. He had been all day. His lip swollen from biting it so hard, his temper shorter than ever, going crazy with the waiter who brought him a pasta with the olives he'd asked to be left out.

'I hate olives. I can't stand them,' he'd said to me by way of an explanation. It was clear there were other things bothering him more. It was the deal. Sparse conversations with his dad, edgy questions, trying to control the excitement in his voice.

'You've done the hard work Zim, you just need to go in there and sign it. Try and keep calm.'

He nodded nervously, tried to take a breath.

The casino speedboat jumped the currents, smacking hard down on the black water. No one spoke. It was a short, dark journey. I wasn't in a much better state then Zim. Taut and nervous. There was as much at stake for me tonight as him.

That morning I'd called Inspector Srinvasen, told him I had information on Ram Kumar from his Russian girlfriend and a gang member. They'd told me it was him that was responsible for the head – and the rest of the smuggling. Paulo Mendes had nothing to do with it. Would he be interested in talking to me in exchange for an exclusive interview with Touchstone? He wasn't interested.

'Why should I change my story for a couple of Russians? Paulo Mendes owns the warehouse. Paulo Mendes is going to take responsibility. It's high time Goans took responsibility for Goa. It's a mess. It's a shame on India,' he said.

Things had gone just the way he planned, he didn't want to change his story now. I called David. He agreed with Inspector Srinvasen.

'It's rather tabloid, ex-girlfriend dishes the dirt. Doesn't really stand up. How do you know to trust these two? You need it from the horse's mouth, I'm afraid Ruby. You need real evidence.'

David revelled in concocting a plan for the night. His flair for drama was excellent and he enjoyed it all the more, I'm sure, for the lack of direct consequences he would have to face, sitting in London, thousands of miles away. It was me who was gnawing myself up with worry about delivering what he called a masterful impasse.

'Sometimes Ruby, you have to create the news. It's not enough just to describe,' he told me airily.

But David still wanted an interview with the police, not the Inspector, but someone. I was loath to get in touch with Inspector Ferreira but I did. He loved the news. It was obvious he couldn't stand the Idol Squad.

'Who do they think they are? Waltzing in here like this – judging us all – giving us more bad press. We're such a welcoming place, we're so tolerant. Of course people want to come here. They're all just jealous. They see us as different and we are. Who would want to be part of that mess? We didn't want to join India, it was forced upon us,' he said.

And so if New Year's Eve went to plan, I would have all the interviews I needed – the police included.

The Marbela Casino boat party was supposed to the best in Goa. Beautiful, tasteful. Perhaps it had been early evening, with little gambling frissons, a chic gold bar, bottles of champagne. But it was after one when we arrived, people were trashed and the place was a mess. The debris wasn't pretty at all. Two terrible dancers in short black dresses were waving their arms and moving their legs on the bar, with a vague notion of sex. Their heels scuffed and swilled around the spilt beer and sticky drinks lying across the top. Smeared old glasses, empty bottles and crushed beer boxes piled up. The night had started with mojitos and wine in stemmed glasses. Now everyone was drinking vodka from plastic cups. Women and men crowded raucously on to the small dance floor. Only the gamblers seemed half-way sober.

I turned to Zim. 'Why the hell are you doing a deal in here? It's crazy.'

'Tax. We play a poker game, I win, Paulo transfers the money, straight to my account. Winnings, off-shore, no tax,' he said.

'Who's idea was that? Isn't he in enough trouble?'

Zim shrugged. 'I've not got a problem with it. I've done worse things,' he said.

The manager ushered us into a private quiet room,

quite apart from the New Year mayhem. Paulo, Ram, Galina drinking green cocktails. Galina was wearing a tight silver dress and snakeskin heels. She looked fantastic at night, away from natural light, glittering and sleek.

Three packs of cards stood on the table, around which hovered a straight-backed waiter. Galina was biting her nails and smoking. Paulo was tapping on the table. Ram was leaning back in his usual relaxed position.

'Hey, I'm so, so sorry I'm late. It's the traffic. It's crazy out there.'

'Please, don't worry. We're still waiting for Paulo's wife, coming up from Vasco. The final decision will rest with her,' said Ram.

Paulo laughed too loud. 'She's the one with the taste apparently!' he said.

His eyes flicked out to the side as he said this. The waiter asked us for our orders.

'Mojito. Double shot,' said Zim. I asked for the same.

Galina didn't look at me much, neither did Ram. Everyone seemed preoccupied.

Paulo's wife arrived in a rush, neat hair flying up at the edges. She apologised to us all for being late. Her daughter wouldn't go to sleep. She'd never seen the roads so bad.

'I honestly didn't recognise the place. Terrible. What's happening to Goa?' she said.

A petite, pale woman with American English and a deep twang of Mumbai, she had dark circles round her eyes. All this shit with the smuggling, the arrest, the newspapers; it was drawn across her face. She slipped into the booth beside Paulo, kissed him on the cheek. He bristled, kissed her back. He looked at her carefully, searching for signs of the upset he had caused her. He frowned, guilty.

Zim passed the folder he had been working on so hard to the couple. The Goan Modern Art Investment. That had been a new idea – from Zim.

I felt sorry for Paulo, but his problems were Zim's lucky break, and he was doing everything he could to rise to the event. I'd heard him on the phone to his father, more confident, happier sounding. He had a bright concentrated look in his eye as he worked. He was having his own ideas and they were getting the go-ahead. Everyone had loved the Goan Modern Art Investment – including Raoul Moon who said he'd wanted to shift the lot out of Blue Moon for several moons. Bad jokes seemed to run in that family.

If the deal went through, the collection would be sent straight the Goa Art Gallery, on loan from the Mendes family. If Paulo's charges did end up in a sentence, his good work for the state, including the recent donation of his new modern art collection, might be taken into account.

There was a file on each of the five works; an HD picture, a profile of the artist, a profile of the piece and an independent investment advisory. This had been written by a friend of Zim's father at Christie's salesroom in Beverly Hills.

Paulo's wife went through each file slowly, nodding in places. Paulo looked over her shoulder, one hand placed in her lap. Galina ordered another drink. So did Zim. Ram's phone went. He said he had to take it. I excused myself and said I needed to go to the bathroom shortly afterwards.

I found Ram on the deck, leaning over the side, talking gently in Konkani. This was a good start. It would never have worked, talking to him inside, with the music and the screeching laughter. I leant up against the rail and waited, looking out to the far shore. Silhouetted cargo ships slid past, filled with mounds of rubble. You wouldn't think piles of dirt could be turned into all this casino wealth. Lights from the casino showed up a sailor, leant over the side of his ship and washing out his dinner dishes. Thin yellow curry spilt into the water. I don't know why I was feeling sorry for the Mendes family, whatever they had was more than that poor guy.

Ram saw me, nodded his head but didn't stop his conversation. After sometime he finished, with what sounded like many goodbyes.

'Sorry to interrupt,' I said.

Ram glanced up at me. 'My father's been taken into hospital again. More pains in his chest. I'll have to go up there after this meeting . . . Are they waiting for me?'

'Shruti's going through the portfolio. There's time. I came out to talk to you.'

Ram nodded, invited me to continue, not really listening, thinking of his old father, up in some countryside hospital.

'I think I know where the bull's head is.'

He jerked into life, looking at me afresh, frowning hard. 'What? Where?'

301

'I am not totally sure. I haven't gone looking myself. But I think it's a good guess.'

'Where?'

'I need you to answer some questions for me first.'

'What?'

'I know you stole the head. I know you framed Paulo. I know it's you who's been in business with Sister Michael, Dorothea Caperelli, since the beginning.'

There was another, denser expression of surprise over the accountant's face. I handed him the letter he'd written to Sister Michael years ago. He read it very carefully. He didn't hand it back.

'I didn't think she'd kept this. I wouldn't have thought she was so emotional. I wouldn't have thought she cared enough.'

'I know you did her accounts too.'

'It was how I met her. I offered to help her with finances after Francis died. It was the least I could do to help. She had nothing then. She was helpless, very poor.'

'And you helped her make some money. A lot. She had one million pounds in a savings account. Ten thousand in last year. This isn't a church pension. How much did you smuggle out of here? There must be stolen pieces of Goa all over the world.'

'Who told you?'

'She did.'

'Sister Michael?'

'In so many words. Ram, will you talk to me?'

'What do you want to know? What are you planning on doing with it? You'll go to the police? Srinvasen won't believe any of it.'

'No. No. I'm not going to the police. I just want to know. I just want to know why she did it. I didn't know her well. But . . . we spent some time together. She told me a lot of things. I think she saw something of me in her. She wanted to warn me about life, I think. She told me not to turn away from help, because when you need it, it would be gone. She was talking about you. She was very sad, before she died.'

'She wouldn't let me love her. She was seething with anger. Blamed everyone for Francis dying. She wouldn't love anyone else. Only her dogs and her things. She loved to find the most beautiful things. But it's not enough. Human beings get twisted up when they live alone in their heads.'

'Did you kill her? Did you kill Sister Michael because she stole the bull's head?'

Ram's face crumpled slightly.

'I didn't kill her, of course not. I don't know who did. I don't know. She killed me, she killed herself.'

'What do you mean? She killed herself?'

'She brought it on herself. It was her fate, her karma to die like that. I told you, she'd always pursued beauty. I loved her for that. I knew she had changed, become a different person, when she hacked off the bull's head. She destroyed something ancient and beautiful; violated it, made it ugly, for money. And she was killed the same way, in an ugly, violent way. I don't know who by. Maybe Father Jonathan, he hated her. But I don't know. Maybe it was Maria. All I know is she brought it on herself.'

'You sent her a note saying she'd gone too far. That was a warning.'

303

'A warning. Not a death threat.'

'And you took the head? You took the head to punish her?'

Ram shrugged, looked out to sea.

'Not just her. Everyone, everything. I used to find starfish and crystals washed up on this beach. Now it's only condoms and whisky bottles. I'm to blame as much as anyone. I've been making money from Goa, balancing the books, weighing up the profit for each holiday home we build, each bar we begin, each ship we send off with some of our history. But it doesn't add up anymore, it's not worth it. This rampant, unchecked tourism, it's malignant and its killing Goa. Greedy people, buying up land and houses, building like there was nothing in the world but money. Pushing us out and making our home into some giant play-park for cheap drugs and cheap drink and free sunburn. I needed to shake everything, everyone up. And stop the Arambol development, stop Paulo.'

'By framing him?'

'He won't listen. I tried to stop him, persuade him to reconsider, to think of somewhere else, something else. But he wouldn't. There is nowhere else left, that's what he said to me. It didn't worry him.'

'Why Saint Francis? Isn't he supposed to protect Goa? Isn't he supposed to be your patron?'

'That rotten old saint? You know how he converted so many of us? You know how he became such an icon of the church? He'd take a hunk of beef and an army of slaves, grab every Hindu he could and smear their mouths with the meat. They were untouchable then. Their families wouldn't let them in the house. They had no choice but to become Christians. And he'd simply bayonet the people who still refused. It isn't a wonder, with him as our patron saint, with him as our saviour, that the place has turned into such a hell. Rotten for centuries. He didn't manage to get up to Tambdi Surla. It's stayed as it is for centuries. But now, Paulo, the bull's head. I needed to do something. It was time to balance the accounts,' he said.

Ram gave this speech still looking at his hands, in careful measured tones. When he had finished he cracked his knuckles and looked down into the slapping black waves.

'I don't know if I did the right thing. Sister Michael dead. Paulo about to go to prison. What has more value? A human life or a swathe of unspoilt land? But she started it. And my father won't survive. Unless we get the bull's head back. Where is it? You said you know?'

'I met a Russian. Alexander. He couldn't look me in the eye when I asked him about the head. He stole it.'

'No. Galina's asked him. He didn't. She used someone else. Is that all you know?'

'Are you sure? Are you completely sure? I think that he has the bull's head. Maybe he was still working for Sister Michael.

Ram hit his hand on the rail.

'No, Ruby. Galina spoke to him. He wouldn't lie to her. He didn't take the head. Is that all you have?'

I shrugged.

'Maybe you should talk to him yourself. His English isn't too bad.'

Ram shook his head.

'I'm tired Ruby, and worried about my father. I haven't got time for all this. If you'll excuse me, there's a rather important game of poker going on inside that I'm needed at.'

He began to walk away but turned back once more.

'Also – if you care about your friend – about this deal that clearly means so much to him – you'll keep quiet about what I told you. If anyone finds out, it's not only the whole of North Goa that disappears, but the Goan Modern Art Investment too.'

I waited until Ram had disappeared from sight. A group of girls from Mumbai were shouting and discussing what to do with one of their friends, throwing up over the side of the boat.

I took out the iPod. It looked like it had recorded it all. I hope the retching sounds and the subsequent squeals hadn't interfered too much with the recording. I'd picked up a pocket mike at the Majestic Boutique before leaving tonight. They did high-quality electrical goods as well as beauty products. I took out Zim's phone. I'd told him I'd take any calls for him while he was busy with Paulo. I logged on to the wireless network, on to Facebook, messaged David.

I did it.
You recorded it?
Yes.
And he confessed?
I guess so.

You got it down? With the recording facility, like I told you?

Yeah. But you know I'm not sure it's the right thing to do. Maybe we should wait.

Ruby. You are not God. It's not your place to decide what information to withhold and what to publish. We have it all set up. Nothing either good or bad, but thinking makes it so Ruby.

Don't try and woo with me Shakespeare, David. I did the same tragedy course as you, remember? I'm just not sure that coming out with all this now is quite the right time.

Do it, Ruby. Knowledge which is divorced from justice may be called cunning rather than wisdom.

What? I don't know that.

Your problem is you didn't learn Latin.

Neither did you.

True, but I at least read the Penguin Cicero. Ruby, it's a cracking story. We go to print in three days and I'm holding the cover for you. Just make the call and get that interview. That's all you need now.

OK. OK.

I logged out and called Inspector Ferreira.

'It's Ruby. I've got it. I've got him admitting it on tape.'

'Excellent, excellent. The Idol Squad won't know what's hit them.'

'I'll email you the mp3 of the recording when I get to an internet terminal.'

'Good.'

'And I'll get an interview with you tomorrow?'

'As we agreed.'

I walked through the debris of the casino hall, the ghoulish party still going strong. Back in our private poker room, the atmosphere had lightened. No more green cocktails. Champagne and Martinis. A game of cards laid out. Paulo had regained his bonhomie. His wife was smiling too, sipping carefully from her flute. Zim was leaning back in his chair, smoking heavily on his cigarette. Ram read carefully over some papers from his briefcase. Galina had disappeared. The manager of the casino stood waiting with a card payment machine in his hand.

'It all looks in order,' said Ram. 'If you're happy then so am I. I've checked everything over. If you want to both sign here then Marcello can begin his card tricks.'

'I'm starting to like the idea of being an Art Don,' said Paulo, a bear-like hand curled round a Martini glass, the other round his wife's bird-like shoulders.

'Great. Yeah, it's a lot of fun. Good way to get girls. Openings and all that shit. Er . . . have you got a pen?' said Zim.

Ram handed him a steel biro.

'I should just look through this too right?' he said to Ram.

Ram shrugged. 'As you wish. If I were you, I'd take some time to look at it.'

'Just get on with it, Zim,' I said, in a burst of impatience.

Everyone looked at me.

'Ruby, it's New Year's Eve. We've got all night to celebrate,' said Zim, smiling. He was nearly there; he'd nearly done his legendary deal. The nerves were gone. His body had expanded triumphantly.

'Let the boy have his time. I remember signing my first contract, down at the Vasco Dock Office, for a ton of iron ore I bought down from the north. I got good money for it too. You remember when I got that, Shruti? I said we were going places?'

She smiled at Zim.

'I think the paintings are lovely. I'm looking forward to seeing them myself. I just hope Paulo is here to appreciate them too.'

Her voice rose at the end.

'Come on, Shruti,' Paulo growled.

'I'm sorry. I just, I'm just nervous. I just wish they could find who is really responsible for this mess, instead of blaming someone as honest as you,' she said, wiping her eyes.

Paulo rubbed his wife's back, bent in towards her whispering. We all looked somewhere else. Zim went back to studying the contract. It was all I could do to not rip the pen out his hands and sign it for him myself. I thought this would have all been over by now. There wasn't much time.

It was the casino manager who saw them first. His eyebrows went up high on his face. The card machine he had been brandishing so suavely was suddenly behind his back. We all turned around to a flash of white light. When my eyes adjusted I saw Inspector Ferreira standing in front of an entourage; photographer, reporter, assistant. Paulo's wife gave a little quivering wail.

'Don't worry, Mrs Mendes. We're not here for

your husband. We'd like Ram Kumar to come with us for questioning.'

'Ram?' said Paulo.

'We've evidence to suggest Mr Kumar is the man behind the smuggling ring and the theft of the head of Saint Francis.'

Inspector Ferreira turned to the reporter.

'Did you get that?'

He nodded.

'The Idol Squad thought they had this case wrapped up, but all they've proved is the vendetta they have against Goa and good Goan businessmen. The only thing Paulo Mendes is guilty of is successful enterprise. Mr Kumar, I'm arresting you on suspicion of smuggling, robbery and perverting the course of justice. We'll also be questioning you about the murder of Dorothea Caperelli. You have the right to remain silent but anything you do say may be taken in evidence against you.'

'It's rubbish,' said Ram. 'But I'll go down to the station. To cooperate. Don't sign anything till I get out, Paulo. I'll look after all this.'

Ram walked out the room quietly, holding his head straight ahead, looking smaller than usual. Inspector Ferreira held the door for him before following him out. The sound of the party blasted through the open door before it closed once again to dead quiet.

PART 5

1

The room was dark. The thick hotel curtains kept out the midday sun and cooked the hot sleep smell. Zim refused to face the world; a deadened lump wrapped in white linen sheets like a corpse. I arrived back from the station to see him in the same position I'd left him in. His failure had crumbled him. It was an awful start to the New Year. It was my fault.

A rush of heartache came over me, seeing him lie there. I would have done anything to make him feel better. I cursed myself for listening to David, for calling Ferreira.

'Zim,' I said quietly.

He didn't answer. I went over to his bed, put my hand on his shoulder. He shrugged me off a little.

'Oh Zim, please. Get up?'

Still no answer. I took off my clothes and climbed into bed with him, burrowing myself into the thick covers, holding my hands out to find his skinny arms, his slender chest. I wrapped my legs around him and hugged him, pressed my face to his back. He smelt of hot body, of sweat and of night breath, not his usual brash aftershave and soap. I'd never known him not wash. I felt such a swollen pain for him in that moment that I knew I loved him. I loved him because he was human and fragile and because he tried and he often failed. I loved him because I was beginning to understand him. How much he wanted to prove himself, how he struggled with who he was. His temper, it flared so badly because he found the world so hard to cope with. But he'd done what he'd said he'd do, outside the police station. He'd helped me get over Stephen. Not by taking me away to paradise, like he'd said, but by showing me himself and beginning to need me.

I hadn't really known, up till now, if I would really go to LA with him. It seemed too crazy, too whimsical, to take such a chance. But now I knew I would, not just for the change, not just to see what it was like, but because I wanted to be with him. I wanted to see what could happen to us. I wanted to calm him down, bring out the kindness I'd seen. The humour. The love. He could love. That was clear. I didn't want to end up lonely, bitter, crazy. I didn't want to end up like Sister Michael or Saskia or Galina.

Zim moved slightly, pulled my arm around him. Pressed his back on to my chest. I spread my fingers out across his stomach, whispered in his ear.

'Zim. Will you get up please?'

He pulled himself round to face me, under the covers, black but for our eyes.

'I don't want to yet. I just want to stay here.'

314

'Please. You're making me feel terrible. I can't see you just lie here.'

'Don't worry about me. This isn't your fault.'

'I am worried about you. I can't help it. You know, I like you. I like you a lot. I care for you. I'm going to come with you to LA.'

Zim looked at me for a moment, happy, surprised. He kissed me.

'I didn't think you were the kind to do one night stands. I'll get up. I need to book those tickets back home anyhow. You won't regret it, Ruby.'

The curtains were open, the bed a twisted, harmless heap, the shower full blast, Zim taking one of his marathon scrubs. Steam seeped out through the cracks around the bathroom door, making the whole room soapy.

I'd made him happier, but I wasn't happy with myself. A worm of guilt wound round and round in my stomach. I'd meant to tell him I loved him. I'd meant to tell him that I was sorry. That it had been my fault that his deal had fallen through. That I'd called the police just as he was about to sign. That if it hadn't have been for me he wouldn't be going back home empty-handed, that he would be going home having proved himself to his father, the formidable Raoul Moon.

What was I going to do? I switched on the TV. Take my mind off it. I rolled my eyes when I saw Inspector Ferreira, giving yet another quote to local TV. I had got my interview this morning, but it wasn't worth much. He was talking to everyone. Unlike Inspector Srinvasen, Ferreira did not shy away from the camera. He was everywhere, in newspapers, online, on TV, gleefully explaining how the Idol Squad had got it wrong and there were strong reasons to believe that Paulo Mendes was completely innocent. At least he hadn't given away the story or what was on the tape. He wouldn't do that yet. And hopefully not until Touchstone got their next issue out. Three days. I still had to write the damn thing though. I switched to NDTV.

The new developments on the story had made headline news nationally. Paulo was giving a press conference outside Government House. He was introduced by the Minister for Tourism Development, who said how pleased he was that Mendes, who had done so much to develop Goa for tourists, was now able to continue with his biggest project yet.

Paulo stood side by side with his wife, one arm around her shoulder.

'I'm not saying this whole business is over. But the problems seem to be more the police's than mine now. The onus for me to prove my innocence has shifted and the Idol Squad are delaying pressing charges. I hope to restart my plans for the north of Goa as soon as possible, bringing more job opportunities, investment and holiday fun to this under-developed part of our state. I want to thank my wife, who has supported me and looked after my family throughout these dreadful weeks. As a present to her and a gesture of my continuing love for my homeland, I will be donating a large M.F. Husain canvas to the Goa Art Gallery,' he said.

'Zim, get in here,' I shouted. 'Good news. You're going to sell a painting.'

Maybe I didn't need to tell him about calling Ferreira after all. One painting or five – did it really matter?

I left Zim to call his dad with the news, went down to the hotel coffee shop to begin writing the article. I put off starting and read the international papers.

The press at home, they weren't so interested in whether Paulo or someone else had stolen the antiques. They were more concerned about corruption in the auction houses and were busy questioning Sotheby's Director in London, who denied all knowledge that anything in any of his auctions could possibly be stolen. He blamed the Vatican.

'I know that India has had terrible problems with Temple raiders and we've been working with the Government to contain this problem. But really, one should look after their own stable and it seems the Vatican and the Roman Catholic Church in Goa have just not being paying enough attention to their rich treasure of colonial art. Every little village church in this country has an inventory. Not even the Basilica of Old Goa, a UNESCO World Heritage Site, has a brief list of the treasures it contains. I really think the responsibility for this lies with the Church there. There seem to be a lot of questions surrounding the late curator of the Museum of Christian Art there,' he said.

Asia Today on CNN was playing downstairs. Somehow they'd managed to get an interview with Paulo, sat in his penthouse suite in Vasco, cigar and drink in his hand. With the charges against him slipping away, Paulo's largesse and humour had renewed with greater gusto. He didn't seem to question why it was that his trusted advisor had betrayed him, had tried to get him framed. He didn't question the development in the North or the anguished cries from the environmentalists that had begun once more. He didn't see life from any other point of view but his own. It was a generous point of view and filled with a kindness of its own, but its complete bulldozing confidence made standing in his way lethal. I could see why Ram would need to resort to framing to stop the development of his beloved home. The man would not, could not, see a point of view that was not his own, that placed other values higher than profit, lunch or immediate family.

I rubbed my head. I felt guilty. It seemed to be a constant these days, this slow drawn feeling of not doing the right thing. I'd contributed to spoiling a whole swathe of beautiful coastline. I was keeping quiet that it had been me who had fucked up Zim's deal for him. And I had no idea who had killed Sister Michael. Maria? Ram? Father Jonathan? One of Alexander's boys? Or a stranger? Just an unlucky, fated break-in like Ram had said? But how could that have been? The whole place was supposed to be sealed off, though that hadn't stopped absolutely everyone from coming and going without trouble. Any one of them could be lying, except Maria of course, she wasn't around to deny anything. I guess that's why it was easy to blame her. Even her husband said she wasn't quite right.

I opened my notebook. I hadn't got a laptop with me. I'd need to write out the article longhand, type it up on Zim's computer later in the day. I wasn't used to working without a computer, working from longhand notes. My writing was almost illegible.

The coastal state of Goa has a slightly
different flavour to the rest of India, with
a different history and different ages. It
was the ancient seat of the Hindu Kadamba
dynasty. The Portuguese turned it into a
colony centuries before the British Raj ruled
the rest of India. The Jesuits and sailors
made sure the native population were
distinct too; with Christian names and
forefathers mixed into their original Hindu
blood. And independence came at a
different time; in 1961 as opposed to 1947.
Indian Independence was marked by the
end of World War II, Partition and a
massacre of Hindus and Muslims.

Goan independence seemed more to
coincide with the summer of love and the
coming of the hippies. Its sandy beaches, its
palm trees and its beauty have drawn
people to its shores for centuries and in the
sixties it was an essential part of the hippy
trail. Full moon parties, Indian mysticism,
good charis and LSD. Later, when India was
taking the IT world by storm, was becoming
an Asian economic powerhouse; Goa was
hosting rave parties and kids on ecstasy.
And now? It's the age of the package
tourist, the Russian holidaymaker and the
rich city-dweller. It's the age when the
extent of corruption, the drugs, the irre-
sponsible land deals is revealed. It's all
destroyed practically. It's all destroyed.

I closed the book once again. This wasn't the article I was supposed to be writing. This was something else entirely. I needed to start again. Where? At least I had that iPod recording. But there was this big gaping hole that was the old nun's death – and the head of the bull. The story, it still didn't make sense to me. Maria getting angry at her boss, smacking her over the head and then committing suicide. It just didn't seem right. Father Jonathan? But could Father Jonathan have concealed something like that? At the height of his rambling madness? Unless it had all been an act I didn't think so. Ram? Ram had said it was her fate. Ram said it was robbers. That didn't make sense either. Who the hell were these mystery robbers? No one had been caught. Nothing had been stolen. The only thing that was missing was the statue of Saint Michael. And Ram had been so surprised at me finding it in the warehouse. Upset. Unless he was an excellent actor, I didn't think it could be him who put it there. So he hadn't been to the house recently. Who then?

I wished I had got more out of Ram when I was talking to him. I wouldn't get another chance. He was in Panjim police station. And with Inspector Ferreira questioning him, I didn't hold much hope for any new information. He wasn't the finest interviewer. I'd called Galina; her phone was off. I couldn't get in touch with her. She seemed to have disappeared at the casino. Saskia? She seemed to know something of what had been going on. But I didn't think she even had a phone. She knew Alexander. Knew he was dangerous. Could he have killed Sister Michael? Could it be his gang the Diamond Dogs? Why? To stop her giving them away?

She'd worked with them for years, she must have known a lot. But then she would have been giving herself away too – and Alexander didn't look particularly stressed or worried about his situation. Maria's husband? Maybe he could tell me more; but he was wound up in his own grief, devastated and angry at himself and his wife. He wasn't a clear thinker.

Maybe I should just forget about it. I had two days to write this article. I should just start. I sat there for a while, staring at the notebook. I needed something to get me going. I needed a coffee. Maybe a cake. Something sweet and reassuring.

There was a huge selection of frothy concoctions on display in the cake cabinet; creamy layers piled high with bright cherries, innocent pineapple slices, childish chocolate drops. I knew someone who would appreciate one of these. Father Jonathan.

2

The cupcakes I had bought at the hotel didn't look as sprightly after their hot journey. The sticky icing, which had been piled up so perkily, had drooped and melted into the paper.

Father Jonathan didn't mind at all. He reached his large hand into the white box and popped one into his mouth in two bites. He leant back on the bench and chewed happily.

'The cooks here, they don't bake,' said Father Jonathan.

'It's nice though, here. Very peaceful.'

The Panjim Institute was outside the city, on the banks of the Mandovi. The garden faced the sea, where patients could watch the boats and ships steaming out. If I went mad this was the kind of Psychiatric Unit I would like to end up in.

Father Jonathan nodded.

'I feel quite happy, different.'

He seemed different. The pained, wretched look in

his eyes had gone. His hands were still on his lap. His face was as pale as before but calm, without the twists and the frowns that had accompanied his whining voice.

Doctor Calisto had told me he was on a combination of medications to prevent psychosis, panic attacks and possible hallucination.

'Is he that mad?' I had asked.

The doctor had shrugged.

'He tried to confess to his crimes when he came in to us. Thought we were the police. From what he was saying it was clear he'd been suffering from delusional disorder for some time. He's been under incredible mental stress. The drugs alleviate all that. Psychiatric medicine has moved on a lot recently, we don't need to sedate the man, these new medicines work on just the conditions under which a patient is suffering. He's quite lucid. He'll be pleased to talk to you.'

Father Jonathan took another cupcake. I took one myself. The icing melted to pure sugar in my mouth. I licked it off my teeth with my tongue and savoured the moment. It really wasn't bad, sitting here, watching the sea, eating cakes. Once you've lost everything there's not much to worry about.

'It must be quite a relief being here. Not having to worry about Saint Francis,' I said. He nodded.

'Yes. Yes. I think that saint was driving me mad.'

'I spoke to Maria's husband. Do you remember me telling you?'

'Not really. I know him though. How is he?'

'Not very well. He misses his wife. He said that Maria had depression, had been very ill with it. He blames himself for her death, for not stopping her working.'

323

'That's very sad.'

'He told me she had done some strange things. She stopped all the family going to the exposition of Saint Francis, soon after she started working with Sister Michael.'

'How sad.'

'And in her confession book she'd scrubbed out the prayer to Saint Francis. I think she would most often pray for protection from evil souls, for protection from Saint Michael.'

'Ah. Saint Michael the Archangel. Always there to save us when death comes. Whatever you have done, whatever sins you have committed, he is there to hear your repentance. To help you into the kingdom of God. I am looking forward to seeing him.'

'Father Jonathan, do you know why Maria was so against praying to Saint Francis?'

'Yes, yes I do.'

'Why?'

'It's rather a long story.'

'It's OK, I have time.'

'You have to understand. I did it for love. I only did it for love.'

'Did what Father Jonathan?'

'Ruby. You know sometimes, you love someone so much, you do bad things? Things that people would say are wrong?'

I could think of a few examples. Saint Francis Xavier himself for a start. All those poor Hindus he accosted with hunks of beef, all in the name of love of Goa. I nodded.

'And sometimes, you have to keep things a secret.

324

You have to keep things quiet because people rely on you. People, many people, could be very hurt by the truth.'

'What's the truth, Father Jonathan? What truth?'

'You won't tell anyone will you, Ruby? I'm telling you because I want to explain why I did what I did to you. I'm so very ashamed of myself. I am very ashamed.'

'Tell me, Father Jonathan.'

'It's hard to know where to begin. When Francis died, I suppose. Or before, in the seminary. Francis and I were special friends. From the moment I saw him I knew we would be special friends. People have bad names for it. You're not supposed to love your friends, but my love was very pure. I wanted just to be like him.'

I'd been right. Father Jonathan, he'd been in love with Francis. This man seemed to have turned everyone's head. Perhaps it wasn't Sister Michael that was the snake but her husband.

'Of course, Father Jonathan, go on.'

'He wasn't interested in women. Ever. He was a good priest, a very very good priest. He was due to become curate of the shrine. You know that? It's only when he left the church that I got the position. Things would have been different if he hadn't died. Of course they would. It was like a death to me when he left the priesthood. Hearing the gossip around the halls at dinner. It would make me sick. Really, I would have to leave, to go to the toilet sometimes, when I heard them talking about Francis and his wife.'

'What about?'

'They spent so much time in the confession box.

Before anyone knew what was going on. Some priests thought they'd heard sounds. They made jokes about it. Sister Michael on her knees. It was all untrue of course. Francis only acted with God in mind. It was her that was the viper. The mother superior found her bed empty one night. And what could he do? He had to leave the church and marry her. He only did it to save her. She would have been thrown out the convent with nothing if he hadn't. I was devastated. I begged him not to leave.'

'But he did. Where did they go?'

'They didn't go far away. He wasn't far. In that old house of his. I would visit as often as I could without people talking. When it was cooler we would sometimes go for walks, after tea, around the old churches. It was much quieter then. None of these tourists. I loved those moments. My vocation was going well, I'd been given curatorship of the shrine. It usually went to a youngish priest, someone the cardinals thought would make a good bishop of the Basilica. It was supposed to be a training in responsibility. I never got further than curate of the shrine. If things had been different, I would have been bishop by now.'

'What happened Father Jonathan?'

'It was soon after Francis died, about a year or two after. I wasn't in a good state of mind. I wasn't at all. The exposition was coming up. I hadn't been in charge of the exposition before. It's so much work. So many people coming to see the saint. So many people to look after. So many visitors from Rome. It's very stressful. I wasn't in the right frame of mind at all for it. You know, I wasn't. But I still think I did the right thing. It wasn't right, but it was. Do you see? And perhaps I wasn't the first. No, I don't think I was the first.'

'What did you do Father Jonathan?'

'It was about a week before the exposition. We were due to dress the saint. It's a woman who does it, that's the tradition. Usually the housekeeper of the priest's house, but that year the housekeeper was very ill. She had chicken pox, I think, she caught it off her daughter. I asked Maria to do it instead. She had been working as a cleaner in the Basilica; Francis took a shine to her. He liked her. He felt sorry for her he told me; she was a sad soul he said. He took her with him to keep his house and she stayed on there with Sister Michael, Dorothea, after he died. I liked the idea of having her dress the body. But, you know, she's a big woman. Maybe she was clumsy. One of the arms came off the saint when she trying to get the habit on to him. She came straight to me, crying, sobbing. I told her not to tell anybody. I went down to the shrine. The arm was lying on the floor. Papery. The whole body was falling apart. Xavier, he was just crumbling.'

'He'd had his day.'

'Yes. No wonder the old curate of the shrine had been so keen to retire. He knew the saint wasn't going to last another year. And now it was up to me to tell the world that the miracle was over. Xavier couldn't be exposed this year. He couldn't be touched because he'd crumble under all that faith. I went to the bishop. I told him what had happened. He didn't help. All he said was the exposition must go ahead. I explained it couldn't. He said it would. He said that our whole church in Goa rested on the exposition, the Jesuits rested on the exposition and the good name of Saint Francis rested on the exposition. It must go ahead. I asked him what I should do. He just shrugged and told me to pray harder.'

'What did you do?'

'I prayed. I prayed very hard. And Francis came to me in my prayers. To help me. He said I should take him back to the church and that he could help me. He could help me. And I made a plan but I didn't know how to begin. I had to speak to someone about it. I needed help. I spoke to Sister Michael. At first she was angry. She said I was sick, I needed to go to hospital but something changed her mind. Then she said she would help me.'

'What did you do Father Jonathan?'

'It was rather like a phoenix you know? Rising from the ashes. And once we had done it, once we'd managed to do what we needed to do, it was so beautiful to know he was up there. That people were worshipping him. That no one had to lose their faith.'

'What did you do?'

'We swapped the bodies. Sister Michael, Maria and I. Maria didn't want to do it. But we needed someone else; we couldn't do it alone. And she knew the body was falling apart, she could have told anyone. Sister Michael said she needed to take part to keep it a secret. We convinced her that she must do it with us. We took the body of Saint Xavier and we replaced it with Francis.'

'Oh God. Poor Maria, it must have been terrible for her. You made her do that?'

'But there was nothing else to do. The old saint was just dust. There was nothing else to do with him,'

'Didn't anyone notice? Didn't Francis smell?'

'He'd been buried a year or so already. He was quite dried out. But he wasn't dirty. The coffin hadn't started to rot yet.'

'But surely, people saw he was different?'

'A few of the priests remarked that he looked a bit fresher that year. And you know, you've been yourself, you can't see much. Just a hand, a little of the face. Most people are so overwhelmed with the experience they don't really notice the saint.'

I didn't know what to say. Poor Maria, living with that. I wondered if David had gone to print yet.

'And no one knew apart from you and Sister Michael and Maria?'

'No one. The bishop, he didn't mention it again. He told me over tea it had been a fine exposition, that was all. But you know. I don't think we are the first. I'd started to get worried about Francis just recently, he was beginning to get crumbly, dusty. I don't envy the priest who takes my position.'

'But why did Sister Michael do that? Why did she?'

'The same reasons I did it. Because she loved Francis? Because she loved the people? She didn't want them all to stop believing in the saint and the church. She told me soon after she wanted to get more involved in the church, in different ways. It was her idea to set up that Museum of Christian Art. She asked me to help with the set-up. To propose the idea to the bishop. He thought it was an excellent idea. Things just went on from there.'

Had Sister Michael done it from love? Or to get a hold over the curate? To help her smuggling plans along? Who was she? The only person I really felt sorry for was Maria.

'Poor Maria. Poor woman,' I said.

Father Jonathan nodded.

'Sister Michael, said Maria was never the same after that. Never the same. I think she had medicines though. I think they helped. We all went through bad memories because of what we had done. It's been so stressful. So stressful. We really thought someone was going to find out about the whole thing, when the head was stolen. We did. We talked to Maria, asked her if she had told anyone. She said she hadn't. We were rather stern. Then we worried that they would do a forensic test and find out the age of the corpse. But it turned out for the best. Everyone assumed it was God's grace keeping him young.'

'It's . . . it's crazy.'

'But I did it for love, Ruby. You have to remember that. If you do something with love, for other people. It can't be wrong.'

'Did you kill Sister Michael, Father Jonathan? To keep the secret?'

Father Jonathan looked at me.

'No, no. I didn't kill Sister Michael. I didn't. I didn't like her. I hated her sometimes. But I loved her too. We'd been part of each other's lives for so long. I needed her. I just wish I hadn't left her alone that day. She had a delivery she said, that I should go back.'

'Do you know the people who made the delivery?

Was it Ram? Do you know Ram? He has a grey beard, trimmed. Small man. Goan, from the North.'

'No, no. The only person I saw about that day was a tourist. I couldn't see his face though, he had some kind of hood over his head.'

3

Trees lined the road back to the centre of Panjim, flicked shadows across the car and across my eyes. In and out of shade, in and out of light. My head flickering. This was surely bigger than the smuggling. The head of Saint Francis. It wasn't really *Saint* Francis. The beloved saint, the founder of the Jesuits, was a fake. Millions of people had worshipped at the feet of an ex-priest with a weak, impulsive heart.

Maria's suicide, it now made more sense. She hadn't killed herself because she was angry, because she'd done something terrible to Sister Michael or because she was just plain depressed. She'd killed herself because she was scared, because she couldn't cope with the memories of grave-robbing a priest and stealing a saint. Because Father Jonathan and Sister Michael, they had scared her, told her they were in danger, that the church would find out.

And something else. The tourist with the hood.

Zim was out when I got back to the hotel. There was

a note. He'd gone shopping; presents for the family. He bought tickets back to LA for us both on the fifth leaving from Mumbai. We'd need to there by the third, to sort out a visa at the Embassy. His dad had a client in Washington, they were going to help us get it fast-tracked. Paulo was buying two paintings. Zim had recovered part of his homecoming pride at least. I really should just forget about telling him. Forget about all of it. It wasn't anything to do with me. I just had to write this article and get out of here. I was looking forward to LA, but I had to try writing up what Father Jonathan had told me before leaving. I couldn't just leave it sitting there in my head. I logged on to the computer. Facebook. David.

Hey
Ruby . . .
David are you on Skype? Can you talk? I need to talk
to you properly.
Of course. Should I ring you?
I'll log on to my account.

The bleeping theme tune came on immediately. David Dryden calling. I pressed accept. The video blinked into life. It was the first time I had seen him since Oxford. Floppy hair, blue shirt, black hair with a couple of grey hairs streaked through it, deep lines beginning around his eyes. He didn't look healthy.

'Ruby. Have you finished the article? We should be going to print tomorrow. I've told Bukowski the outline of the story. He's very pleased.'

'I think I've got something bigger. You'll never believe it.'

333

'Oh really? Go on.'

I told him what I'd heard. He sat back in his chair.

'The problem is, Ruby, the man is clearly mad. Is anyone going to believe us?'

'Yes – why not? I mean it makes sense of Maria's death right?'

'Perhaps.'

David clicked on his keyboard, I could tell he was checking his emails.

'David – are you taking me seriously? Don't ignore me. This is a great story.'

My editor stopped what he was doing and looked straight at me.

'I'll be honest with you Ruby, Bukowski won't like this. He's an incredibly open-minded man. His two blind spots are his daughter and the church. He won't stand for something like this in his paper. I'd like you to just keep to the outline we discussed before New Year's Eve.'

'David. You're a journalist. Can't you see how good this is?'

'I don't really care, Ruby.'

'What do you care about then? What's your motivation? Don't you want to get the true story out there? We still don't know who really murdered Sister Michael. It's all been brushed over.'

David rubbed his head, rolled his eyes slightly. He was losing patience with me. I could see that.

'Ruby, I grew up on a housing estate in Rhyl. There were seven of us living in a three bedroom flat. My father beat me up when I was seventeen for wearing nail polish. My sister is a heroin addict and her dealer is also her pimp. I know this because my cousin drinks with him in the local pub. My motivation is to get as far away from my reality as possible. Journalism? Stories? They're just games. Money. That's what really matters – and this job gives me money and influence and camouflage. Would you ever know where I came from? The truth hasn't ever mattered to me. I rather dislike it.'

I didn't know what to say. I shook my head.

'Ruby, you don't know these people. You really don't owe them anything. Goa, from what I can see, it's Paradise Lost. It's gone. Anyone of them could have killed her. But I didn't ask you to write on that anyway. Step back from the story. You're not scared. I'll give you that. You're brave. But you never employ logic. You stumble around impulsively, following one gut instinct after another. That isn't any way to write, to get anywhere. What are you doing in Goa anyway? What are you doing in India? Where is all this leading? You're nearly thirty, wandering around like a gap-year student. What are you living on? The way you work isn't professional. It's amateur.'

I couldn't speak. I had a lump in my throat. I wasn't any match for David. He was ruthless and he was right. I wiped a tear away. He sighed with forbearance.

'Look. You'll get two thousand pounds if you finish this article in the next couple days. Why don't you just get on with it and then come back to London for a while? I could use another London reporter. And you can actually write, which is something in your favour. It's not fun being single and lonely. It must have been hard after Stephen died. Seeing your friends and family will do you good.'

I shook my head some more, took a breath.

'No. I'm going to the US. I'm not alone. I've met someone out here. He's from LA. We're leaving in a couple of days.'

That surprised him.

'Oh, well, that's great, Ruby. He's a lucky man. What does he do?'

'He's an art dealer.'

'In LA? Nothing to do with Raoul Moon is he?'

'His son.'

David sat back impressed.

'Well, that does sound promising. Good luck. We could do with some seedy stories from Los Angeles. That's one city that's always seething in vice. Just get this finished first.'

'OK. But if you won't let me write the story of the head, at least give me another day to do a couple more interviews. I just want to try and work out what happened to Sister Michael.'

David rolled his eyes again.

'You should forget about the old nun. But OK, if you agree to just concentrate on what we agreed, I'll give you another day. Who are you going to talk to?'

'I wanted to talk to Galina, Ram's girlfriend. The Russian. But she's disappeared. I'm thinking where she could be.'

'Just follow that gut instinct of yours, Ruby. It does seem to get you places after all. But if you don't get the words to me by the fourth, I'm writing it myself,' he said.

I sat back in the hotel chair, rubbing my head. It had been an exhausting conversation. There was a loud smack on the window that juddered through the room. I jumped up in shock. It was a pigeon. I could see it flapping outside the window, concussed and confused. I felt sorry for it. I understood how it felt.

Trust my instincts David had said. I hadn't even known I had any. But something was making me uneasy, stopping me writing up the story. Something didn't make sense. Maybe David had been right, maybe the best thing was just to forget about Saint Francis, Sister Michael. Just write a simple easy story and take the money. Ten paragraphs, each with a main point and a quote and it was done. I was leaving the day after tomorrow anyhow – and Galina still wasn't picking up her phone. I wondered if she was all right.

But I still didn't begin. I thought about packing my bag. But I didn't have much anyhow. My sundress, a few other clothes, the bag of toiletries I'd collected, the iPod Zim had given me. I still hadn't got back my old rucksack, with my old iPod, with my photos of Stephen. I wished I could at least get the photos back. Stephen had an old film camera. He wouldn't buy a digital one. He said it wasn't the same, seeing images on a screen. He liked them in print, in your hand. But there were no copies of those photos. They were gone. I'd never find them. The one of us both, sitting on top of Humayun's tomb, leaning back in the pink sunset heat. Or the picture of him drunk, a careless cigarette hanging out his mouth at a party. And the photo that haunted me most. Me brushing my teeth, frowning into the sink, and Stephen behind, a slack outline just visible in the bathroom mirror, his camera held up to catch me unawares. I'd looked at that photo so many times since he died. It made me think. He really must have cared for me, to creep out of bed, take a photo of me that early in the morning, that undone. More than that, it was how I liked to think of Stephen now, standing just behind me, watching me.

What would he have thought of all this? What would he have thought of Zim? I'm not sure he would have liked him. He would have laughed. He never thought my taste in men was up to much. But he would have approved of going to America. He'd always go on about how I didn't know the world properly because I'd never been.

And he always told me to do a headstand if I needed to sort out problems; that it helped turning things upside down.

I lay down on the floor and began to prepare. I hadn't done any practice since I'd arrived in Goa. I shook my head from side to side to loosen up. Closed my eyes. Lay there for a while, trying to blank out my mind. I opened them again. And saw something I recognised. Under Zim's bed. It looked like my rucksack. The one I had lost; navy, Eastpack, squashed up in a corner. I crawled under the bed, pulled it out, heavy, opened it up.

Everything was crammed in. Someone had pushed everything down to make it as small as possible. I began taking it all out. My iPod. My change of clothes. My toothbrush. My wallet. My photos of Stephen. All there. My book too, even, *Strangers on a Train*. And something else. A screwed up piece of paper. I unfolded it carefully. It was an address, written in heavy-handed joined-up writing, sporadically thick and thin. Fernando and his felt-tip calligraphy pen. Sister Michael's address, with directions how to get there. The blood rushed to my head.

'Hey, hey, Ruby. Look what I got you in the market. Fake Louis Vuitton. But it isn't bad, look. A travelling bag, for LA.'

Zim crashed through the door loaded with bags and saris and spices. He fell on my bed and threw his goods across the floor. It took him a few seconds to understand what was going on.

'I can explain, Ruby.'

'Can you?'

'It's like, you know when you were missing, I came back here and I booked in and I went down to the police station and I said that something had happened to you. Inspector Ferreira came out, I think he was pissed off 'cause I disturbed his lunch. He said that there was nothing he could do, but your bag had turned up just today. He had wanted to phone you but you hadn't got a phone. Right? You hadn't. It's true. Some priest had found it in under the seat of a confession box, he said. I said I was with you, I'd take it. I signed for it. He didn't mind. He knew we were together. I took it, but I forgot about it, you know with everything that was happening. You were missing and then you were in the hospital. Everything's been so fast.'

I wanted, I so wanted to believe him. But I didn't.

'Really?'

'Yeah, yeah. Honestly.'

He couldn't look me in the eye. He was starting to sweat. Little shiny beads above his lip.

'Zim, you're not telling me the truth. You hid it.

Why did you stuff it under your bed like that if you didn't want to hide it from me?'

'I don't know all right, Ruby. Jesus!' he said.

He stood up, turned away from me, banged the wardrobe door. The sound made me jump. I got that lurking feeling back again. The one where I felt that I was next. That whoever had got Sister Michael was going to get me. Fear.

'Zim. Please don't. You'll scare me. Please, just tell me the truth. Why did you hide the rucksack?'

'Because . . . Because . . . I didn't want you to get that iPod back OK? I wanted you to have mine. I bought you that as a gift. I bought it as a symbol. I didn't want you to get all your old things back. Your old photos. I looked through them. He didn't look trustworthy, your friend. You didn't need to be reminded of him. I wanted to help you. I wanted to help you forget your old life and give you a new one.'

'That wasn't your place Zim. You shouldn't have done it Zim. It's not right.'

'Why not? Why isn't it right, if I did it out of love? If I did it to help you? Sometimes you do bad things for good reasons right? I didn't want you to go. I wanted you to stay with me. I wanted to look after you. I didn't want you to just go away.'

I still had the piece of paper in my hand. The piece of paper with Sister Michael's address on it. I clenched it harder, looked down. I was shaking. I needed to keep calm, at least calm enough not to disturb Zim anymore. Calm enough to convince him to talk to me.

'Zim. It's OK. All right. It's OK. Just tell me the

truth, that's all I want. OK? We can't go away together if you can't trust me and I can't trust you.'

He was contrite. Sat down, put his arm around me, leant in too close. I could smell him, a mixture of hot skin and aftershave and something else. I don't know how to explain it, just this smell that exuded from him, that was just Zim.

'Did you slash your girlfriend?'

He clenched my shoulder, face screwed up, angry again. Those same mood swings I'd seen since I'd known him, intensified. How could I not have thought about this before? He wasn't in control of his emotions. It was so clear. He was capable of anything when he was mad.

'Why? Why are you asking me about this? We've talked about it.'

'Zim. I need to know. Please,' I said. I could hear my voice wavering, getting higher. I needed to keep control.

'OK, yeah, once. I went for her once. I didn't mean to, I just meant to scare her. I didn't want her to leave me. I was scared. She was all I had. She was all that was special to me. I didn't mean to hurt her, it just happened.'

'Oh, Zim.'

He still had his arm around me. I could still smell his smell. But I was suddenly so far away from him. He wasn't the person he said he was. I shrank inside my body. I had begun to put my trust in him, invest him with my dreams. What a mistake. What a terrible mistake. He put his hand over mine, still gripping the address, getting wet from my sweat. He stilled the shaking.

'Look – does it matter? We're going tomorrow. I've got some money now. I've made the deal. You've got your bag. We're not suspects anymore. We're free to go. We're free to have a beautiful life.'

I pulled my hand away from his. Spread out my palm in front of us. Sister Michael's address opened up like a greasy flower.

He looked at it. Recognised it. Flushed deeply. He stood up, trying to distance himself.

'This is Fernando's writing. I recognise it. He used his calligraphy pen. The felt-tip one. You didn't tell me Fernando gave you the address. You told me you hadn't known where I was. But you did. You knew I was at Sister Michael's.'

'So? Does it matter. I forgot, OK. I forgot.'

His voice went high and loud.

'So how did you get this address, Zim?'

'I went to Fernando's. To ask after you. He wrote the address down for me. Said he knew who you were staying with. I tried to find the house but I didn't. I just didn't, OK?'

'Father Jonathan saw you, near the house. A tourist with a hood on. You were wearing that damn sweater of yours when I saw you in the church. The same one.'

'The priest. He's mad. He's a mad one. Why are you listening to him?'

Zim was scratching his arms now; acting weird. The bones in his face were moving under his skin. He was clenching his jaw together.

'Zim, please. I just want to know the truth. You know that's all I want to know. So tell me. Did you hit her over the head? Please tell me.'

342

He put his head in his hands.

'I'm telling you the truth,' he shouted.

I forced myself to put my arm around his shoulders, calm him down, rub his back. Incredibly, I could feel my insatiable curiosity rising up. I wanted to know what happened. I wanted to know what happened and I would do anything to persuade him to tell me.

'Zim, come on. You say you love me. Well trust me. Tell me the truth. I'm not going to let anything happen to you. I'll protect you.'

He didn't take his head out from his hands. I continued to rub his back.

'Zim?'

A long pause, but I could feel his back relaxing into my hands. Then he talked.

'OK, OK. I knocked, but there was no answer. The old woman, she didn't have a doorbell did she? I tried it and it was open. I just walked in. I wasn't going to do anything. I just wanted to have a look around. It looked a nice old house, I hadn't seen a place like that before. I was quiet. There didn't seem to be anyone in at all. It was cool. Really cool. I walked through the library. She had all these old books. You know there isn't anything old in my house. It's all steel and blasted stone. I got to the ballroom. There was no one around. Just this half-set-out nativity scene. I was just looking around. I picked up this nice vase. I really liked it. I was just looking at it. She walked in the door, these two figures in her hand, Mary and one of the wise men. She started screaming when she saw me. She just screamed. I thought she was scared but she was just crazy about the vase. It was just a fucking vase. She kept yelling at me to put it down. That I wouldn't get away with it. I just got angry. You know, it was just a damn vase, I wasn't going to steal it. I wasn't. I tried to explain to her, to calm her down but she was just going mad. Then, I don't know, it's like, I can't explain, sometimes I see red. You know that. I just get, just mad and I always do something wrong. Something I can't control. It's not me, you see Ruby, doing these things, it's someone else. I said to her, "it's not going to fucking break. Look at it. It's as thick as my fucking arm." And I threw it at her. She went for it, tried to save it, but it got her head instead. It didn't kill her. It just made her stumble. That floor, it was slippy. That wasn't my fault. She went right over; hit her head on the floor. And it was really hard. I turned her over, her head was bashed in but she was looking straight at me. I didn't know what to do. I wanted to help her but what if she had told on me? What if you had come back and she'd told? I knew I wouldn't get away with it. I knew I'd be going to prison. I had to hit her again. I dropped the vase on her head. I had to. She was done for anyway. It wasn't really murder. It was just an awful accident. And I called the police. I called the police afterwards.'

'It was you who made the call?'

'Yeah. I felt terrible about it. And you coming back finding the body.'

'You said you didn't know the number.'

He shrugged. 'I didn't want anyone to know it was me that had called. I found the number on my phone, before going to the church.'

Such a weird sense of right and wrong. He called the police after he'd killed someone. He went to the church to pray. He wasn't crazy though. He knew how to hide it. He knew what to hide. I shook my head at him.

'You went to church after killing someone?'

'I went to the church to pray. Of course. I'd done something terrible. That's when I saw you. You were praying too. I'd wanted to see you again. I'd really liked you, at the airport. And then we'd met again, just when I needed you. I knew things would be all right from then on. And when you rang me after? You were so shocked. So scared. You needed someone to help you. I had to come back. And I did. And I helped you as much as I could here. I liked you more and more. We got on so well. And now we're going to LA together.'

The thud in my ears turned to a roar, a fuming thunder. Zim had killed her. Ferreira. He'd been right. I'd been defending a murderer. I'd fallen for a murderer. I'd thought I'd seen into his heart, but I hadn't. I thought I'd seen past his crazy temper, his impetuousness, his spoilt frustration at the world and everything in it. But that was him. He *was* who he seemed – it were these things that allowed him to do what he did. He didn't live in the real world. I tried to wrench myself away from him. He grabbed on and I let him. I began to cry, sob. He cried too, pulling me into his arms.

'I didn't mean to Ruby, you have to believe me. I would do anything, just to go back. To change what happened. It wasn't me who did it. It was someone else. It wasn't the real me. This is the real me, here with you now.'

I couldn't talk for crying. Hysterical crying. He grabbed my face, tears streaming down his cheeks.

'Ruby, please. You can still trust me. I know I lied to you. But I just, I blocked it out. I felt so terrible I just had to block it out. I stuffed the address into my jeans. I didn't even find it till I was packing up to leave. I should have told you about it then. I don't know why I didn't. I just stuffed it into the rucksack with everything else. I don't know why I did that. I've fucked everything up. But you know, I love you. I really do. I want to be with you. Please don't leave me now.'

I shook my head. 'Of course not.'

'Ruby? What does that mean? No, you won't leave me?'

He grabbed my face harder, stared into my eyes, trying desperately to find some forgiveness there, some connection. I couldn't give it to him. I tried to push him off, still sobbing. He wouldn't let me go, brought my face to his and kissed me hard. I let him. That touch again. Hot and sickly down to my stomach. That's what it was about, fear and desire, mixed up together. But more fear than ever before. All this time, I'd tried to bury this terrible feeling, that I was next, that the murderer was close by, that whoever had killed Sister Michael was watching me. I'd been right. I was right. It was Zim, he was with me all along. I'd shared a bed with him.

Was I really next? Would he let me walk out of here? Would he get too angry to let me go? I wasn't tied up, I wasn't bleeding but I was in more trouble than ever before. Zim moved his hands down to my stomach and I let him pull my waist towards him, let him pull my top. He wanted to have sex. I closed my eyes. I could feel a sickness rising up my throat. Revulsion. How could I stop this?

I leant back. Put all my energy into giving him an easy smile.

'Zim, I hate to tell you this. But you smell.'

He was obsessed with washing, with being clean. He couldn't stand bad smells, he'd told me that the first time I had talked to him. He pulled his head up, frowning.

'Really? But I showered, two hours ago.'

I made a face. 'Maybe you need another one.'

He smelt his armpit, wrinkled his nose.

'I think you might be right. God. It's so fucking dirty in this country. I'll just take a shower. You want to come with me?'

'No, I'm all right. I'll stay here.'

'OK, I won't be long. I'll just get clean.'

Of course he would be long. He couldn't have a shower that lasted less than half an hour. I waited till I heard the rush of running water, the hot smell of soap. I picked myself up, got into my clothes, grabbed my rucksack, stuffed everything back in it and left. I took the fire exit and got out the Majestic Panjim by the bins, rotting and smelling and swarming with flies. There was a few rickshaws waiting in the slip road nearby. I got in the nearest one.

'How much to the airport?'

'One thousand rupees.'

'OK, go. Fast. And stop at an ATM on the way.'

The airport flags waved limply in the hot air. White taxis, black and yellow cabs, rickshaws and huge charter buses lined the mile towards it.

'What flight ma'am?' asked the rickshaw driver.

'I don't know yet. Just get me as close as possible.'

I weaved through the parked cars and the waiting drivers and the tourists coming and going to find the information desk.

Are there any flights to London this evening?'

'Yes ma'am. New Kingfisher flight, direct to London, 10:55.'

'Is it full?'

'Let me just check for you.'

See clicked on her screen a few times.

'No, there are places left. Just in business though ma'am.'

'How much is that?'

She clicked a few more times, looked at her screen, clicked.

'One thousand eight hundred pounds, ma'am.'

I winced, despite everything. Thank God I'd got the bail money back.

'I'll take it, thanks.'

'OK ma'am. You'll get priority boarding. Here's your pass to the VIP lounge.'

There was wine and beer and phones in the lounge. I took out my notebook, phoned Inspector Ferreira. Enya, 'Sail Away' was playing. He'd gone home for the day. I'd have to call Ferreira from London now. That gave Zim some time.

I lay my head back in the airseat. Someone handed me a glass of champagne. I took Stephen's iPod out and put it on shuffle. 'American Pie'.

4

STEALING SAINTS IN GOA

HOW THE MIRACULOUS SAINT FRANCIS LOST HIS HEAD AND EXPOSED A PARADISE OF CRIME

By Ruby Jones
GOA – Panjim

Every year, around Christmas, thousands of pilgrims descend on Old Goa for the feast of Saint Francis Xavier. The usually quiet peninsula of tropical churches and monsoon-blackened convents transforms into something like a religious Glastonbury. Pushing, shoving crowds are hemmed in by stalls selling plastic Rosary beads, shiny stickers of the crucifix, wax models of legs or heads or even babies, to help with supplication to the saint.

Revered and worshipped in Goa, Saint Francis spent much of his life converting locals to Christianity and is said to protect the state. He's also a huge international

figure, spiritually speaking, as one of the founders of
the Jesuits, the largest single religious order of priests
and monks in the Catholic Church.

But the unique draw to his shrine, the thing which
makes it the most visited Christian site in Asia, is a
fascination, perhaps morbid, with his miraculous corpse.
Saint Francis is said to be 'incorruptible'; his dead body
will not rot . . .

And so the article began, written in a fug of jetlag
and shock and just in time. But it wasn't hard to write.
I just wrote what happened. Well, part of what
happened.

Bukowski didn't want Father Jonathan or Sister
Michael mentioned. I was too exhausted to argue. If
I had written about Sister Michael, I would have had
to write about Zim and I couldn't bring myself to do
that. And she had suffered enough, so shockingly
murdered, without running her reputation into the
ground.

There was more than enough to write about
without her. Paulo Mendes, the framed victim who
was innocently destroying Goa and making a fortune
in the process. The resident Russians: running gangs,
making money, dancing in Bollywood, or simply
washed up and lost in Anjuna. The rivalry between
the Idol Squad and the local police. I used one of
Inspector Srinvasen's most offensive quotes, from his
first press conference.

'Saint Francis, from what I have read, isn't such a
saint. He is the man responsible for the Goan Inquisition,
where hundreds of lapsed Goan Christians were

sentenced to death. His letters show a deep disrespect and revulsion of Hinduism. He was known to destroy temples and statues. This seems a perilous reputation in a country where Hindu politicians have called for the death penalty on missionaries,' he said.

I didn't think Saint Francis was such a saint either, a blood-thirsty evangeliser and a vicious iconoclast. But I didn't want to upset his holiness Bukowski too much – I wanted more work. I thought it best to have Srinvasen point out the saint's possible faults.

Then there was the trove of Indo-Portuguese art that Saint Francis had led the police to. The unique blend of Christian and Hindu artwork found only in Goa. The ivory angels with the tails of holy Hindu snakes, statues of saints squatting like Sadhus, paintings of baby Jesus surrounded by gods such as Krishna and Parvati. The shocking discovery that a whole landscape of heritage had been systematically removed. Another bottle of Claret and David Dryden's friend at Sotheby's was happy to be quoted, albeit anonymously.

'Indo-Portuguese art is so desirable because it is rare and it is beautiful. By the sixteenth century, Goan craftsmen were famous for their skill throughout Europe. Because so little care has been taken of these pieces there has been a steady stream of Goan antiquities coming through our auction houses for many years. Although not much valued in India, they have become prized pieces with European collectors interested in Colonial history,' he said.

And of course, there was Ram. The man behind the crime. The accountant who had wanted to settle his accounts, who remembered catching starfish and

351

crystals washed up on the beach but now found only condoms and whisky bottles. Who had looked around him, disgusted, and had wanted to make amends for profiting from his homeland.

David was keen to explain how Touchstone had helped in the arrest, but I was happy to leave the glory to Inspector Ferreira. I didn't feel so good about it. There were no real winners in this story, it seemed. Not the church, not the police, not 'innocent Paulo', not even Saint Francis, either of them, both crumbling old fakes. And of course, not Ram, charged and waiting trial. But somehow, as I was writing, the quiet accountant began to appear almost heroic. He had at least stood up for his flailing state when everyone else seemed to be looking the other way or holding their hands up in helplessness.

There was a last interview I wanted to do. Not an interview for Touchstone but for me. With someone who might know where the bull's head was. I couldn't stop thinking of Casa Bonita, concreted over. Or poor Ram's father, dying of a broken heart. Or Ram, in jail, for wanting to rescue Goa, for having convictions, however strangely executed. Perhaps if I found the Tambdi Surla bull, if it could be returned, there would be some small protection from Paulo's bulldozers.

154, Bimney Street, not quite on Bond Street, just off it, on a small street, discreetly placed between jewellers and designers and cheese shops. Edward Jones Antiquities. Flaking gold lettering and a window full of dusty chairs, crude pictures of saints in ornate frames. Hard to believe this was the place that had caused all the trouble; this fusty, quiet-looking shop.

A bell rang when I opened the door. It was hot inside, airless. Loot was piled up, but nothing that seemed of much value: a brutish looking statue of Jesus, a few silver plated crucifixes, nothing beautiful.

'Just browsing? Or looking for something particular?'

A middle-aged man, fraying shirt and furring eyebrows idled through from the back.

'I am looking for something particular. But nothing I see here. Is this all your stock?'

'No, not all of it.'

'Where's the rest of it?'

'Most of it is at auction.'

'So this stuff, it's all the bits you can't move? The bits that don't sell?'

'Is there something you want, Madam?'

'I'm Ruby Jones. I think you've already spoken to my editor.'

The man's eyebrows went up and then down into a deeply pissed-off frown.

'I told Mr Dryden I had nothing to say to him. Nothing at all. If you have any questions, direct them through my lawyer.'

'Look, I'm not here to interview you. I just, I want to know about Dorothea.'

'What do you want to know? Hounding us like this. It's not on. Neither of us were rich. We were just trying to make a living. It's not easy you know. We didn't do anything so wrong. If it wasn't for these antiquated Indian laws there wouldn't have been any need to be so covert. We're not temple raiders. Just antique dealers. Nothing more.'

'Are you sure? Raiding temples is what started all

the problems. Because temples started to get broken into, because a bull's head was stolen.'

'You know we're not stupid. Of course that's trouble. Who wants a visit from the Idol Squad? Well, I've got one coming now, thanks to you. We'd had a tough year last year. The market had bottomed out for Eastern Christian Art here in London. Nothing was selling. All the buyers that usually love this kind of thing, the Portuguese, the Spanish, the Catholics, they'd lost all their stocks, half their savings sometimes, in this crisis. We needed to find another source of sales. And we found it. In Russia. Dorothea got the idea, seeing so many Russians coming to Goa, buying up the rosaries and the prayer cards at the Basilica. She suggested we look to selling there, or even simply selling in the Russian sale. And it worked. They loved what we had.'

'So you never traded in Hindu idols?'

'No. I only deal in Christian art. I met Dorothea in Rome, on a History of Catholic Art course. That was our interest, that was our expertise. And we'd amassed a huge amount of goods. We didn't need any more. Dorothea, she was wanting to wind it all down anyhow. She wanted to come home. She'd had enough of living out there. I said I might be able to get her some kind of consultancy work. She knew a great deal. She was passionate.'

'I saw her statue, of Saint Michael, in the warehouse. I thought whoever had killed her had taken it there. I thought Ram Kumar had killed her.'

'No. She had the statue there to ship back to England. Waiting for her return. She told me, its strange now,

354

but she felt she didn't have long, that she'd die in England if she moved back. She wanted Saint Michael over here, protecting her at that hour. She misjudged her timing, she sent him away just as she was about to die. It's really horrible. But I hope, I'm sure he was there.'

'What's happened to the bull's head? The one that was stolen? Ram Kumar, he says Dorothea stole it. She was the only one who had the knowledge, the experience to smuggle something like that out of India. She was the only one who knew the right people to do this.'

Edward shook his head.

'Don't we all want to find that head? The Idol Squad are flying over here next week to scour the auction houses. They have a special Interpol warrant to search my premises, which I'm not looking forward to at all. I have nothing of theirs here.

'She didn't take it. She would have told me if she had. She had no idea who did. We talked about it. It was one of the few times she called me. She was dreadfully upset. I didn't know much about Ram, I didn't deal with him, but I knew he existed. I knew he was a solace to her. She told me he accused her of stealing it, of stealing from other temples. She swore to me that she didn't. She wanted me to call him, get in touch, let him know that I hadn't received any of these things. I sent him an email. He didn't reply. He didn't believe me I don't think. I think this was one of the reasons she decided to come home. She was scared. She didn't feel in control anymore. She couldn't find out who had taken the bull and neither could Ram. And then Saint Francis . . .'

'The one person who she relied on, who loved her, turned his back on her. Wouldn't trust her.'

'I don't know about love. We didn't speak of that,' said Edward.

'Someone played a trick on the two of them.'

'I don't know about that. I just don't know. I'm very tired of it all. But we're all in trouble, me and Ram and Sotheby's, because of it. And are we really that bad? Surely India would be better spending its money on cleaning up corruption or battling against child labour or something else. There are more than enough problems in the world without bothering us,'

I'd finished my article but the story wasn't finished. Everyone had been wrong. Sister Michael hadn't taken it after all. Who had? It was a mystery I had no leads for.

It was raining, cold hard rain, as I walked to the tube for the first time in years. David had a spare room in his flat, above a delicatessen on Gloucester Road. He said I could stay there for a while in exchange for some work at Touchstone.

I was doing the menial job of editing letters to the editor as well as working on a piece about avant-garde theatre happenings in London. It wasn't my kind of thing but most of these new directors were David's friends and he'd promised them a little something in the magazine.

I couldn't leave Goa or Zim or the bull behind. I kept up a newsfeed on my computer. Bits of information filtered through among items on land reclamation, football and illegal mining. Work had begun on the Arambol Complex. Simon Moon would not be extradited back to India for trial. His father was quoted as saying that, like every man, Simon was suffering from untrue accusations from the female race.

I tried to block him out. Guilt and sadness and anger. Mournful loss and deep distrust of myself barraged down upon me when I thought of Zim. Of course I should have hung on the phone, got to Inspector Ferreira before leaving Goa. It was my fault he had escaped, for waiting till London to call the police. I couldn't help wonder if I hadn't known, deep down, what I was doing. That I'd wanted to give Zim a break.

Maybe because I could imagine precisely how Zim would have felt when he'd come out the shower and seen me gone. A horrible, sinking realisation. I wasn't with him. I wasn't going to be there. He must have known I would report him. He'd got a taxi all the way to Mumbai, got on a flight from there. Clever. He didn't use the local airport in case people were looking for him. Clever. He was a murderer. He'd been able to fool me. I'd almost been in love with him.

I would have felt terrible guilt, but I tried to remember Sister Michael, her advice. It was a useless emotion. Maybe that was the only thing I'd learnt, over the whole damn holiday. Holiday, it was funny, calling it that.

At least I'd found Touchstone. David was a good editor. It was a job. Maybe things could get interesting here. Bukowski, apparently he was pleased with the story I'd written. I hadn't rocked any boats. I hadn't mentioned any of the really awful stuff. The body swapping, the murder, the suicide.

Ram was out of jail on bail and was pictured attending his father's funeral. Inspector Srinvasen cropped up occasionally. He seemed to have been jolted from his winning streak by Saint Francis. He was having as little luck as me finding the Tambdi Surla bull.

A Russian woman believed to be in her late twenties washed up ashore on Anjuna beach. There wasn't much fuss. I thought it could be Galina. It turned out to be Saskia. Of course. It was clear how fragile she had been. There was a small photo of her in one of the local newspapers. It had been taken when she first arrived in Mumbai, around Colaba by the sea. She had been startlingly beautiful, looked straight into the camera with the confidence that she was going to be adored. Beside her, I recognised Galina, a little chubby, softer in the face, looking to one side, unsure of herself. Who would have known what would happen to those two Russian girls? There were no winners in this messy sprawl. Everyone had lost.

Or so I thought. A few days after starting at the Touchstone office, I received an envelope, written in sprawling spidery copperplate. I opened it up to find a heavy card, embossed with an ornate crucifix. Edward Jones Antiquities.

I don't want to get involved. But I thought this might interest you. Page 14.

I flicked through. Page fourteen. A small strip of writing accompanied by three colour photos.

'Relo's Auction House holds first Indian Sale.'

'The Moscow Auction house Relo's held it first

Indian sale 'A Taste of the Eastern Gods,' on Wednesday. The auction house had seen a surge in sales thanks to Russia's recent economic boom. The sale was set up to capitalise on the new interest Russians have in travelling abroad.' said Vladmir Molotov, director of Relo's.

'India has been growing in popularity as a holiday spot for a number of years now. We have a taste for beautiful and religious objects in Russia and tourists often like to bring souvenirs of their travels back with them. However, due to the strict antiquity laws in India it is difficult for individuals to purchase objects within the country. Relo's has worked with a number of antique dealers in Europe who have Indian pieces for sale in order to bring "A Taste of the Eastern Gods" straight to our customers here in Moscow.'

The sale was well attended and there was a notable young presence in the audience. Most of the lots were sold for above their asking price. Of particular interest to buyers was a Himalayan Bronze depicting Parvati and Shiva locked in tantric yoga and the polished granite bust of a Nandi, or bull, of unknown origin. Both were sold anonymously.

Three pictures accompanied the piece. Shiva and Parvati locked in an embrace, arms and legs. Smiling passion, simple and apparently holy. A picture of the Tambdi Surla bull's head, polished, eyes closed. Serene. A photo of the auction audience. It was small, difficult to make out. I reached across for a heavy magnifying glass that sat on David's desk.

'What do you want that for?' he said.

'Just wait.'

I peered into the audience and found what I was

looking for. Different clothes for a different climate, a green wool coat and a fur muff sitting by her side. But those same Chanel sunglasses and those same emerald stilettos and that same poker face.

David drew up behind me.

'Galina,' I said.

'Ah, Hell hath no fury like a woman scorned,' he said.

Acknowledgements

Thank you to Marika Ohtani, Jess Hamilton, Sophie Lewis, Terry and Elizabeth McCaul, Charlie Viney, Emma Besthewick, Lucy Icke, James Ellroy and Harriet Sergeant.